Dear Reader,

I am delighted to share Soho Teen's June 2014 title: *I Become Shadow.*

Debut author Joe Shine not only has the distinction of being the first male on Soho Teen's list, but also the first Soho Teen talent that we discovered in a very happy accident.

In 2012, before Soho Teen launched, Soho Press Publisher Bronwen Hruska and I met with film executive Tia Maggini, to pitch our plans for the new imprint. We were surprised when she had a pitch for us: a YA thriller by an unpublished author, a manuscript she fell in love with— which by her own admission almost never happens. The premise sounded very cool: A teen girl gets nabbed in the middle of the night by an organization that can see into the future. They foretell that she's going to die shortly, so they intervene and "save" her, removing her from her normal life (where she is assumed to be dead) and training her to be an elite bodyguard/assassin . . .

That was enough to pique my interest. Needless to say, I fell in love with the manuscript, too. But what Tia didn't mention—and what sets this novel apart from so many other high-concept thrillers—is the voice of its protagonist, Ren Sharpe. Tough, vulnerable, hilarious, and always honest, Ren shares her creator's plainspoken and unsparing wit, especially when it comes to herself. She is so refreshing, so tragic and funny, and yet she delivers the attitude and action you expect from classic bad-ass YA heroines like Katniss, Clary Fray, or Clarke from *The Hundred*—that I know I'll spoil her if I try to describe her any more. Only Joe can do Ren the justice she deserves.

So please enjoy this extraordinary first offering from author Joe Shine. You're in for a wild ride.

Sincerely,
Daniel Ehrenhaft
Editorial Director, Soho Teen

I BECOME SHADOW

JOE SHINE

SOHO
TEEN

Published in the United States by Soho Teen
an imprint of
Soho Press, Inc.
853 Broadway
New York, NY 10003

Library of Congress Cataloging-in-Publication Data

CIP TK

ISBN 978-1-61695-358-4
eISBN 978-1-61695-359-1

Interior design by Janine Agro, Soho Press, Inc.

Printed in the United States of America

10 9 8 7 6 5 4 3 2 1

Dedi TK

CHAPTER 1
MILKSHAKE

What if I told you that we already know who the President of the United States will be in 50 years? (William Stinson, if you're wondering). Or that the world's first trillionaire is currently only three years old, lives in Manchester, England, and has a pet turtle named Labooboo? You can doubt me all you want, but it won't stop us from knowing these things.

How we know is not relevant to this story, at least not at this point. Who these future bigwigs are and how we protect them is. I say this because I will soon be one of the protectors. Today, after four long years of training, exhaustion, and pain I will officially become a Shadow. But I'm getting ahead of myself. For any of this to make sense we can't start now. I mean, we could, but you'd be confused, and I'd be annoyed by your interruptions for explanations. So *beep, beep, beep* goes the truck as we back this sucker up.

For everything that's about to happen to me to make any sense we'll have to go back four years to when I was just fourteen years old. It was then that I lost what was left of my childhood. Scratch that. Lost is a poor choice of words. It implies I had something to do with it, like it was my fault.

Stolen. Yeah, that's the word I'm looking for; it was then that my childhood was *stolen.* It's no five-dollar word, but it'll do. That's where this whole thing really begins. Four years ago almost to the day.

So from here on out, everything is in the past. I'll let you know when we're back to the present. In fact, let's have a safe-word cue so there's no confusion. Our finished-with-the-past-back-to-present-safe-word-cue will be—wait for it—"Milkshake."

CHAPTER 2
A LIFE QUITE ORDINARY

The Pap smear was easily the most embarrassing moment of my life. Nobody should *want* to do that for a living. You always hear the saying, "Do what makes you happy." Well if doing *that* makes you happy, you've got issues, major ones. Plus, who came up with the name? Pap smear? There was *no* smearing. Should have called it a Pap probe.

So after I was Pap probed, the doctor told me the last step in our little meeting was a blood test. Not quite sure what that had to do with anything, but who argues with a doctor?

He left me alone for a moment to get dressed, but quickly returned through a side door holding a needle. I hate needles. He said, "This won't hurt a bit." I call BS on that because it did. It stung, and then it hurt. Whenever something leaves a bruise, that means pain. I had to look away because the sight made me light-headed.

I was sure he'd taken a little more than necessary to

add to his Dexter-like blood collection of "trophies," only he wasn't nearly as good-looking as Michael C. Hall and didn't have a clever inner monologue full of witty puns and sarcasm.

After that I was free to pick up what was left of my dignity and leave. Trust me, there wasn't much after all of that. Being a gangly, pasty white teenager with low self-esteem is tough enough. Now this had happened? Way to pile it on, society.

I was too disgusted with the whole process to respond to my mother's question about how it went. She knew exactly how it went. I could see her and my father having a good laugh about it later. And for some reason I saw that my ten-year-old brother joined in there, too. Ridicule should be shared by the whole family. Makes you stronger.

The ride home was long and awkward. Mom kept asking me stupid questions about the appointment.

"I don't want to talk about it," I said.

"It's all part of being an adult," she said off-handedly as she changed the radio station.

Like she would know. My name is Rennes Sharpe. She and Dad named me after the town where I was conceived. (Another truly disgusting moment in my life when I found that one out.) Thank you, "adults." I guess it could have been worse. I could have been named Fort Stockton or Baltimore. But as if having a bizarre name weren't enough, they nicknamed me Ren. Bizarre real name; nickname sounds like a boy. Yes, this is what "adults" do. At age one hour, my life was already going to be an uphill battle.

"I'm not an adult," I said. "I'm only fourteen."

It was an argument I'd been making for quite some time. I rolled my window down and let the booming of the wind act as my shield against further questioning. She got the not so subtle hint and left me alone to my thoughts. You see, I know it may come as a shock to you, but I was actually happy being a child. This girl was in no hurry to grow up. Being a grown-up was something I wanted no part of, and today's Pap smear had only strengthened that belief. Being an adult seemed way too complicated. I knew high school started in a week. With it I was sure I'd change, but not yet. I still had time.

The road we were on was my favorite. I knew it like a beloved old book. The trees, the houses, the smells. It was home. If we drove right, we'd hit Main Street in our small town, starting down the path that would take us to our house. I closed my eyes and let the wind and sun do their jobs as I zoned out. Zoning out is something I could do really well. Easily a top five skill. You know what? Scratch that, it's number one by a mile. I'm *really* good at zoning out. It's something one picks up from a father who is an engineer and loves talking about his work.

I counted the turns in my head and opened my eyes just as we pulled into the garage. The wind had blown my black hair into rat's nest, and one look in the mirror told me that the battle to fix it would have to take place in the house, not in the car. I was feeling better but I couldn't let my mom know that, so I trudged out of the car with an "I'm still not happy about earlier" mug.

Before I could open the door and go inside, she grabbed me and wrapped me up in a full-on mom hug, complete with the feeling of total comfort and safety. Teenage Kryptonite.

"I'm proud of you, sweetie," she said as I melted. Man, why had she waited until now? Where had this been before we drove home?

"It sucked," I blurted out in her shoulder.

She gave a snort and added, "I know. Come on. Let's go figure out dinner. Can you help me out with it?"

DINNER WAS UNEVENTFUL. I think my mother had forbidden my father from bringing up the afternoon's probing, and my brother was as oblivious to my life as I was to his. What did I have in common with a ten-year-old boy? *Nada mucho.*

I spent the night barricaded in my room, hoping my parents wouldn't stop by to see how I was doing. At about nine there was a knock on my door.

"Hey, honey. Can I come in?" came my father's deep voice.

Sorry, Dad, not gonna happen. I mean, I guess he could be coming in just to say goodnight, but I wasn't going to risk it. No way.

"I'm on the phone," I lied. Well, not a total lie. Texting is on the phone, right?

He left me alone to continue my marathon texting tear with my best friend, Beth. She had heard that there was a party, and "everyone" was going to be there. I wasn't a part of "everyone," but she was, and she constantly tried to include me in this group. They tolerated me because of her. But I didn't mind being dragged along because Trey, a boy I'd had a crush on for most of my life, was part of "everyone." He was ridiculously good-looking and probably going to be the first ever freshman starting quarterback at our high school. Oh, I know how cliché it all is. Suck it, I was fourteen. He was beyond out of my league, I knew this, but a heart wants what a heart wants.

By the time Beth and I had hashed out our plans, I was sure we had broken our record of 500 texts in one hour. A quick check of the time log confirmed it. 502, hey yo!

I spent the rest of the night quietly practicing my cello (have I mentioned yet how truly uncool I am?) before calling it quits and going to bed.

So if you're counting, that's zoning out, texting, and playing the cello that I'm really good at. Okay, soul-baring time since I doubt it will change your opinion of me. The other two things things on my top five list of "things I do well" are, drum roll please: being annoying and loving horror movies. Is that really a skill? Watching horror movies? Fine, we'll put an asterisk by that for reconsideration. I mean, it's not like I keep an official list of these things in a well-worn, green journal I hide under my bed. And it's not like I edit said list periodically ensuring that it's up to date and accurately reflects the most current me. That would be crazy. (Insert awkward laughter here.)

I AWOKE ON SATURDAY as I always did, sleepy. I would sleep all day if they'd let me. I *love* sleep. But Saturday is chore day in these parts, and a good daughter must oblige, especially one that wants to go to a party that night.

I stumbled downstairs in my pj's to the predictable *da-na-nah, da-na-nah* of ESPN SportsCenter. If my father could have bought stock in that show, we'd be part owners.

I sat down at the table next to my brother. He was eating cereal and playing a video game. Next to him was a fresh bowl filled to the brim with Golden Grahams. I don't know why he did it, but every Saturday morning there it was, a fresh bowl waiting for me. Maybe it was to make up for being such a little turd the rest of the week. Who knows? All I know is I love me some G-Grahams, and with a quick pour of milk I was in cereal heaven.

Our chores were easy enough even though I would never admit to it. Complaining the whole time was a strategic plan. I had to make them think I hated it. But really, taking out the trash? Easy. Vacuuming? Secretly loved it! Weeding the garden? Oddly satisfying. Easy money.

I'd used chore time to fashion the plan of attack to get my parents to let me go to the party. It was simple. I chose to believe honesty would be the best path.

I'm lame. I don't drink. Nothing is going to happen to me, I'd tell them. It was true—pathetically so.

I took a shower and found them sitting on the backyard porch talking. They looked up at me as I walked toward them.

"Hey," I said nonchalantly.

"Hey, honey," my dad said. He motioned for me to sit in a chair by them, but I stood instead. I never chose to hang out with them so they knew something was up. Like ripping off a Band-Aid, I decided to just go for it.

"So, there's a party tonight," I started smoothly but then began to ramble, "and Beth and I were thinking about going and you know I would never do anything stupid and we're only fourteen so there won't be any liquor there just soda, not that I drink anyway, plus, you're always telling to me to expand my horizons and meet new people which this party would be and it's me getting out of the house to hang out with more people my age which I know you guys want me to do more often." I took a deep breath when I finished, realizing I had probably just rattled off the longest run-on sentence of my life.

My parents sat in silence, either thinking about it or maybe just trying to process all that had just spewed out of my mouth. I had prepared up to six different responses for what I predicted they would say.

My dad looked at my mom, then turned to me and said, "Have fun."

Wha-wha-what?

"Be home by ten," my mother added with a smile. She took a sip of her tea and leaned back to relax.

Confused, I wandered back inside. I wasn't sure what had just happened. Wasn't there supposed to be some kind of push back, or an argument or something? That was just too easy. And then I realized it. They *knew*. They knew I was lame, that I didn't drink, and that nothing would happen to me. How sad is that?

I went upstairs to text Beth the good news and that I'd head over to her house after I got dressed. I never knew what to wear to these things so I just put on a pair of shorts, a tank top, and my ratty old USC hoodie. I slipped on my flip flops, hopped on my bike, and fifteen minutes later I was at Beth's door.

She met me outside and yelled, "Bye, Mom." Her parents were the coolest people in the world. They had invented some restaurant software that a theme park chain had bought a while back, which meant they pretty much got to sit around and do whatever they wanted all day. Also, they could go to said theme parks for free, forever. So jealous.

I was glad to see that Beth was wearing similar garb. Sometimes I would be overly dressed or extremely underdressed in anticipation of hanging out with "everyone." At least I'd fit in dress-wise tonight. The party wasn't very far away but was still too far to walk, so we rode our bikes.

NOW, CONTRARY TO POPULAR belief, high school parties are not three hundred people strong with loud rap music. If you're looking to get busted, that's the recipe. No, most parties are more just glorified hang-out sessions of twenty to thirty people. I only sound so knowledgeable because last year, when I went to my first "party," I was sorely disappointed it wasn't like in the movies.

Beth immediately ran over to some kids sitting by the small koi pond. Then I was alone. I'd been expecting this, but the sudden reality didn't make it easier. Beth became a whole different person around "everyone." She spoke like an idiot, cared about garbage TV shows, and was basically the annoying popular girl we had hated when we were younger. I never told her this because I was sure she knew and wasn't proud of it. Why rub it in, right?

I scanned the yard. Across from the pond there was a fire pit. *There.* My eyes zeroed in on Trey, who was surrounded by girls and even a few guys, playing the guitar. Did I also mention he was an amazing musician? He finished his song to raucous clapping. I almost clapped myself but resisted. He laughed off the over-enthusiasm with a wave, and then gently put the guitar down. He was standing and stretching when his eyes found me. He gave me a nod and a smile.

I did what any other sensible girl in my position would do. I turned beet red, wondered if I smiled or just gaped, and then sprint-walked toward Beth. I pretended to be hanging with her group while I snuck peeks at Trey, walking over to the coolers to fish for a drink. Bad idea to choose this spot. I had to get away from their stupid conversation before I grabbed my bike and ran home. But by this time there was no one by the fire pit anymore.

The wood had burned down to coals by now, so I headed over and tossed on a few logs. The flames climbed in a shower of sparks, and within a few minutes the fire was roaring again.

Fires are relaxing. I don't care who you are. It's primal: the warmth and watching the flames. It transcends "everyone." It didn't take long for me to lose myself in it, forgetting where I was for a bit. Then there was the sound of someone sitting down on the other side. I glanced up. It was Trey. He was smiling as he sat there drinking a beer.

"How're you doing?" he asked me.

I'd spoken to him before in classes, so if you were hoping for a speechless moment, sorry to disappoint. But damn, those eyes. Big and blue. What my mom called Bette Davis eyes, only on a dude.

"Okay," I answered, trying to be cool.

"How was your summer?" he asked genuinely.

"Fun. Slept a lot. You?"

"I wakeboarded all summer. It was amazing. Only one more week left though," he said, sighing.

"One more week," I echoed like an idiot, and hated myself for it.

Behind me I could hear loud talking. Strangely, I heard my name a couple times, too. I turned around to see what was going on.

Loudly, and overly animated, Beth said, "Oh, she drinks! Watch." She made eye contact with me, smiled, and said, "Think fast."

I saw her arm do a tossing motion, which usually meant something was being thrown at me. But Beth knew I had the reflexes of a no-armed blind person so she knew better then to do that. Didn't she? I only had enough time to realize she'd tossed a beer can at me before it slammed square into my nose. .

The pain was instantaneous. I gasped and stumbled backward, then pulled my hands away from my nose and looked down at my hands. Blood. A lot of it. At this point in my life, I was normally okay with the sight of my own blood. I was clumsy and accidents happen, but this was more then I'd seen in a long time. I got light-headed and stumbled, but a thick bush seemed to rear up and catch me, holding me up in some strange levitated state. My vision went fuzzy.

I was vaguely conscious of Beth, suddenly at my side. "Oh, God, I'm sorry, I'm sorry, I'm sorry!" There was laughter coming from all over. And I guess it could have been funny if you weren't the one who'd been hit. But it *had* been me, so I rolled out of the bush, away from everyone.

When I stood up I was facing Trey again. Through watery eyes I saw that he was laughing too, but when he saw I was bleeding he made a sickened face and turned away. Embarrassed and covered in blood, I pushed Beth away and ran out of the backyard.

I ran out to the street, sat down on the curb, pinched my nose, and put my head back. I'd seen it in a movie once. Not long after, someone put a hand towel on my nose and held it there. An arm wrapped around me in a tight squeeze.

"You okay?" Beth asked.

"No," I growled, muffled through the towel. I reached up and took her hand and the towel away. "How bad is it?"

She looked at me and said, "Bloody, but," and she looked closer, "doesn't look broken. So that's good, right?"

I made a sarcastic cheer with my arms.

"I'm so sorry," she whispered. Her eyes were wide. She not only sounded sincere, she sounded frightened.

"It's okay," I said. She desperately wanted her other friends to like me and vice versa. It was important to her. I loved that. I offered, "Maybe if I ran track or something, that would help." A few of her friends were runners.

"Huh?" Beth said.

"You know, so your other friends don't see me as total loser. I'd do it if you think that would help with merging the groups?"

"Can you run?" she asked, even though she knew the answer.

"No. Well, I ran from a dog once and I felt really fast while I was doing it."

"Oh, right, the big dog incident of third grade. I totally forgot about that. But wasn't the dog really, really old?" she said with a smile.

He'd also been mostly blind too, but I wasn't going to remind her of that since the running feat was already dangerously unimpressive. We sat in silence for a few seconds before I tossed out, "Cheerleader?"

All she had to do was look at me, and I laughed. We both did. But then it hurt. After a minute of solid, semipainful giggling, I took the towel off my face again. The bleeding had basically stopped, but I knew it was still all over my face and clothes. "Do I look badass?"

"Totally," she said as she helped me up. "Come on. Let's get you home and cleaned up."

CHAPTER 3
SO IT BEGINS

After the beer can incident, I stayed inside the house for the last week of summer, icing the bruising away. I told my parents the truth about what happened. Why lie? Beth had actually been looking out for me. They just nodded, and mom gave me a bag of frozen peas. Man, my parents were weird but kind of mellow and cool, too. I turned down the rare parent-paid-for clothes shopping, telling my mom I had everything I needed. Okay, *that* was a lie, but one I could live with to avoid running into anyone I knew while I still looked like a plastic surgery casualty.

By the first day of school most of the bruising was gone, and concealer basically hid the rest. You could see it if you really looked, but you really had to know it was there to even notice.

While I walked to school, it didn't surprise me to see everyone else was wearing spanking new first-day outfits. It's what you do. Not me. I wore some old friends, an old pair of jeans and a faded T-shirt. Classic, comfy, neutral. I wanted to draw as little attention to myself as possible, and this outfit could only help me do that. That was my goal for the foreseeable future. Be invisible until something embarrassing happened to someone else and they'd forgotten all about the beer to the face.

Yes, I was hoping something embarrassing would happen to someone else. I'm not above admitting that, like you're any better.

The one-mile walk was uneventful and thankfully sweat-free thanks to the cool morning. The walk home in the end of summer heat would be a different story.

Once inside, I avoided the main hallways to find my locker. I'd had some orchestra concerts here during middle school, so the place wasn't a total maze to me. Honors US History first. The history wing was on the second floor, and the only possible route was the big staircase in the middle of the school. The problem was: there was a massive open space in front of the stairs that served as the main hang-out area. If you were "everyone," you were there. If you were loosely associated with "everyone," you were trying to be there. If you were anyone else, you weren't welcome. From the outskirts, I spotted Trey and his friends, standing right in front of the bottom step, making it impossible for me to get by unnoticed.

I did get a good snigger in though. Yeah, Trey was saying hey to some older football players and looked the part, but his freshman entourage looked out of place and—could it be—uncomfortable? I was never a big fish in middle school, so being a little one again in high school wasn't

going to be much of a change for me. But I could see how
irked they all were, back at the bottom.

"Yo, Ham-bone," I heard a deep voice call out to my
right. One of the largest men I'd ever seen was waving to
some people in the main hallway. There was no way he was
a student. He looked thirty at least.

Quick as you like, I followed him. He was easily four
times wider then me and kept me shielded from view. I
was a little fish—exactly like one of those little fish you
see hanging out below a shark in nature videos, for protection. My human mountain got me to the stairs safely,
where I skirted up unnoticed.

I took my seat in the second row right in the middle of
the class. You're probably thinking: *Wait. A nerd like you
belongs in the front row, right?* Normally, you'd be spot-on,
but rumor had it that the History Teacher, Mr. Floyd, spit
when he talked. He also apparently had a third nipple,
but that's beside the point—the spit was the issue. Beth,
through her connections with "everyone," had told me
that the front row of his class was nicknamed "the splash
zone," like at Sea World. I had a thing about drool. I wasn't
germ-a-phobic, but drool rubbed me wrong. Beth knew it.
If I saw spit fly out of his mouth I'd probably gag. If any
of his spittle ever actually landed on me, I'd vomit. So I
fought my nerd instincts and took my seat in row two.

Class slowly filled in around me. I got a few head nods
and a "hey" from a girl I had Geography with in eighth
grade. When the class was all but full, Trey, of course, came
in. (Oh yeah, he was wicked smart too.) The only seat left
was right in front of me, in the middle of the splash zone.

He pretended to look around, but there wasn't a choice really. I pretended to be reading an inspirational poster on the wall to avoid eye contact. He dropped his bag and sat down in front of me just as the two-minute warning bell rang.

There was light chatter between friends all around. I just kept quiet and stared at the empty teacher's chair in the front of the room. A twist of Trey's shoulders gave me just the slightest heads up he was turning around. I focused once again on the inspirational poster on the wall, really pretending to be into it.

Leadership. Yes, a bald eagle sure does look like leadership. So majestic.

"Hey," came the quietest, sweetest voice I'd ever heard. All the anger I held toward him vanished. "Hey," he repeated.

I turned to look at him, pretending I hadn't heard him, you know, because I was so into the poster. I doubt he bought it.

"Oh, when did you sit down?" I tried to say coolly. So aloof I am.

"You have fun at the party?" he asked.

"Uh, yeah. Until . . . you know." I followed it up with, "You?"

"Awesome. Had a blast."

"Cool," I said. Man my voice sounded so high-pitched and annoying in my head. I hated the sound of my voice.

We sat there quietly for a few seconds. Had he forgotten about what happened? Or did he not recognize me? Had he been drunk? I didn't have long to dwell on it because in the most dreamy voice imaginable, he whispered, "Hey, so I've got this problem with my eyes. I can't see middle distances very well. The board's right in my blind spot. Would you mind switching with me?"

I stared into those deep blue eyes. All speckled with gold. Maybe this middle vision thing was his penance for such beauty.

"Sure." I was mesmerized. The word came forth without my knowing it.

"Great, thanks," he said.

In a daze I stood up and grabbed my bag. We slipped past each other as we swapped places. As I was sitting down reality set in. *What the hell was I doing?! The splash zone, you idiot! Middle vision? Blind spot? It's not even a good lie!* I had to switch back. I turned to him.

He smiled, his beautiful eyes flashing. Before I could say a word, his cell rang. "Hey," he answered. "No, second row, all good. Thanks for the heads up. Yeah, that would have been nasty." He hung up and put the phone back in his pocket, his eyes never leaving mine

I was too shocked to care that my mouth was wide open. I stared at him. *He knew?! He played me?! That sneaky S.O.B.* I wanted to say something. I had to say something. But of course I didn't. It's not what I did. So I just turned around, defeated.

I was vaguely aware of the sound of a door closing to my right. Then an adult called out, "Eyes up front, please." Mr. Spittle aka Mr. Floyd was walking toward his desk.

"Hope you all had nice long summers. Welcome to Honors US History."

But that's all I ever heard him say. When he hit the 's' in history, I saw it coming.

THE REST OF THE day was awful. After bolting for the bathroom, I was pushed back out into the wild, and trust me, no matter how many times you brush your teeth or no matter much gum you chew, your breath still smells like vomit. Beth even wrinkled her nose when I saw her between classes. Following her advice, I refused to speak the whole rest of the day except to say "Here" during roll call. Even then I covered my mouth. No one had actually seen me throw up, but by last period the rumors were circling and people were pointing. I bet it was Trey who ratted me out. What a turd bucket.

IT'S FUNNY HOW YOUR brain will latch on to the most mundane details when it comes to memory. I couldn't tell you anything in particular I did that last night before it happened. And there was probably nothing of note that happened anyway, but I remember everything about that last dinner with my family. The ketchup on my meatloaf kind of looked like Elvis. I remember showing my dad, who sang a little ditty *a la* the King. Mom commented it was too bad it didn't look like Jesus, because then we could sell it on eBay. We all laughed. Then my little brother successfully got me to gag when he opened his mouth like a bowl and let the dog drink gravy out of it. Like I said: drool rubs me wrong.

It had never occurred to me that I should have cherished each second. Who thinks of something like that? I wasn't a mind reader . . . yet. Just kidding. Still not a mind reader. But maybe my brain, after the fact, catalogued that dinner as something I would want to look back on. And it was right. Way to go, brain. You're tops.

After the meal I watched some TV, texted Beth that I'd do better tomorrow, brushed my teeth extra hard, and went to bed.

The last vision I have of my room is muddled. It was dark. I don't remember why I woke up, but for some reason I did. Something just didn't feel right. I sat up and looked around. I was too old to cry out for my parents, right? The moon cast shadows across my filthy room, but nothing seemed out of place. I squinted at the clock. 3:13 A.M. Whew, still plenty of time to sleep.

I took a sip of water from the glass I kept on my nightstand, took one more look around the room, and shrugged. *Must have been nothing*, I remember thinking. Nothing my ass.

The last thing I remember about my room is seeing my old USC hoodie at the foot of my bed and how comfy it looked. I started to reach for it, and that's when the blackout bag was dropped over my head and zipped tight. A hand clamped over my mouth preventing my "Hollywood horror movie worthy" scream from reaching anyone.

I struggled, but more hands pinned my arms behind my back. I kicked hard and caught one attacker in the face. If it did any damage, there was no response. My foot hurt like hell, so I hoped it had done something. In an instant, my arms and legs were zip-tied together, a gag had been forced in my mouth, and I was being carried. Screaming did no good. Only a muffled squeal made it through the gag and the hood. There is no feeling like true terror. I was choking on my own freak out.

Hadn't my parents heard something?! My mother used to check on me at night when I was young. Where was she now?! Help me please!

I kept trying to fight even though it seemed pointless.

Someone with a fed-up, whiney voice said, "Gas her." I barely had time to comprehend the words before there was nothing.

IN THE MORNING MY parents would wake up to find me gone. At first they would think I just got up early to go to school. Eight angry phone calls and ten texts later, they would give up threatening me and become frightened. They would contact the police. They would file a missing persons report. Fear would become panic. After twenty four hours *their* true terror would set in and never quite disappear. God only knows how much time they would spend looking for me. Both of my parents would develop any number of psychological and emotional issues because—regardless of what I believed—they did love me more than I could ever know.

About a month after my "disappearance" a burned body would be found in the woods about seven miles from my home. This dead girl would be unrecognizable but the teeth would identify her corpse as mine. Whoever she was (I never found out) would be the same height—similar build, similar everything. The identical teeth would be the clincher, though. There would be no point in continuing the investigation.

And thus the case of the missing person that was me would be officially closed. I was dead. Gone. Nonexistent. And thus: perfect for the task at hand.

OF COURSE, I DIDN'T know any of this at the time of my kid-napping. No, I would be told this information later when they took out four of my teeth. I asked them, "Why?" They told me about teeth-as-positive-identification and then proceeded to steal them from me. There was no malice, just stating fact.

But I'm way ahead of myself again, and that fun stuff would happen soon after I woke up. I was only justifying a tangent about what happened to my family once I was gone and, alas, I got on another tangent about teeth. I'm done here.

CHAPTER 4
MY NEW HOME

I woke up strapped to a chair by my arms and wrists wearing only a hospital gown. The room looked like the Pap smear office, only whiter and cleaner and without any free samples. I could smell the bleach that was used to keep it so spotless.

I instantly regretted my past love of horror movies because my mind suddenly filled with all of the greatest hits of the gory death scenes I'd once laughed at. They were so obviously fake. That's what made them safe. Only now, they all served as education. My brain worked overtime to come up with the most painful, disgusting death scene of all time. I tried to convince myself that this was all a really bad dream, a movie. But for some reason that bleachy smell triggered something in my head. This *wasn't* a movie or a dream. No, this was very real and very scary.

I started to hyperventilate as I struggled against my bindings. I wasn't very strong, so what I was hoping to accomplish I didn't know. But going down without a fight seemed sad. Tears poured out of my eyes. For the first, true time in my life, I was absolutely helpless.

The door slid open. It made the futuristic hiss like in sci-fi movies. In any other circumstance, I would have gotten a kick out it. But at that moment, it paralyzed me with fear. I watched, frozen, as an elderly man in a white lab coat entered. Behind him was a smaller, younger woman.

The man was holding what looked like a tablet of some sort. But it was too thin to be an iPad; besides, it was transparent—it looked like a sheet of clear glass. I could make out a picture of my face and some backward writing all around it. I saw my birthday, height, and weight before the glass went blank. Or clear, I guess is more like it.

"And how are we doing this evening?" he asked me.

It was such a casual question and asked with such honest interest that it caught me off guard. Did he not know I was just ripped from my bedroom and taken here against my will? Could he not see the bindings? My tears?

Something beeped. He looked back down at the glass, now flashing red.

"Great," he muttered sarcastically. He looked at the younger woman and asked, "Can you do this one alone?"

She nodded. He returned it with a curt nod of his own. The door hissed shut behind him.

With her short red bangs and porcelain skin, the woman looked like Beth, only older. Maybe mid-twenties. She even shied away from making direct eye contact with me like Beth did when she was about to say something that would make me mad. Only I think this girl didn't want to look at someone who was about to be [insert horrible death here]. I cried harder. I wanted to go home. I wanted my mother.

Not-Beth busied herself at a small medical fridge making much more noise than necessary. Her back was to me but I caught her looking at me through the reflection in the fridge window. Her eyes darted back to her work.

"Please help me," I begged. "Please." I didn't care that I was sobbing uncontrollably; maybe that would get a rise out of her. I knew she didn't want to turn around and face me, but I could tell she was finished with whatever she had been doing at the fridge.

After a deep breath, Not-Beth turned.

She held a metal tray with a massive syringe on it. I'd seen horse shots smaller than this one and got light-headed. My fear of needles was about to be tested to the limit.

"Please. Don't do this," I continued. "Just let me go. I won't tell anyone."

Her face was set, determined to do her duty regardless of my pleas. The syringe was filled with a jet black liquid. She took it from the tray.

"I know you can hear me. Please don't kill me," were the words I could squeeze out before the sobbing completely took over.

Not-Beth looked at the syringe. She sighed and placed the needle back down. She shifted her body slightly and then finally looked directly at me. Her eyes were green, like mine.

"I'm not trying to kill you," she said. Her voice was

surprisingly strong, considering her seemingly shy demeanor. "None of us are. You're safe here."

Safe? I felt anything but safe.

"Why are you doing this?" I asked.

"That's not my place to say. You'll find out soon enough."

"But . . ."

She made the slightest of eye motions toward the corner and whispered, "There's always someone watching, listening."

My panicked eyes flashed over her shoulder, focusing on a small camera pointing right at us. She quietly continued, "I can't tell you what you want to know. Not now."

She picked up the needle again.

"What is that?" I asked.

"There's a technical term for it. But *we* call it fire."

"Why?" I asked.

"You're about to find that out," she said.

I turned my head as she slid the giant needle into my arm. Searing pain surged through me on contact, intensifying the farther into my blood stream it went. I tried to scream but the torture was too much. I clenched my jaw. Time slowed to a standstill.

"I'm sorry. You'll understand soon enough." Not-Beth left, and outside the door I heard her say, "She's ready. Take her to her room."

Two beefy guards unstrapped me from the chair. I wanted to fight them off and run. But there was only agony. My body began to vibrate and spasm. Whatever she'd injected continued to spread in waves. Each new jolt of pain was more excruciating than the previous. I felt like I was burning alive from the inside out. *Fire.* The word echoed through my head. Not-Beth had lied to me, I was sure of it. This was how it was going to end.

When the two guards plopped me into a wheelchair, I let them, though every touch felt like hot coals on my skin.

I wondered where they were taking me. Was this the plan all along? Inject me with some poison and then take bets on how long I'd live? It couldn't be long. I kept waiting to black out but never did.

They pushed me through a maze of hallways and into at least two elevators. Even thinking seemed to hurt now. I could hear the unmistakable sound of others, all around me, crying in pain. It filled my ears. I tried to shut it all out. I closed my eyes. I mentally began to say goodbye to my life. My family, my friends. It was over.

And then I was being lifted out of the chair by the guards. Their hands like hot pokers on my skin. I opened my eyes as I was carried into a dark room. I couldn't make out anything particular since the lights were off. All I remember is they laid me down on what felt like a bed and left.

THE DING OF AN alarm woke me up. Whether I'd fallen asleep or passed out, I couldn't remember. I didn't have to open my eyes to know that there wasn't hope; it wasn't all a bad dream. The blanket and pillow didn't feel right, smell right. I wasn't home.

At least I wasn't dead, which I took as a small victory.

I opened my eyes and found myself staring at a gray cinderblock wall. All at once I was energized, panicked again. I jumped to my feet and ran across a cold linoleum floor toward the door. I banged on it as hard as I could, screaming for help, fresh tears falling. But the rush of activity made me dizzy and I stumbled back to the bed and sat down on the edge. My whole body was sore but I didn't feel like I was burning alive anymore. I had scabs on my palms from where my nails had dug in. Lovely.

I took a look around at my new digs. A single ceiling light illuminated the room, *my* room. Not-Beth had called it my room, but let's be honest here. It was ten foot by ten foot, tops. Cinderblock walls painted asylum gray, a tiny bed, a toilet-sink combo where the sink sits above the toilet water tank, and a desk. All of this does not a "room" make. I'd seen enough TV to know a prison cell when I saw one. So why was I in prison?

Folded neatly on the desk was a stack of yellow clothes. Realizing I was still wearing a hospital gown and nothing else, clothes seemed like a good idea. I slowly stood up on sore, wobbly legs and crossed my room to the overly fluorescent yellow pile.

Strangely, at that moment, all I could think of was how horrible I looked in yellow. I had jet black hair with orange freckles and I rarely saw the sun. Yellow and I were not pals but bitter fashion enemies. But since I was cold and being practically naked was uncomfortable, I began to get dressed. On the plus side, there was no mirror to be found.

Yellow underwear. Yellow sports bra. Yellow shorts and tank top. And a nice set of yellow warm-up pants with (you guessed it) a yellow jacket. Even the socks and shoes were yellow. I looked like a giant French's mustard bottle.

Clothed and warm, I felt slightly safer. I brushed my teeth with an unlabeled tube of toothpaste and tried to break through the tangles in my hair with a generic brush, but I lost that battle. With nothing else to do, I sat back down on my bed just trying to keep it together. The down comforter sank around me. I wanted to curl up and shut down again, but something told me not to. Something told me to be aware, to be ready.

My ears hummed from the silence. I tried to think of a single reason for what had happened to me and how it would end. But I couldn't. So I stared at the door doing what I do best, zoning out. There I was, Ms. Mustard, a broken human clock ticking toward something truly horrible. What that was, I didn't know. I just knew I wanted to be ready when it came.

"Good morning, I hope you slept well."

The smooth male voice came from nowhere, from everywhere. I snapped out of the haze and jumped to my feet.

"Who's there?!!?" I shouted.

It was a silly question.

"I see the clothes fit well. Good."

I looked around for the source. My eyes spotted a small speaker in the ceiling above the door, placed next to an even tinier camera, focused right on me. They'd probably watched me change. Violated again.

"Hello?" I called out. "Please, help me."

Mr. Speakervoice continued, "I am sure you are bursting with questions, my dear, most of which will be answered now."

Directly to my left a cinder block slid out from the wall like a dresser drawer and stopped. Inside, resting on velvety black fabric, was what looked like a pair of clear plastic sunglasses.

"The answers to all of your questions will be found when you put those on. We'll speak again once you are finished. Hurry along now, there's no time to waste."

Eager for answers, I didn't think much past getting them. I didn't wonder if this was a test. I wanted to now what the hell was going on. Besides, if they had wanted to kill me they would have done so by now. The injection had proved that. I got up, walked over to the wall, and picked up the glasses. They seemed to have no weight to them whatsoever. I raised them to my face and put them on.

I CAN'T DO THE experience justice. It was like watching eight different movies all at the same time, and at one hundred times the speed. But strangely, when it was finished, I somehow understood everything I had seen and knew exactly where I was and why. Overwhelmed, I pulled the glasses off and managed to stumble back to my bed before completely losing my balance and eating it onto the mattress. As I fought the nausea, I began processing what I had learned. I took comfort in the knowledge that they really *weren't* going to [insert circumstances of my horrible murder here].

Because the irony? The best bit of info I got from those super specs was that apparently I was dead. Or, I guessed, would have been soon. Had I not been so rudely taken from my bed I would have died shortly thereafter. How did

I know this? How did they know this? Because my grave said so, silly.

IN 1992, A HOTSHOT NASA scientist designed a satellite that was supposed to be able to take super high resolution photos of whatever part of the Earth it happened to be over at the time. We're talking read-the-paper-from-space close-ups here. Anyway, the satellite took the photo of whatever it was pointed at all right, but the pictures were not of the present. The pictures that were taken were of 2042.

Minds were blown, jaws dropped, large bonus checks were given out, yada, yada, yada. And with the ability to see the world fifty years in future, they knew *who* was important, *who* was not, and, in my case, *who* was dead. In 2042, my gravestone said I died when I was fourteen. Thus I was volunteered for what was named the Shadow Program.

As terrifying as my new reality was, all locked up here against my will, I guess it was better than death, right? And I wasn't alone, which was comforting. The moans and groans I had heard the night before were from hundreds of other fourteen-year-olds who, like me, would have been dead had we not been taken.

Every year a fresh batch of the not-quite-dead-yet were snatched for training to protect the future leaders of tomorrow. We would make sure those leaders remained as safe as possible while still living the lives that would define them, that would shape them into whoever they were to become that was so damn important. We would be trained to be their protectors. To shadow their every move and breath. To keep things simple, probably, we were called Shadows.

Now don't get me wrong: understanding one's situation and accepting it is not the same thing. But with the other option being death, even a crappy situation like this is a step up.

I was now at the official headquarters of the Shadow Program, a facility known as the F.A.T.E. Center. The acronym stood for Future Affairs Training and Education. It was beyond classified, beyond secret. It was *unknown*, even among intelligence agencies like the CIA. Only heads-of-state and their most inner circle knew, the kind of people who could shuffle funds around. The entire operation was funded by them, by every major government in the world. All had agreed that the future had to be protected. All were willing to not only pay in cash, but also to allow the periodic kidnapping of soon-to-be-dead teens for the program.. The price you pay for the future safety of your best and brightest.

To make sure no government held sway over the program, a new international agency was created. This agency had no allegiance to any country and answered to no one but its members. Donor governments had collapsed since its founding, but the agency remained. It was unique in world history, its own entity. An extremely powerful one at that.

With nothing else to do, I lied there in my bed, working through the information dump. Man, I wish I'd known my old life would end. My texting record seemed a rather colossal waste of time now. I should have gone for 1000. I also didn't like that my life was suddenly not my own.

But the worst part about it was that there was no escape, except maybe dying (again). There wasn't even a whiff of hope, the dream that some super-secret group could find me and free me. This *was* the super-secret group. It was the end of the line.

"Feeling better?" asked my old friend Mr. Speakervoice. "Now please sit up and listen carefully to what I am about to say."

I shot the camera a go-f***-yourself glance before I sat up. I knew they weren't going to kill me, so maybe that's why I suddenly felt braver then I should have.

He continued, "Precisely thirty seconds after I am finished speaking, the door to your room will open. Please exit and follow the markers toward the Echo room. The correct path will be obvious. Do not stray off course or attempt to escape. Any deviation from the path will result in severe punishment. Chin up, back straight. You have nothing to fear if you behave."

The door slid open.

I knew I should stand. But my body was unwilling or unable to move. Then I saw something. Someone. A boy.

He was much taller than me but dressed in the same lovely, stylish yellow. It didn't look too terrible against his tan skin and blonde hair. He moved down the hallway, too afraid or too focused, so he didn't give me a second glance. He was followed by another boy, and then another. A girl, petite and gerbil-like, soon followed them. She looked scared out of her mind, like me. Her eyes connected with mine for a half-second, but she scampered on. I wanted to will myself to stand but my body was not cooperating. What would happen if I never got up? Could I just go home? As if reading my mind, a hulking figure in black police riot gear stepped in front of my door. In his right hand he held a baton. That was all it took. Finally on my feet, I urged myself to walk. I approached the door one small step at a time.

His muffled voice said, "Good choice." He then strode off down the hall.

Flashing rows of soft green lights were telling me to go left and follow the others. But every fiber in my being was telling me to go right. Following the lights meant admitting that I was supposed to be here. Heading against the lights represented the chance of going home. *They're wrong*, I told myself. *You aren't supposed to be here.* I had to try, didn't I?

A yellow blur sprinted past me, heading in the opposite direction. A fairly large boy in total panic mode. He ran like a child, reckless and awkward. I wanted to join him, and others were pausing to watch him go. You could tell they had the same thought.

WHAM!

From behind a doorway a metal baton slammed into his chest, hitting him so hard he did a complete backflip. Unseen hands dragged his limp body from the hall and the door hissed shut.

Needless to say, the thoughts of fleeing vanished. Maybe that was the point of such a brutal display. Maybe it had been planned; maybe the boy had been planted here to do it. Either way, it worked. The door to my room slid shut behind me.

No one spoke as we walked. I wondered what they were feeling. My legs shook with every step. It took most of my concentration not to fall over, but I managed to keep upright and moving. I guessed there were at least twenty kids in front of me and another twenty behind me. But who knew how many more there were, in how many other hallways, on how many levels?

But there was no point in wondering anything. I followed the flashing lights toward wherever and whatever this Echo room was.

CHAPTER 5

WELCOME TO YOUR NEW LIFE

The long walk helped calm my mind down. They weren't going to kill me if I obeyed. I was going to be okay. The realization didn't quite rid me of all my fear, but it did help me relax a little.

A pair of massive double doors hissed open on a cavernous room, bigger and more intimidating than anything I'd expected. Wall to wall it was probably 500 feet across. Giant, and I mean *giant*, LCD screens adorned the walls like wallpaper. Satellite images, news displays, and an array of global camera feeds flooded the monitors. The entire place was pitch black, save for the screens and what looked like hundreds of little half-bubbles hovering about eight feet off the ground. Each bubble shot a perfect three-foot circle of blinding white light on the floor. Within each circle was a name. Our names. Or so I presumed when I saw mine.

I noticed that the first boy, the blonde I'd spotted in

line, was cautiously tiptoeing his way under one of the strange bubbles to my right. The name read Junie Miller. I think a lot of people were watching his progress with interest. This Junie kid was a lot braver than any of the rest of us, for sure.

I don't know what we expected to happen to him. I know I was half-expecting blow darts to come screaming down from some exotic booby trap above like in a treasure-hunting movie. But without incident Junie stepped right into his circle of light. As if confirming his identity, the light changed from blinding white to a mellow blue.

I looked around as the rest of the mustard army followed his lead and began to find their places. Our names were arranged alphabetically by surname—at least those in the alphabet I recognized. Every language of the world seemed to be represented. It was easy to lose your place.

Rennes Sharpe.

I closed my eyes and stepped in.

"Well done, Ren" said Mr. Speakervoice.

How he knew my nickname was a bit unnerving, but then again, should I have been surprised given the circumstances? Not really. I opened my eyes. The soft blue light had turned my drab yellow outfit a nice green. Go primary color wheel. *Wait, was the internal joke I just made a telltale sign I was coming to grips with it all?*

"I told you there was nothing to fear." His familiar voice was almost comforting.

I looked up into the bubble. I had seen the poor man's version of this at a local electronics store. I glanced around to see the other kids looking up and quickly realized that

Mr. Speakervoice was cheating on me. He was speaking with the others, too. It was pathetic, I know, but I felt a little pang. I really was just another calf for the slaughter and not unique at all. My guardian angel, looking out for me and guiding me, was a glorified Speak & Spell.

"Please wait patiently while the others find their places. You're doing very well."

My legs were still shaking from nerves. I tried to keep still but suddenly I lost my balance and took a big step to my left to keep from falling. Half of me was suddenly outside the bubble. There was nothing but silence outside of it, but almost instantaneously my cool blue light turned red—

Pain.

Electricity shot up into my feet and through my body, riveting me to the floor. I tried to jump back but I was frozen like a statue. Five seconds passed, maybe ten (though it seemed a heck of a lot longer), and it stopped. I immediately stepped back under my bubble, and the light returned to blue.

"I'm sorry, I'm sorry," I whispered to anyone and no one.

I looked around, expecting that hulking guard to come pummel me with his baton, or worse yet, for them to crank up the power on whatever shocked me. But it didn't happen.

Mr. Speakervoice said, "Please do not leave your assigned spot, Ms. Sharpe. The consequences won't be so pleasant next time."

And then I saw it. We all did.

In walked that boy who had tried to run. My stomach bottomed out at the sight of him. Streaks of blood came out of his right ear, both nostrils, and his bottom lip. His left eye was swollen completely shut. He walked gingerly, not necessarily with a pronounced limp, but as if his whole body hurt, as if every step was agony.

He didn't have far to go to reach his light, but it seemed as if it took him hours to get there. At one point he fell. A few lights suddenly turned red and I knew that a few more of my fellow prisoners were experiencing the lovely jolt I was now familiar with. Silly kids, trying to help someone. But I learned something. Sympathy was not tolerated here. The beaten boy picked himself up and eventually made it to his space. All the lights were now blue. Three hundred or so walking dead, ready and waiting.

Like a school of fish we were all facing the same direction, even though no clear "front" of the room had ever been established. Normally, I would have turned a different direction just to be unusual, but I was already on the "tried to leave her bubble" list. So with all of the little fish bundled together, the only question in my mind was: where are the sharks?

A spotlight illuminated a man standing in front of us. *Had he been there this whole time?* He wore a military type combat outfit—fatigues, boots, some armor—that I would later learn had no distinguishing connection to any of the major armed forces. Obviously. He looked especially dangerous and impressive compared to the frightened tweens that made up his mustard army.

His head slowly swept the room, taking us in. Then he spoke.

"Have a seat."

His voice was surprisingly warm yet still had a tinge of "don't fuck with me." Serial killers, I've since learned, seem to have the same type of skill. Before my brain could ask *"Sit where?"*, blocks rose up from the floor behind each one of us. My legs welcomed the relief of it. The blocks were hard and cold, but it was nice to be sitting.

"I first want to apologize for what you've been put through. I understand it has been, and probably still is, the most frightening experience of your life. And I'm not foolish enough to think that a glorified slide show has earned your trust. But please believe me when I say you have nothing to fear here. You are the special ones, and we are only here for you. I am Lt. Colonel Shane, and I will be overseeing your training at F.A.T.E."

He began to walk among us, making eye contact with everyone he passed. His boots clomped against the hard floor.

"You will be tested here beyond the limits of your mental and physical abilities, challenged like never before. You *will* hate us. You *will* want nothing more than to hurt us, maybe even kill us. We don't take it personally."

He paused next to a younger-looking Asian girl and gently touched her on the shoulder as if to emphasize the last part. It seemed way too rehearsed.

"We understand none of this has been or will be easy for any of you. But you have been chosen for something noble, something beyond all of us. In time you will understand this and accept it."

He gave a large boy an encouraging nod and a slap on

the shoulder, as if to say *I know you're already there, champ.*
The boy gave a slight smile. This Shane guy was good.

"A lot of you are probably thinking there's been a mistake."

Now he was speaking my language. *Where's the exit for satellite error?* I squeezed my eyes closed, imagining being allowed to go home.

"Ms. Sharpe. Am I boring you?"

I opened my eyes. My light was no longer a soft blue but bright white again. *Gulp.* I looked to my right. He was there, right beside me.

"Am I?" he asked.

I shook my head. "No. Sorry . . . sir." I added the "sir" at the last moment. It seemed appropriate.

He stepped closer to me, his black combat boots skirting the edge of my light zone. His nose was slightly crooked, obviously broken a few times. He also had a scar across his forehead I hadn't been able to see earlier. "Well, what has you so preoccupied?"

Was I being given the opportunity to ask anything I wanted? I wanted to ask about my family and if I could go home. I wanted to tell him I was still terrified and that they were wrong about me. I wanted him to promise me they weren't going to hurt me. But I didn't want to look weak in front of my new peers. I'd been weak my whole life and look where it had gotten me. No, I wanted to look tough, smart, and totally accepting of the situation. Someone everybody could count on. Ren Sharpe, everybody's buddy and one tough cookie. So I asked something I felt a lot of us were wondering.

"Why was I given that shot last night?"

"That's an excellent question, Ms. Sharpe," he said. "Never hesitate to ask questions or say what's on your mind here." He smirked, and I knew he understood there was a lot more I had really wanted to say. "The shot you were given is called "fire." It is a drug you will be given every night after training, so get used to it. Over time it will kill all of the nerve endings in your body until you feel no pain." He turned and looked at an Indian girl next to me and said, "If you do not feel pain, then there is nothing left to fear but death." He grinned before continuing, "And all of you are already dead.

The treatment cycle takes four years to complete."

My stomach bottomed out. Had I heard that right? I thought this whole thing would take a month or two tops. Four years was an eternity. Four years from now, I should be starting college somewhere, high school already behind me . . .

I now understood why people in court hung their heads when told the length of a prison sentence. It absolutely defeats you. That was me. That was us. The Defeated. We may have been saved from death but would this really be any better? On the bright side, with a shot of fire coming every night my fear of needles would be quickly snuffed out. Silver lining, anyone?

Shane turned toward me and asked, "Anything else on your mind?"

Before I could stop myself I blurted out, "Where to begin?"

To my surprise, he chuckled. A few others in the room

did too but only after they heard him. He spread out his arms as he graciously said, "I'm all yours, Ms. Sharpe. Begin where you see fit."

I paused, deciding which of the numerous questions racing through my head I should ask. I'd already asked a question to look tough, now I wanted to ask one to show I was a thinker too. Brawny, yet brainy.

"Why do you need us?" I asked. He gave me a look that showed he thought I was an idiot, so I elaborated. "No, I mean, I know *why* we're here; I just don't see the point. Down the road these people are important, the satellite shows this. But if they didn't have us protecting them before, why do they need us now? And what are we protecting them from?"

Shane nodded. "The world is a cruel and unpredictable place, Ms. Sharpe. It's ever-changing, creating new threats and removing old ones. Something minor that happens in one place can have ripple effects thousands of miles away. These threats are unavoidable, tied up with the nature of time itself. It will be your job to stand in the way of them. And also, who's to say we are the only ones with knowledge of the future? Would you agree that others may not be as honorable with that knowledge?"

I swallowed. That actually hadn't occurred to me.

There was a soft but audible ding that seemed to come from all over.

"That is all the time we have today," he said. "Thank you for your patience. Thank you for your sacrifice. Good luck." And with that he took his place directly in front of us.

A new light shone down on a hard-nosed, drill instructor. He barked, "Do not move until directed!"

From above I heard Mr. Speakervoice say, "When your light is extinguished, you are to exit through the designated door. Do not attempt to leave before then. Best of luck over the next four years, Ren Sharpe. I'm rooting for you."

You suck, Mr. S, I thought. I bet he was some Hollywood voice guy who had no real idea what his work was for. He collected a fat check and ate avocados all day long.

Across the room a door opened. Randomly, fifteen bubble lights turned off. Those under the lights began to move.

Soon enough, my light went off. *So, the first day of the rest of my life, huh?* The open door for me was directly in front of everyone, behind Shane. My legs barely had the strength to stand up, and the walk toward the door was slow. As I passed Shane he gave me a grin and a nod before whispering, "Have fun."

CHAPTER 6
LET'S HOLD HANDS, NOT GRUDGES

I entered a hallway and followed the other kids. We ended up in a room about the size of a tennis court with white padded walls and floors as soft as a yoga mat. Half of me laughed. Maybe I had really lost my mind, and this was the mental institution room I was stuck in. The other half saw a group of seventeen yellow-clad kids all standing together in a white room and thought we all looked like bath ducks.

On my left was Junie Miller, that tall blond boy, the first one of us to dare enter a bubble. He had already proven himself to be much braver than I was. I wanted to hate him for it. But when I glanced up at him he caught my eye, shrugged, and gave me a "well, we're really in it now, aren't we?" look. It was the perfect combination of goofy and serious and sad and lost. He also made me do what I never thought I would again: smile.

He whispered out of the corner of his mouth, "I'm Junie."

I whispered back, "I'm Ren."

"Cool name," he responded.

"No, it isn't," I said.

"Better than mine. Mine's like a hillbilly who can't say June," he said. Then in a thick hick accent, "Ma' name's Joonee."

I almost laughed again. Okay, this Junie kid was all right. He could be my wingman anytime. Totally bro hug with fist bumps on a flight deck. I saw that no one else seemed to be talking to anyone and I caught a few of the others sending us dirty looks.

Was I a cool kid?

"Oh my God," I heard Junie say, and I snapped out of it. "Did you just zone out? Can you pay attention to anything for more than three seconds?"

I scowled. "My mother always said find what you're good at and stick with it. I'm really good at getting distracted and lost in my own awesome inner monologue."

His smile widened, revealing a dimple. "You're gonna get me in trouble, aren't you?"

"I'm pretty good at that too," I said. I was trying not to smile back. This place was not for smiling. I felt a little tingle in my stomach. *What the hell are you doing?* I thought. *He's messing with you. Snap out of it, Sharpe. Get your head in the game.* But I couldn't. I guessed if I was running the gauntlet of emotions why not let this one have a shot too? Even if he was messing with me it was so much better than anything else I'd felt in so long. I didn't have the will to squash it. But I didn't see the need, either.

Strangely, that was easily been the best conversation I'd

had with a boy my entire life. I'd been witty and aloof, too. Why had talking to him been so easy? I had never been able to do this before so why now? Why here? What had changed?

"Your attention!" shouted a whiny and oddly familiar voice.

A wiry, long-haired, pasty guy with a rat face appeared from a hidden door. He had two blackened eyes and what looked like a recently broken nose. Crooked noses seemed to be a reoccurring theme around here. I instinctively touched mine. I liked my nose. I vowed to do my best to keep my sniffer straight.

Thinking of noses reminded me of something. I vividly remember kicking someone in the face . . .

"Line up over there," the man squeaked.

My heart thudded. No doubt: it was the same voice I had heard snap, "Drug her!" Fan-freaking-tastic. He motioned to where Junie and I were standing and the others quickly lined up along with us to our left. I was at the end. My stomach was full of butterflies again. Big ones.

The man walked to the far end (*so I would be last*, I couldn't help but think) and began to move down the line. He took a good look at each faces as he passed. "My name is Cole. I will be your instructor. I will do my best to train you but many of you will fail to make it through the program. You will succumb to the pain of fire and break mentally, or the injuries you sustain will render you unfit to continue." He sounded like he didn't want to be here, that this was some sort of demotion and he was being punished.

When he finally reached me he smiled. His breath smelled like cat food. "And some of you will die."

I blinked. *Did he just threaten me? Seriously? What happened to all that you're-safe-here crap that Shane had promised?*

He stared at me. I wanted to apologize for what I'd done. But the more I thought about it, it didn't make sense. Wasn't it better that I had fought? That I wasn't completely useless? That even if it wasn't much, I had some fight in me?

"But we will do our best to avoid that."

He turned and marched away. A block rose from the floor behind him, and he took a seat. With a glance at the biggest girl in the room, he said, "Katie Jones, please step forward."

Katie took three shaky steps forward and stopped. Unsure what to do she stared at the ground, a solid technique I'd used many a time myself, but it leads to zoning out, so use it with caution.

"Ren Sharpe, please step forward," he commanded.

I had been expecting it. But that didn't mean I responded. I was glued to the floor. My mind was telling me to step forward, but my legs wanted no part of the action.

"Now," he said in a tone that gave me goosebumps.

I swallowed hard, took a deep breath, and managed a wobbly lurch so that I was in line with Katie.

"Turn and face each other," he said.

I turned to face Katie, and she me. She had a light scar on her jaw and a small piece of her ear was missing. A dog bit her as a kid maybe? Who knows? But otherwise she was a cute girl. I wondered how she was judging me at that moment. Probably checking out the freckles. Everyone stared at those.

"Bow to each other," Cole said.

Katie and I shared a confused look.

"Formalities should always be followed," he added, but he sounded bored.

We bowed. Why not?

Cole smiled. "Good. Now fight until one of you is unconscious."

Huh? I froze, still half-bowed, not quite sure I had heard right. I blinked at Katie, whose lip was quivering. Her eyes widened. We turned to Cole. His smile hardened. "Is there a problem here, ladies? I'm not joking. Fight. Now."

I looked back at Junie for support, but he only shook his head, as frightened as we were.

"Now!" Cole spat.

I had never been in any kind of fight, ever, and judging by Katie's non-reaction she wasn't too eager to obey Cole either. So unless Cole's idea of fighting was a brutal stare-off he was going to be sorely disappointed by this contest. Given my new occupation, I got that physical confrontation was something we should be ready for, so the idea of having to train for it was understood. But I figured a fight-off like this would only be appropriate after some extensive training, right? Not day one type stuff. Did Mr. S. know about this?

Cole stood up and glared at the two of us. Then he did something I don't think anyone expected. He reached behind his back, pulled out a gun, and pointed it first at Katie then at me.

"Fight or I'll kill one of you," he said.

I froze, terrified. If you've never had a loaded gun pointed at you, be happy. It's not a pleasant experience. Combine that with a death threat from someone whose nose you'd broken. But this was only a scare tactic, right? How would killing either of us make any sense? It would be stupid and defeat the whole purpose. He couldn't be serious. *We'll be safe here as long as we obey—*

BANG!

Katie crumpled to the ground.

Crimson blood began to pool around her lifeless body. I stopped breathing. This couldn't be real. It was a trick, an illusion. I looked at Cole. His eyes were blank behind the wisp of smoke still creeping out of the barrel of the gun.

Now here is something that I've never told anyone. To my fellow snatched tweens it looked like I charged Cole, ready to attack him for what he'd done. But the truth is that I knew that somewhere behind him was the hidden door. It was that simple. I wanted out of that room. My only thought was to run. It was pure panic, nothing more. I never told the truth to anyone because after that they all thought I was some crazy brave girl. It gave me a dangerous reputation I would carry through my time at the center, a certain level of totally undeserved respect.

So here I was, charging Cole (wink). His eyes narrowed as I barreled toward him, and he looked confused, then oddly amused. The last thing I remember before everything went black is Cole's grinning face. That, and terrible pain.

Waking up after passing out was becoming a regular thing in my life now. It was strange that I had been knocked out more times in the past twenty-four hours than I'd brushed my teeth.

I was back in a hospital gown and lying in a pretty comfy bed, but my head was killing me. I guess you can't lose consciousness without consequences. I'd only been drunk once when Beth's older sister had given us some gin so my hangover experiences were limited, but this seemed pretty similar. Curtains were pulled around me, but I could hear other people out there. Moans of pain and anguish, mostly. There was also hushed chatter, the beeping of machines, and someone snoring not too far away, but mostly it was agony. I saw the shadow of a pushcart pass my curtains.

I took a deep breath but choked. My throat was killing me from where I think Cole had rammed his knee. It was all a little fuzzy. His sadistic smile popped into my head. And then, just as suddenly, Katie's face was all I could think about. I remembered her confused face as she looked at me, then the image of her body. I could feel her warm blood spray across my face. Here came the waterworks. I tried to be quiet about it, but everything I'd been fighting since minute one of my kidnapping came pouring out. I was a blubbering mess. The scales had tipped; I was no longer in control of my emotions. I covered my head with my pillow to muffle the sounds, but that did very little.

"Are you okay?" came a soft, sweet voice.

"Yes," I barely choked out.

There was a snort of laughter. I tried to collect myself

and was able to control my gasping and sniffling, but the tears kept coming. *Better than nothing.* I removed the pillow, expecting to see a nurse, or maybe even Not-Beth. I was not expecting to see Katie's face grinning back at me.

CHAPTER 7
BACK FROM THE DEAD

A sniffled and shocked, "What?" was all I could muster.

Katie arched an eyebrow. She was actually quite pretty when not confused, terrified, and dead on the floor.

"May I?" she asked and motioned toward my bed.

I nodded and scooted over. She sat next me, and we looked at each other for a moment.

"Those aren't for me, are they?" she asked pointing at the tears.

"Not all of them," I said as I sat up. "I saw you die. Am I imagining this?"

"Ha. No, I'm really here. Never assume you know everything in this place," she said. "That was part of my final test."

She pulled down the collar of her own gown to show a strange, hard patch to the right of her heart.

"Show no fear in a situation that could mean death," she said. Her eyes twinkled. "I passed!"

"Does it hurt?"

"No. Fire acted pretty quickly on me. Been pain-free for about six months now. But feeling no pain and having no fear aren't quite the same thing. This showed I was capable of both."

She looked around the room before muttering "I won't miss this, that's for sure." She glanced back at me. "They said you charged Cole after he shot me? Gutsy. Stupid, but gutsy."

Remember that lie I mentioned earlier? When I nodded it began right then and there.

"What happens now?" I asked.

"I wait to be linked to my FIP," she said.

"FIP?" I asked.

"Sorry, slang for who we're assigned to. Our Future Important Person, F-I-P."

Then in a mocking, highbrow voice she added, "*Individuals whose safety and protection are essential to the welfare of the human race* is such a mouthful. So *we*," she motioned between the two of us, "call them FIPs. It's easier. We made T-shirts."

I made a mental note to remember this useful windfall of hip so I could share it with Junie and the others to enhance my rep.

"How long will getting your FIP take?" I asked.

"Could be tomorrow, could be a year," she said flatly. "No one knows. Hope it's soon though. I want to get linked and get out of this place."

"What do you mean by linked?"

"When you get your FIP, you're linked to them. It's hard

to explain. Their safety becomes more important to you than anything else on the planet. Make sense?"

I shrugged, "Kind of."

"You don't really know what it's like unless you've it done, which I haven't." She shrugged her shoulders. "How are *you* feeling?"

She had kind eyes, but you could tell they'd been through a lot and had barely come out the other side.

"Fine," I lied.

"Riiiight," she said sarcastically. "Trust me I've been there."

"I hurt everywhere. Happy?" I said.

"Beyond," she said with a grin. "Thirsty?"

There was a glass of water on a nightstand to my left. I started to reach for it, but Katie reached across and got it first. Her movement was fast, almost unnaturally so. Curious, I took the glass from her.

"A pleasant side affect of fire," she said. "Since your body knows it will never feel pain, there's no hesitation on movements anymore. Makes you faster than you were before."

I drained the water. *When was the last time I'd eaten or drunk anything?* My stomach gave a growl. Katie took the glass and put it back. I really watched her this time. The movement was faster-than-normal enough to be notice-able, but not fast enough to raise suspicion.

Knowing I was watching, she smiled. "Now you keep taking your medicine and you'll be just like me."

I gave a light laugh. There was the clang of a tray being dropped nearby. Katie stiffened, alert and ready. There was something about her that sent a shiver down my spine. She was no longer my older confidante. The façade was over, and the look on her face was that of a stone-cold killer. Realizing her mask had fallen away, she quickly joked, "Looks like you'll probably take my place as the regular here."

"Let's hope not."

She took a deep breath as she absentmindedly touched her wound.

"I thought you said it didn't hurt?"

"It doesn't. It itches," she said. A few seconds of silence passed before she announced, "I better get going."

"Please don't go," I said, fighting fresh tears. I didn't know this girl; I didn't trust her. But she gave me hope, like maybe I could actually get through this. I didn't want to be alone again.

"No. Stop that," she scolded, as if I were a child. "You can't do that anymore. Not here. The girl you were can't survive here. She won't make it. You need to become someone else."

"Okay." I sniffed and wiped my eyes.

She held my hand and whispered, "I'm trying to give you advice I wish someone had given me." She gently let go before continuing, "But I gotta get going. They're moving me to new quarters while I wait to be linked." Her eyes twinkled again. "I get to have a TV and a radio. Man, I miss TV."

When she reached the edge of the curtain she turned. "They'll try everything they can to break you. They'll hurt you. Threaten you. Threaten your friends. The worst of anything and everything you can imagine. Don't let them win. If you believe you can get through it, you will. Good luck. Maybe we'll bump into each other in the world."

And with that she turned and slipped past the curtain.

I WAS TO STAY in the hospital wing that night for observation. I didn't argue. For dinner I was given some kind of mush that "had everything I needed in it." It tasted like grits, which means it tasted like dirt. Halfway through the bowl one of the nurses snuck a pinch of cinnamon on it which helped immensely. It was a small gesture, but I appreciated it. From then on the search for and barter of spices for our breakfasts and dinners of mush would become a fun distraction from our other everyday activities. The nurses always had the best stuff.

As I was dozing off, Not-Beth returned for my nightly dose of fire. I thought being in the hospital would get me a night off. Silly me.

I WAS AWAKENED THE next morning by a nurse and told to get dressed. Sitting up proved difficult. I was sore from the fire, and from Cole's abuse. Finally vertical, I found a nicely washed pile of yellow sitting on the stool next to the bed. Stupid yellow. This place sucked.

Since I'd spent the night in the hospital, I got to eat my breakfast there instead of my room. Today's mush was seasoned with rosemary. When the nurse came to take my clean bowl she dropped a twisted-up baggie full of rosemary on my bed and winked as she left. Big fan of that one.

Fully dressed and fed, I was instructed to return to training. On my way out

I saw others like me. Most were nursing minor injuries, cuts and bruises, that sort of thing. Others weren't so lucky. One kid had his lower body in a cast. I passed one girl who was missing what looked like half of her face. What little skin remained was charred black. She stared at her hands, lost and alone.

I couldn't place the location, but somewhere I could hear wailing. At the time I had no clue what it was, but later found out that behind the hospital wing was where you went if you broke and completely lost it. The wails were the animal cries from those whose minds were gone. If you went in, you never came back out. A lot of people I would come to know and call friends never did. I still want to believe that they eventually recovered and got to lead normal lives. But why believe a lie?

I hurried the rest of the way out. The door slid open. I was at the end of a hall with nowhere to go but straight. As I approached my first intersection I got nervous. I had no clue where I was, or where the room I was supposed to be in was either. How would I know where to go? If I got lost would they think I was trying to escape and punish me? Or would I become some hallway hobo, begging for help? The image of myself in tattered yellow rags popped into my head and made me laugh. But to my very pleasant surprise, when I reached the intersection a green light softly pulsated on the hallway wall leading left with a pleasant *ding*.

Left it is. At the next intersection my good friend the

green light and his trusty companion *ding* told me to keep going straight. Four left turns, two rights, one elevator ride, and who knows how many keep-on-truckin' straights later, brought me to a door with no windows. I knew I had to go inside, but the idea was like a punch in the gut. My eyes began to tear up, but then I remembered Katie. *Not here. Not anymore.*

I triggered the sensor on the door and it slid open in front of me.

Cole was holding some boy down with a move that looked way too familiar. The bruises on my arm and throat tingled. But there was no malice in Cole. It looked like, could it be, he was instructing? My appearance was met with a grin; it was not comforting.

"Welcome back, Ren," he said. "Come inside."

My eyes immediately found Junie and we shared a smile, both happy to see the other was okay. Four long nail marks were visible across his neck but otherwise he looked fine, especially when compared to the others. They looked like the bruised and battered survivors of the zombie apocalypse. The shooting of Katie and my quick dispatch had worked. Nothing like the threat of a bullet to motivate you. Everyone had fought when told to and fought hard.

I started to take my place with the others, Junie was scooting over, but I stopped when Cole said, "No, no. Stay where you are, Ren." That grin again. "How are you feeling today? No lingering injuries?"

I shook my head and said as nonchalantly as I could, "I'm fine. Tip-top." I didn't want him to think he could hurt me. Big mistake.

Cole smiled wider. "Excellent to hear. I was afraid you'd be unable to complete your assignment from yesterday. But since you're 'tip-top' . . . you still owe me a fight."

He helped the other boy up; a hulking kid who, unlike the others, looked completely unscathed from the previous day's battles. "Young Tom here will fight again, right?"

The boy looked down at Cole—yeah that's right, looked down on him because he was freaking huge—and shrugged as he said, "Sure." He kind of sounded like Voldemort. I could have fit into one of his pant legs. I looked around for the tank I would need to beat this kid.

Katie's voice was in my head again, *You need to become someone else.* So I unzipped my tracksuit jacket and tossed it to the side, pretending to be unafraid. That was definitely 'someone else'. *Do I make fists? Karate chop hands?* My hands were visibly shaking.

Tom looked disinterested in the whole process.

"Whenever you're ready," Cole said from his customary fight seat.

Tom took one step forward before Cole interrupted him by saying, "Remember, bow to each other."

Tom stopped and bowed to me which lowered him to my height. My bow put me eye-to-eye with his kneecaps.

To say I was about to get my ass handed to me would be selling ass-handing short.

Now it was on. He took a big step forward and raised his fist. I failed to do anything except scrunch my face up and raise my hands His knuckles felt like a boulder as they smashed into my cheek and sent me flying across the room onto the floor. His foot slammed into my stomach before those two massive hands hurled me into the padded wall. Love ya, whoever padded those up.

My head spun. I landed in a sitting position to see Tom striding forward for more. I knew I didn't have much more time in this fight and wanted to do something on the offensive before it was over, so as Tom reached down to grab me I kicked up. My foot caught him square in the face. I think it surprised me almost as much as him. He back pedaled, grabbing his nose. "Damn it," he hissed.

I rose to me feet and put all of my strength behind what I knew would be the finishing blow. Unfortunately, my accuracy was off and I wound up hitting him directly in the right tit. But it was a vicious tit shot; I knew it. Totally left a bruise.

I heard Cole snort with laughter. Tom didn't find it funny though. He grabbed me by the throat and picked me up in the air. My would-of-killed-a-normal-man tit shot had really pissed him off. My feet dangled helplessly two feet off the ground before he slammed me down onto the ground onto my back. It knocked the wind out of me. Tom's grip around my neck didn't falter; it only tightened as he crouched on top of me. I couldn't breathe. The only things I could see were Tom's snarling face and his crotch, which was way too close.

My eyes rolled and the lights were going out again. I only had one move left in my arsenal. Call it dirty, call it cheap, it's all I had left. I reached up and grabbed his junk like a fistful of cash. I gripped and twisted with all my might. There was a scream of pain, and the grip on my throat weakened as I kept on squeezing and twisting. But it was too late. The lights were still going out, and every-thing went black. Again.

GUESS WHAT? I WOKE up in the hospital. This time it was not of my own choosing but by a nurse with some vile smelling salts.

"Good," she said as I woke up, trying to brush the smell from my nose.

I looked around and realized that I was in the same bed as this morning. Had they even had time to change the sheets?

She tossed the smelling salts in a trashcan, checked her watch, and said, "You can either go eat lunch with everyone else or you can have it here. Which'll it be?"

Maybe the magic word was "everyone," but I wanted to be with my group. I didn't want to miss out. I was getting a little tired of only seeing them for three minutes at a time punctuated by hours of unconsciousness.

"I'll go," I said.

"Good choice. Food's a lot better in the cafeteria."

"Cafeteria? Food?"

"Well yeah. What, did you think you were going to have to eat that mush all the time?"

My jaw dropped. *Yes, I had. How was I supposed to know any different?! Real food?!* I hopped to my feet, wobbled a bit, and then made a beeline for the exit.

"Wait!" came the nurse's voice behind me. "Take this and keep it on your face." She handed me one of those disposable ice packs. I had completely forgotten about the damage I had taken from Tom. I looked around for a mirror to see for myself, but I couldn't find one. All I could find was a blurred and fun-house worthy reflection in a stainless steel medical fridge. Worthless.

"How bad is it?" I asked.

"Keep the ice on it and you'll be fine," she said warmly. *Whew, still have a shot at Hollywood.* I almost said the words aloud. Instead I mumbled, "Thanks for the ice."

She nodded and said, "See you later."

"Probably a good bet," I yelled over my shoulder as I jog-walked out of there. The thought of food had pushed all thoughts of pain from my mind.

I followed the trail of lights until I reached the cafeteria.

It felt like Christmas morning as I entered what looked like a normal, old-school cafeteria. Except that everyone in it was yellow. I saw kids eating sandwiches and scarfing down pastas. My stomach growled.

I went to the first counter I could find. It was full of pre-wrapped sandwiches. I grabbed one, didn't care what was in it. The next counter was pasta. Got a big bowl of that too. The last counter was a salad bar. Skip-a-roonie.

I grabbed a glass of apple juice and looked out into the cafeteria for Junie. I saw him waving his hand and rushed over to the table. Our whole group was there, and they welcomed me with loud "Heys." Even Tom, who was sitting on a donut cushion.

"No hard feelings?" he said.

"I think I should be the one asking you that," I said, smiling. He grinned and patted the seat between him and Junie. I thunked down and tore into my pasta.

Junie pushed a bowl of untouched cereal in front of me and said, "I'm stuffed. You want this?"

"Sure," I was able to blurt out.

But that gesture had instantly flashed me back to my brother and how he would always have a bowl of cereal ready for me on Saturday mornings. At that moment I wanted to go home so badly it hurt. I shoveled more pasta in my mouth to hide my sudden lapse. If anyone had noticed, they didn't say.

We all ate in silence. Maybe like me, they were all content to be doing something normal after the craziness of the past forty-eight hours. Kidnapped from home? Check. Crap beaten out of us? Check. Witnessed a murder? Check, or check for the others, I knew the truth of it. So forgive us if we didn't really want to chat.

Junie had other ideas though.

"Okay, I can't take this anymore," he blurted out, tossing his fork onto his plate for good measure. It clanged loudly. "It's like a morgue in here. Doesn't anyone have anything fun to talk about?" He looked around at the table and was met by blank stares. He turned to me last. I shook my head.

"Come on. Ren, you literally tried to castrate Tom as you passed out. And now you're eating lunch with him and he's sitting on a donut. That's kinda funny." He laughed when he said it. My face went red. I couldn't help but smile. Even Tom smirked. "Come on people. We can do this."

Some of the other tables were now looking our way. Junie fed off the attention. "Okay, game time," he said. Everyone listened to our de facto leader. "It's called '*looks like who?'* I used to play it with my brother all the time at the mall. Here, I'll go first."

He scanned the room and then said, "Easy one. Goth Justin Timberlake."

We all exchanged looks, silently trying to figure out if we were actually going to play. That answer came in the voice of Stacy, an Asian girl at the end of the table as she quietly said, "Three tables over." She pointed for good measure.

We followed her gesture and found him. He had black hair, was paper white, but totally looked like JT. The resemblance was uncanny.

"Yes! Nice," Junie yelled excitedly. "Now your turn." His enthusiasm was rubbing off on us.

The girl stood up and looked around biting her lip as she thought. When she sat back down she said, to suddenly eager players, "Fat Ryan Reynolds."

I laughed at the thought of it and joined the others as we craned our heads to find him. Mauricio, our Brazilian classmate, found him sitting on the other side of the room. It was totally a fat Ryan Reynolds. Spitting image only, you know, heavy. We all laughed and when I heard Tom's deep ho-ho-hoing I laughed even harder.

"Nice one," Junie said with a nod. "Who's next?"

We all took turns and before long we were standing up and walking around the tables to find our celebrities. Some people, like Junie, were good at the game and named a lot of folks. I only did one. I found a very pretty boy who looked like Anne Hathaway and aptly named him Manne Hathaway. It was a stumper but when they all found him they loved it. I knew I'd never top it and quit while I was ahead. I was having more fun looking for the celebs than naming them anyway.

After that we slid right into a good old Cole-bashing session. We mocked his looks, his skinniness, even made up stories about his parents so we could make fun of them too. We finished on his broken nose. We made up rules for it. Every time it whistled, we had to cough. When it would leak, we had to itch our ears. Whenever he touched it we had to sneeze.

We spent the rest of lunch laughing. As in real laughter. If those in charge were watching (and I knew they were), they kept silent. Would we actually follow through on any of the CNRs, or Cole Nose Rules? Junie was adamant we would. For the briefest of moments it felt like we were all in regular old high school together, that this was a normal place and we'd be off to math or history next.

And that was my first lunch. It was the perfect break. I later came to understand that this was exactly the point. While we were to become killing machines, even *they* understood we were still young and needed time—even if only for a bit—to goof off and be ourselves. Learning to be human weapons was our new vocation, but under-neath it all, we were still just fourteen-year-olds. Every day we would get a one-hour break from the constant training to be ourselves. To be kids again.

IT WAS TOUGH TO leave the cafeteria. But I felt a new strength. I was determined to make a better effort to stay conscious through our morning sessions of hand-to-hand combat with Cole. Lunch was not something to be missed.

We worked our way down the maze of hallways and ended up outside Armory 6H. The numbering made me wonder how many armories this place had. The answer: a lot.

Inside the room and immediately to our right was a short, stocky, young woman. Only the first thirty or so feet of the room were lit; the rest was completely blacked out, but I could tell by my echoing footsteps that it was a pretty big space. There was nothing special from what I could see: rows of long tables similar to what I'd had in my science classes back home, situated between the vast black nothingness and the door.

There was a bottleneck, so we all stopped, unsure of where to go.

"Two to a table, please," said the stocky woman. Her voice was strong but feminine.

Junie and I, without needing to speak, found a table in the middle. Not right up front like brown-nosers, but not in the back like the C students either. The woman watched everyone find their places. Once in place she scanned each of our faces. When her eyes fell on me she stopped. "Ren Sharpe?" she asked coldly.

Crap. Had I kicked her in the face too? Cole's sister maybe? I nodded slowly but kept eye contact with her.

From beside me Junie whispered, "Oh, great."

"You . . ." the woman said. She walked and stopped on the other side of my table. There was nothing but silence as she glared at me. I gulped. It was so quiet I heard some kind of venting system kick on. AC? Heat? Who knows? *Why was I thinking about vents?!*

"On the night you were taken, did you kick someone in the face?" she asked in a calm voice.

I nodded.

"Have you figured out who that was yet?"

"Think so," I said, then quickly added, "Ma'am."

She smirked at the *ma'am* bit. "And then yesterday did you attempt to attack your instructor?" The great lie of my bravery was now common knowledge.

"Yes, ma'am," I said softly.

The corners of her mouth flickered. Then she smiled as she exclaimed, "That's awesome!"

I gaped at her.

She grabbed my hand and shook it. "You have no idea how many times I've wanted to kick Cole in the face."

Was this chick for real?

"You got guts, kid," she said.

I was so surprised by the whole thing I failed to notice her vice-like grip until she let go. I figured it'd be a week till I got all the feeling back in my fingers.

She looked around at the rest of class and said, "Lighten up, folks. It's okay to have fun around here."

As she made her way back to the front of the class, Junie leaned over and whispered, "Being your friend is exhausting."

I shrugged. "Try being me."

"My name is Leslie Tanner. I'll be in charge of your weapons training. Specifically, these weapons." The wall behind her slid apart to reveal a display of guns. Hundreds of them. There were small pistols, machine guns of all sizes, rocket launchers, and everything in between. I have to admit, I felt a kick of adrenaline. It was like an action movie.

She allowed us a moment to take it all in before continuing. "When I'm done with you, you'll be able to disassemble, reassemble, and fire every weapon on this wall. Using them will become second nature to you, as easy as breathing."

She pulled out a black pistol. It looked like the kind of gun you see on cops. She pulled back some thingy and a bullet popped out. She caught the bullet in mid air. Then she removed the clip (I was glad I could at least name that part) and placed both the clip and the bullet on the table behind her. Then she held the empty gun up in front of her.

"This is a standard nine millimeter Glock. It's relatively light, simple, dependable." We passed the gun around, each looking at it. I was surprised at how heavy it was when I finally got to hold it. I passed it along to Junie who passed it to the next table after a brief look-see. Once it got back to Leslie she put the clip back in the gun and pulled the little thing back again. In a flash, she pointed it at us and fired. Instinctively we all ducked. Leslie grinned as she said loudly, "And it's damn accurate."

Even though she'd yelled, I could barely hear her from the ringing in my ears. She nodded and pointed behind us. About 300 feet way, illuminated by a spot light, was a human cutout. Leslie clicked a remote and the target came zooming toward us. She took it off and showed us the hole in the dead center of the head.

She admired her work. "Now let's fire some guns, huh?"

Leslie had us line up across the room and face our own targets—much closer, about twenty feet away. She gave us instructions on the weapon, as well as firing techniques and safety. I don't remember much of what she said because the moment I had the gun in my hand my heart was beating so loud in my ears I couldn't hear anything. My hands were sweaty, and I could barely hold it. I almost dropped it once but luckily saved myself from the embarrassment of that.

When she pulled her ear protectors down and told us to do the same, I was giddy with excitement. Then she gave us the signal to fire away. Holding the gun in my hand meant I had a weapon, and for a fleeting moment I considered shooting my way out. I'm sure I wasn't the only one who had this inner struggle either. But I think we all came to the same conclusion. How far could we expect to get? We'd had a taste of what these people were capable of. None of us wanted to sample the whole dish. Plus, none of us had a clue how to get out.

I cocked the gun, or "pulled the thingy back," as I had been calling it, slid the safety off, and raised it up to eye level. I sighted the target and tried to control my breathing as instructed. Shaky hands were making it hard to aim. Around me the others had begun to shoot. Each pop made me flinch a little. *I can't hit that thing.* I didn't want to be the worst shot in the group, but I also didn't want to be the one who hadn't fired anything either. *To hell with it.* Without really aiming, I gave the trigger a squeeze and gun fired.

I wasn't ready for the kick back though. The gun flew out of my hands and landed on the ground behind me. *How the hell do I play this off?* I looked around, terrified someone had seen it, but luckily everyone was too focused on their own shooting. I sighed from relief and quickly reached down for the gun. When I straightened up I saw Leslie, laughing her butt off near the room's entrance. She mouthed "nice" to me and gave a thumbs-up. I smiled shyly and went back to my place.

I quickly fired off the rest of my clip and holstered the gun. I was one of the last to finish after the tossing debacle. Then we got to see our results. I had fired thirteen shots but had only hit the target once. And it wasn't even the body. It was the white background.

"But that one would have scared the hell out of the person. Maybe even given them a heart attack," came Junie's voice from behind me.

"Is it sad that the safest place for a person is where I'm aiming? How'd you do?" I stopped short. It looked like he hadn't missed at all. He'd even gotten some head shots, the jerk. Junie was far and away the best in the class.

"Being your friend is exhausting," I said.

He laughed and held up his gun. "Wanna shoot our way outta here?" *I knew I wasn't the only one!*

I looked over at Leslie, who was doing some gun tricks to the amusement of some of our classmates and asked, "How far do you think we get?"

"Not very. I don't even know where my room is, let alone the way out."

"Let's reexamine this option later, deal?"

He nodded.

Turned out I wasn't the worst in the group. I know, right? A few hadn't even hit the target. Losers. Okay, now I feel bad. I take the loser comment back. No one else's weapon had jumped out of his or her hand though—that shame was all mine. Queen loser gun dropper, right here.

We spent the rest of the afternoon in the range shooting, varying up the distances. I got progressively calmer and thus better with every shot, which was probably the point of the repetition. And wouldn't you know it, I eventually began to hit the target on a regular basis. I remember I couldn't stop giggling the first time I got a head shot. It was so satisfying. I mainly hit the white part of the target and that was good enough for me on my first day of shooting anything.

The final hour we spent taking apart the guns, studying the pieces, and then putting them back together. I was surprised at how few parts went into making these things. Taken apart and in pieces it looked like a pile of scrap metal. But when put it back together there was something scary about it. So simple yet so powerful. While I played with the weapon in my hands I got a sudden sense of dread. I did not like this thing, but I was destined to wield it for the rest of my life.

As the session came to an end we had to clean up the gun grease from the tables and sweep up the used bullet shells and clips from the floor by the range.

At one point Junie picked up an empty shell and said, "Remember when picking up shells meant you were at the beach?"

I picked up an empty clip and said, "Remember when clips were for hair?"

We didn't know it then, but that would become our private joke for the rest of our time here. Whenever we were doing something odd, dangerous, or just plain nuts, one of us would say something along the lines of "Remember when knives were for butter?" or "Remember when tanks were for fishes?"

What I did know was that being next to Junie felt good. It felt natural. He made me feel warm and safe in a place that was cold and dangerous. Again, inappropriate feelings, feelings that didn't belong here, welled up inside me. I laughed them off though. *Yeah, right. What could it ever lead to? Midnight romps in the used bullet casings pile?* But that didn't stop them. I had no idea how to deal with them.

Back in the world I would have totally put out the vibe as best I could for at least six months: silently waiting for him to talk to me, avoiding all direct eye contact, and keeping my distance before giving up because obviously he didn't like me. But this was not the place for such rash behavior.

I reminded myself that I hardly knew this kid. I only knew his name. Sad since he was already my closest friend here. Scratch that, *only* friend here. I glanced up at him and caught him looking at me, as if waiting to say something. It was now or never.

"Where'd you learn to shoot like that?" I asked. *Good one,* I told myself. Just the right amount of curiosity, but not enough to seem flirty. Innocent would be a good word for it.

"Just growing up I guess. Did a lot of hunting with my dad."

"Ew."

"What?" he asked.

"Hunting's stupid and disgusting."

"No, it isn't. It's a fun sport," he said defensively.

"Football's a sport. Hell, I could even give you golf. But sitting around drinking beer, waiting for an animal to come eat from an electric feeder so that you can shoot it does not a sport make."

"I think the entire South would disagree with you," he said.

"Well the entire South is a hot, stupid place."

"You know you jinxed yourself and you'll be assigned there now, right?"

"Dangit!" He was right of course. Senor Jinx had a cruel sense of humor.

He smiled. "Don't sweat it. I'll give you some pointers, show you where to eat and stuff."

"Deal." I said. And we shook on it. His hands were strong and hadn't been wrapped around video game controllers their whole lives.

We all lived on the same hall. This was old hat to the others but new to me since I'd spent our first night in the hospital. I liked that we were all here, that the whole team of kids without lives was together.

"So where should I hope to be assigned if I really am jinxed to be there?" I asked. A cunning way to ask where he was from, if I do say so myself.

"Falls Church, Virginia."

"Sounds creepy."

"It's awesome. Right near DC, a couple hours from

amazing camping and backpacking. There's everything. It's the best." He choked up talking about his home. He tried to play it off with a cough, but I knew better. I thought about calling him out on it, but figured who was I to do that? I was a crying mess. I'd let it slide for now but be sure to bring it up when I knew him better.

"Virginia's not really the South though," I teased. "It's like the fake South. It's like the Splenda of the South."

"Ouch," he said.

"I mean, Alabama, now that's the South. Mississippi's the South. Virginia? Meh." I added a shrug for good measure.

"Well, where are you from then, all high and mighty?" he asked me.

"A little place I like to call . . . oh look I'm back to my room."

"Not cool," he said, but he was smiling.

I pretended to think about it and crossed my arms. "How about this? You help keep me alive and conscious through the week and I'll tell you then. Deal?"

"An impossible task," he said flatly, but playfully.

"Take it or leave it, smart ass."

"Fine. Deal."

There was the briefest of awkward moments as we stood outside my door. I know what my body wanted to happen, but, again, not cool in this place. *Bad body! Bad!*

Junie gave me a forced smile. I got the feeling, or maybe hoped, that he was dealing with a similar issue. He raised his hand awkwardly and said, "Up top."

Confused, I raised my hand above my head, and he

slapped me five. *Seriously?* Obviously embarrassed, he pursed his lips and furrowed his brow. "Night, Ren," he said before scurrying away.

"Night, Junie," I called after him.

The moment the door shut I began giggling *Up top? Really?* I fell into my bed. That made two good conversations in a row *Up top.* That's something *I* would have done. I was still smiling as I got back up, peeled off my warm-up suit, and tossed it in the dirty clothes bin.

The day was finally over, and I actually felt glad to see my room again. It was the one place I knew my other grunts couldn't see me. Where the mask and lie that was "She Who Attacks Teachers" could come off. I could be me, the real Ren.

I glanced around, really taking in my room. I'd been so scared waking up in here that first morning. It was less intimidating now. Yes, the room was institutional and ugly, but it was mine.

On my desk I noticed a small pulsing light that looked like a button. When I pressed it, a drawer slid open, delivering me a nice warm bowl of dinner mush. I pulled out my tiny bag of rosemary contraband and sprinkled some on top. Not Mm-Mm good, but good enough. Since I knew it was inevitable that I would soon be in the hospital wing again, I made a mental note to try and walk away with some other spices.

The best part about dinner was realizing that the surface of my desk was actually some kind of computer screen. I was so tired of never knowing where I was supposed to be, or how long I was going to be there, that I nearly cried when I found a daily schedule. I slid the bowl aside to look at it.

Every morning I had hand-to-hand combat with Cole. Ew. But each afternoon was something different. Tomorrow afternoon I had Evasive Tactics, or as I would call it, being sneaky. There was some kind of knives training where I'm sure I'd find a way to lose a finger, something on explosives, some surveillance crap, and more time with Leslie at the range.

The smile Junie had put on my face had long since faded. My whole life had not only been decided for me, but it was scheduled out by the hour now too. They really were going to turn me into a machine.

Exhausted, I turned away from my scheduled life and almost missed it.

My eyes widened. I reread the word. Excitement coursed through my weary bones as I said the word out loud. "Driving." It was something I'd been looking forward to since I was ten, and now I was going to get to start two years earlier than was allowed out in the world! And after driving was, *doth my eyes deceive me? Free time*?! I gave an excited "Ha!" I leapt up and did a little happy dance that included a mash-up of three turns, quick hand clapping, and a few mini-jumps. *Driving and free time*!! That day was shaping into the best . . . day . . . ever. Okay, maybe not the best day ever, but when compared to the turd days it was being surrounded by, yeah, best day ever.

All I have to do was make it through the week. Then I'll get to drive a car. Holy Jamolie.

The smile came back. For a good minute I stood in

the middle of my room with a ridiculous grin on my face, savoring the excitement that was this coming Saturday. The smile was still on my face as I showered. Still on my face while I brushed my teeth. Still on my face when the door to my room slid open and Not-Beth walked in with my nightly dose of fire. Smile gone.

CHAPTER 8
DRIVING MISS CRAZY

I want to say the rest of the week went in a blur, that I was so busy it all flew by, but that would be lying. Getting the crap beat out of you every morning tends to make the days drag. The only thing that kept me going was the promise of getting behind the wheel.

Junie took like a champ to the challenge of keeping me conscious. Every time Cole asked for volunteers for something, Junie's hand shot up. We all knew that without Junie, I woud have been Cole's favorite tackling dummy. Oblivious to the real reason Junie was voluneering, Cole must have simply assumed he had gotten a taste for punishment and was all too happy to oblige. But Junie coud take it, he was big and strong and tough, and it felt like Cole was holding back a bit on him. Maybe he figured that once Junie was even remotely trained, Junie would have been able to snap him in half. I posed no such threat.

On the morning of driving day, Cole was showing us a

new hip throw. It wasn't painful, but the landing was. He must have tossed Junie around a good thirty times before letting us team up to practice.

Holding his hip and cringing as he limped over to me, Junie joked, "You better be from somewhere good. Or like the daughter of some rich czar or something."

"Both, and more,.." I said sarcastically.

I grabbed his collar and with all my might tried to do the throw. He didn't even budge. I tried again. Nothing. It was like trying to toss a giant or firmly rooted tree.

"Can't you just tell me now?" he asked.

"Uh, there are like five more knockout-friendly hours ahead of me. I'll tell you after I get to drive, okay?"

I tried to flip him again but was met by the same immovable force. Frustrated, I scolded in my bad-dog voice, "Ju-nie. Stop."

He sighed. "You need to put your hip here." Then gently grabbed my hips and rotated them to where they needed to be, which happened to be against his thigh. His touch gave me goosebumps, the good kind. *I mean, really? Come on, inappropriate feelings. Here? Now?*

He let go of my hips and said something.

I was light-headed from his touch, too busy focusing on reprimanding my body, to hear him. I managed, "Huh?"

"Try now," he repeated.

"Try what?" I asked, flustered.

He smiled, leaned in closer to me. "Anything you want, whenever you want."

Gulp. He straightened up, still smiling, still resting his hands on my hips. I had to do something. I had to act fast before I did something stupid. My body was threatening to win, my mind had . . . to . . . do . . . something . . .

Panic must have given me a jolt of super strength because I hurled him over my hip with ease and he landed on the ground with a thud. The momentum of it made me lose my balance, and I fell to the floor beside him. I giggled. I couldn't help it. My excitement from doing it right had done the trick and I was free from those bad, bad, bad thoughts.

"And what's so funny?" asked Cole's nails-on-chalk-board voice.

I dusted myself off—an odd thing to do since there was zero dust here—and stood up. "Nothing."

"It must have been something," Cole countered.

I decided to be honest, well mostly. No sense bringing Junie and how he had made me feel into it. "I can't believe I did it. It feels good."

"Feels good?" he questioned.

The toss had for sure, not to mention the part-we-shall-not-speak-of, so I nodded. Worst decision of my life.

"Well, then let's make sure everyone gets to feel *good*," he said with a hint of a smile.

The rest of the class was spent letting the other students feel "good" tossing me around like a rag doll. Each one got specific instructions from Cole on how to modify the move in different, painful ways.

"Here's how you do it for more height." And then, "Here's how you do it for more rotation." And so on and so forth. He made Junie do it in the way that caused the most pain. Junie tried to do it wrong, but Cole made him repeat it until he got it right.

Here's the thing, though: I learned to relax my body in the air and land relatively pain free, so after a bit I was almost enjoying myself. By the end of the class I was actually having fun. I egged them on to toss me as high as they could. That odd sense of weightlessness had always made me smile; this felt like when I was a kid being tossed around the pool by my dad. Only the pool was a lightly padded floor now.

Cole didn't seem happy, but I didn't care. He wasn't as scary to me anymore. Refusing to go full throttle on Junie told me that he feared what we (or at least Junie) would become. Cole was just a bully, nothing more.

After the tossing, we had our regular couple hours of circuit training in the massive track center. I left limping, bruised, and exhausted, but holy hell conscious.

Driving, here I come!

MY HEART SANK AS I walked into the class. No cars. None. Just a bunch of big rail car box-looking things spread across the room. I was too furious to pay attention to the instructor. I only caught snippets like "virtual reality" and "immersive." It was crap. *A video game?!?! A freaking video game?!?* The disappointment on my face was mirrored by the others. Everyone was pissed.

Final instructions were to team up and get to it. Today we were to learn the basics of driving while we followed a car through a town. Simple. Easy. Stupid. Oh, and might I add, FAKE! I wish Cole *had* knocked me out earlier to save me from the disappointment of this garbage. I trudged after Junie toward a dumb box.

It was about thirty feet long, ten feet high and about twenty feet wide too. Junie pressed a button on the outside of the box and a door slid open.

Inside sat a full-size black sedan. It looked like a cop car. Not even a fun car to pretend-drive, like a Porsche or something. Lame.

"Want to go first?" Junie asked me. He sounded as unhappy as I felt.

"This is stupid," I mumbled and walked around the car to the passenger side and got in.

"I'll take that as a no," he said and climbed into the driver's side.

Now, I hadn't been at F.A.T.E. that long, but I had been there long enough to know that this place had some pretty amazing gadgets. Why I'd assumed this would not apply here was stupid on *my* part. The moment his door went *thunk* we were no longer in a dimly lit box, but sitting in a car on the side of the road surrounded by a forest.

I gasped. It was so real. If I hadn't known I was actually in a box I would have believed I'd escaped the training center I looked over at Junie and shared a *holy hell* look.

I rolled down the window and felt a breeze that matched the fluttering of the leaves on the trees. Birds chirped. I listened to the trees speak to each other as they swayed back and forth. I took a deep breath. Even the air smelled like forest: clean and leafy and cool. My heart stirred faintly. It was familiar. It all reminded me of home.

"Soooo," I said in that way that means you want something.

"Yeah," Junie said.

I gave my finest sad puppy dog performance as I asked, "Can I drive first?"

Junie rolled his eyes. "Okay. You'll have to climb over me though." He started to slide toward me so we could perform the awkward dance of switching places when a green car zoomed past us down the road. It was the one we were supposed to follow. We froze both deciding if we had enough time to do this. We didn't.

"Nevermind, just go," I said, collapsing back in the passenger seat.

"You sure?" he asked.

"Yeah, it's fine," I lied.

Junie slid back over to the steering wheel and put his seat belt on . . . in a fake car. It was cute. But man, it looked and felt so real! The engine revved, and when Junie accelerated, it felt like we were really moving down a road. The wind rushing through the open windows matched the speed I closed my eyes for an instant. It ruffled my hair. I made a wing with my hand, like I used to in the car back home. I missed this.

I don't know if we were following an old woman, or if it was supposed to be this easy since it was our first lesson, but the pursuit was painfully slow. Within moments, were practically tailgating. So I did what I do best: I rested my cheek against my arm, let the wind blow through my hair, and zoned out.

I was snapped out of it when Junie said, "All right. Pay up. Where are you from?"

I was ready to drag it out, to play coy,. but when we bumped over a small dip in the pavement it hit me. There was a reason this all felt so familiar. I knew this road. I knew it like an old book. *There's a sharp right coming up.* Seconds later we rounded the bend and hit that turn. The trees began to thin, revealing a town I knew all too well.

My throat caught. My eyes began to sting. *Not here. Not anymore.* Katie's words didn't work. A tear fell from my lashes. I shook my head.

Junie, thinking he'd done something wrong, backpedaled. "I'm sorry. I'm sorry. You don't have to tell me." His nervous eyes flashed between the car in front of us and me. "I didn't mean it."

I took a deep breath and choked out, "No. It's . . . I'm from *here*." The dam broke and I began to sob. I never thought I'd see this place again, let alone so soon and like this. I wasn't ready for it. It was a cruel joke. It had to be. This was no coincedence.

Junie didn't know what to do so he focused on following the green car, like he was supposed to. At least he didn't try to calm me down or touch me. But part of me could have used a good hug. I wiped my eyes and smiled as I imagined him trying to give me another high five.

We slowly cruised by the bank that sat on the corner of the main square. The initial rush of emotion had passed. The tears were still flowing, but I was quiet.

"So where are we?" Junie asked me.

I kept looking out the window, afraid to look at him. "Amherst."

"It's pretty," he said.

"It's home," I said softly.

"Where's your house?" he asked.

"To the left," I answered, barely audible.

The car we were following turned right. Junie turned left.

I flinched and sat upright. "Where are you going?" I demanded, whirling to face him.

"I'm taking you home." He flashed a small smile before focusing on the road again.

"Junie don't. We'll get in trouble. Turn around." Part of me wanted him to keep going, of course. But the other part of me was terrified.

"No. I'm taking you home. They can punish me however they want. It's my call, not yours. Now where am I going?"

It was a bad idea. A horrible idea. But in the end, I couldn't say it wasn't what I wanted. If they were going to screw with me like this, I had to see how far they were willing to take it. If they could recreate everything they'd stolen from me with the same accuracy. I reached over and hugged him. Not how I wanted our first non-training physical contact to be, but whatever. He reached over and held my hand, gently squeezing it for support as we drew closer and closer to my house. Each turn that took us closer was an exercise in keeping it together.

When we turned onto my road my stomach did a flip. Would it look the same? Everything else had, but could my own home stand up to that intimate level of scrutiny? Would my mother's rose bushes have the right shape? Would the tree I fell out of when I was nine have the missing branch?

I wasn't sure what I was feeling but as Junie pulled up

outside my house I couldn't breathe. They'd gotten it right, everything, down to the tiniest detail I could imagine. I forgot it was all fake. I forgot I was in a box, no longer living my old life. I forgot who was in charge. I wanted to see my mother. Without thinking I opened the door.

Everything went black.

"No!" I yelled. "No. I'm sorry!" I said again as I shut the door. Fake or not, I wanted it back. But the simulation was over. The inside of the box became dimly lit by some ambient light, and the box exit door slid open.

Junie and I shambled out of the simulator. My legs were shaky. The moment we stepped into the room I knew something was off. It was silent and there was no one else. Where were our classmates?

Three dark-clad attackers rolled out from behind one of the other driving boxes in front of us. I was behind Junie as they approached.

One of them, with a heavy accent I couldn't place, snapped "Should have kept following the green car."

Junie quickly turned to me. "Ren, go. Run."

I shook my head, snapping out of the daze they'd put me in. "I'm not leaving you."

"Please, go."

Maybe I should have listened to him. They attacked with speed, precision, and intent to harm. Two went after Junie. The one who'd spoken came at me. I was no match, not even close, and was tackled to the ground with ease. I was expecting to get punched, elbowed, or worse but it didn't happen. My attacker was suddenly lifted off of me and thrown into a driving box like a rag doll. Junie, eyes flashing with rage, had done it. But that gave his attackers the opportunity they needed. Maybe in a few years it would have been a better fight but it wasn't right now. One swept his legs, as the other kicked him across the chest. He crashed to the ground in a heap.

I got up to help but only made it a few steps before something, I think it was a foot, or a lead pipe, cracked me in the head. For the third time in a week, I lost consciousness. But this time, it almost felt like a blessing.

ONCE AGAIN, I CAME to in the hospital, lying on my back. Three days out of seven I'd ended up in here. At this rate they should just move me down here permanently and give my room to someone who might use it more.

I stared up at the ceiling as I tried to work through how I'd ended up here. It was all very fuzzy after the car chase. Too groggy to think, I rolled over to go back to sleep. When the side of my head brushed the pillow a sudden pain under my ear triggered my memory and it all came back. A flash of Junie being beaten, pleading with me to run.

I shot out of bed and ripped open the curtains to my left. A startled girl nursing a broken arm jumped.

"Sorry," I said as I closed them. I stumbled around my bed and whipped the other curtains open.

Oh, Junie . . . He was a mess. Both of his eyes were swollen shut, and he had a four inch cut stitched-up above his ear. He stirred.

I sat on the edge of his bed and grabbed his hand. He gave a quiet groan through his swollen, cracked lips.

"It's me, Ren," I said softly. "I'm here. It's okay." I gently stroked his hand with my thumb like my mother had done to me when I was a kid. His hand squeezed mine back.

"You okay?" he forced out. His voice sounded like sandpaper.

"I'm fine," I reassured him. "Shhh. Rest."

"How bad is it?" he asked me.

"Don't worry about it."

"Ren," he pushed.

"You look like you shoved your head in a bee hive," I said, attempting to lighten the mood.

He managed a pained chuckle. "Ow. Don't make me laugh. Nothing's broken though, right?"

I looked him over. "Not that I can tell."

"Well, at least I got that going for me."

His breathing was labored, but steady. I thought he'd dozed off but a tear came out of his left eye. "I don't know if I can do this," he croaked. His voice was so soft I had to strain to hear it. More tears followed.

"You can't say that," I said, more frightened than I wanted to admit. "Not you. If you don't think *you* can then what about me?"

He squeezed his eyes tightly shut. "There's more to you than you give yourself credit for."

"There isn't, trust me. It's less if anything." I was crying now too.

"I'm just big and dumb."

"No, you're not. You're smarter than you think. And you're braver then all of us."

"All an act," he whispered, refusing to open his eyes. "I'm as scared as the rest of you."

"You tried to save me," I argued back.

"That's 'cause it's you, Ren. I . . ." He didn't finish.

"We're going to get through this together, okay?" I whispered back, trying to keep my voice from shaking. His last unfinished comment had torpedoed me.

His eyes fluttered open. "Only if you promise me something."

"Anything."

"The next time I tell you, 'Please go,' do it. I don't care what happens to me. But seeing you get hurt is worse than anything they can do to me."

I shook my head. "No, I can't promise that. I can't let you get hurt protecting me. I won't do it."

He took a deep labored breath. More tears. He closed his eyes again.

"I'll give you that one," I said, caving. "But you have to give me one too. We can each say it once, and the other has do it."

"I'll take what I can get." He forced a pained grin. "Now, please go."

"Hey!" I said loudly.

"Shhh, oh, ow," he painfully laughed out. He opened his left eye a slit and looked at me. "Kidding. Will you stay with me for a while?"

"As long as you want."

He squeezed my hand again, eyes still closed

AN HOUR LATER NOT-BETH arrived with a tray of shots.

"No," I said to her seriously.

She pursed her lips. I knew it was not her decision, just

her job, but I was still had to try to stop her. "It'll happen one way or another," she said. Then she flicked her head behind her toward two guards at the far end of the hospital wing.

I gave a defeated nod, so she moved closer.

"Wait." I walked over to my bed and began to drag it over next to Junie's. All at once, it rose from the floor. I looked up and saw Not-Beth helping me.

Junie and I held hands as Not-Beth did her job and left us to suffer through the night together.

CHAPTER 9
THE HUNT

Twenty-two days. I was officially twenty-two days into my stay. I knew this because I had starting marking my walls like that prisoner in *The Count of Monte Cristo*. Curled up in bed I was staring at the four sets of five and two lone rangers. Twenty-two. I rolled over to face the door. It felt like I'd been there for at least a year, but the dashes didn't lie. Unless someone was sneaking into my room and erasing them while I was training. That would be cruel but sort of funny too. This place was like that.

I zombie-swung myself out of bed and lazily put on my yellows. I was sore all over and not just from the dose of fire the night before. Three weeks of grueling training left more than bruises. My bones hurt.

Fully dressed, I pressed the button on my desk that would deliver my piping hot bowl of gruel breakfast. From inside a small nook on the back of the desk I pulled out my secret stash. From the nurses in the hospital wing, I had been overloaded with cinnamon and rosemary. I'd also smuggled out some sugar, salt, pepper, and a few grated Parmesan cheese packets. Feeling adventurous, I added one of the packets to the steaming slop. It didn't do much good.

No sooner had I put my licked-clean bowl back in the drawer than my door opened with a *bing*. Time to boogie.

I glanced at the day's schedule on my desktop to see what was first. *Camouflage.* I groaned. We'd done this last week. It was fun at first, but then extremely painful.

Allow me to explain: An immensely large room had been transformed into a near perfect recreation of a desert landscape. Sand, scrub brushes, mini rock hills, saguaro cactus . . . es? Or is it cacti? (Grammar and spelling weren't high on F.A.T.E.'s agenda.) Whatever, you get the idea. It was even kept at a balmy hundred degrees. We were given thirty minutes of instruction on desert camouflage techniques and then another thirty minutes to camo up and hide.

Cole then hunted us down with a pistol, shooting us with rubber bullets when he found us. Big surprise; he found me first and shot me square in the neck. I looked like I had gotten a hickey from a fire hose all week.

I had a theory that he could literally smell me. I felt it had merit given my history with him. Junie was quick to point out that painting myself green and trying to be a cactus was an awful decision. Funny, yes, but awful. But Junie was wrong, dead wrong. I was a really still fake cactus and totally blended in. Cole had sniffed me out, and I refuse to believe otherwise. This morning's class would be more of the same.

Junie and the rest of my team all gathered together in our hallway before heading out as one. We passed other groups all heading in different directions to different classes. No words were exchanged aside from an occasional head nod. I really wanted to organize some sort of *West Side Story* snap-off with another group but what do you know? I had yet to find the time. It was on my to-do list though.

We were led by our friendly wall lights to a new room for camo class. I instinctively rubbed my neck. The hickey bruise was only now starting to fade. The doors slid open, and a blast of sticky, wet air assaulted me.

As with most rooms in the training center, the front part was dedicated to instruction and learning—tables spread out evenly—but beyond that it was simply . . . beautiful. My eyes feasted on a jungle, a real jungle. The rubber floor of the teaching area gave way to a small grassy meadow about twenty yards deep. After the meadow it was a solid wall of towering trees of all types, bushes, and size-of-your-arm vines. There was even a pretty big creek that snaked its way through the middle of it all. A crack of thunder boomed from above, and rain, actual rain, began to fall. Something *screeched*. I spotted a monkey swinging in the branches trying to avoid the rain.

I heard a few gasps. We practically fought to get inside and up to the edge of the grass. Thoughts of Cole and his rubber bullets vanished.

Movement to my right caught my eye. Had that bush moved? To my left, the branches of a tree were swinging, but there wasn't any breeze.

As if on cue, five figures materialized out of the foliage, as if from nowhere, as if the jungle had come to life before our eyes. One had literally been laying not ten feet in front of me. I wasn't the only one who jumped when he stood.

"Change of plans today," came the whiny voice behind us. "Eyes on me children."

We turned. Cole was sitting on a bench cleaning out his fingernails with the point of a large knife looking, dare I say, giddy. It was unsettling. I glanced back. In my peripheral I could barely make out the jungle ghosts cleaning the mud, paint, and leaves off of their bodies and out of their hair.

"As you can see we have guests today. Special guests with a special treat. Today, you have been chosen to participate in a time-honored tradition here at F.A.T.E. Today you will be taking part in The Hunt. May I introduce you to the Hunters." He nodded and stood, indicating we could turn.

The room filled with a cacophony of excited whispers and gasps from my peers. Only the absolute best of the best were chosen as Hunters instead of Shadows. Once we were out of here, if we ever decided to run, or break any of the F.A.T.E. center's rules, we would be targeted for extermination by the Hunters. Only a killing machine can bring down another, you know? They were legends. Or nightmares, depending on your point of view. They never failed. They were awesome.

A tall, thin man with shoulder-length brown hair walked over and clasped his hands in front of him like a priest. His movements were graceful, like a dancer's. He was young, late twenties maybe, and eyed us all curiously with the faint hint of a smile. The other Hunters soon joined their leader. They were an interesting group. Two of them were massive, almost a parody of comic-book bad guys: rippled muscles and scowls. Then there was a smaller stocky guy with a shaved head and grey eyes that looked through you. He looked bored, which was somehow scarier. And finally there was a woman. She was tall and thin and if she ever smiled she might be called beautiful. Her eyes were black, as if they were all pupil. For a second I wondered seriously if she was some kind of robot.

"I want to thank you all for participating in this," said the leader. "My name is Luka." His voice was soft, and he spoke with some sort of accent—Russian or Eastern European if I'd had to guess, but it could have been anywhere. "I will keep this simple. You will have two minutes to run—"

"One minute," corrected Cole.

Luka turned toward Cole and said coolly, "Two."

I held my breath. You did not question Cole. The look Luke gave him made even me shiver. Cole lowered his eyes and didn't protest.

Luka turned back to us. "Apologies for the interruption." His formality was creepy. He spoke as if he were some kind of living relic from a forgotten age. "You will have two minutes to run. After that time we will come after you. When we catch you, you will return to your room. If you escape, you are free."

The word "free" echoed in my brain. Had I heard that right? *Free? Like, free, free? Like go back home free?*

As if reading our collective minds Luka nodded. "Yes, truly free. We want you to try as best you can to evade us so the stakes must be worth it. All doors are unlocked, no one but us will try to stop you. You have my word that should you manage to escape no one will come looking for you."

Granted, I didn't know the guy, but his word seemed pretty legit. It could frighten Cole, at least. That was good enough for me.

Not one to let us dream, Cole added, "Has anyone ever escaped?"

"Not as of yet," Luka answered. "But there will always be a first."

Nobody said a word. My heart pounded.

"Well," said Cole. Then he yelled, "Run!"

Like scattering birds we exploded into flight. It was a mad dash to the exit and out into the hallways. Half went one way and half went the other. The pattern continued at each intersection until it was just Junie and I—alone, sprinting through the corridors together.

Had it been two minutes yet? Had anyone been caught already? There was no time to stop and think.

"This way," Junie said. He crashed through a door that had never been unlocked before. I'd tried it a few times out of curiosity but it had never budged. There must have been a reason to keep it locked, and there must be a reason it was unlocked now. But I shoved the thought aside. Stairs. And they only led up. One flight. Two flights. Higher and higher . . . Our legs burned and our lungs ached for air when we reached the top, twenty-five flights later.

The corridor we entered was nothing like the ones below. It was carpeted, well lit. It looked like a nice office building instead of our prison. There was no time to think. We kept on running, barreling into some surprised looking people in business suits.

Real people? Here? We found ourselves looking at them like they were some exotic creatures at a zoo. To be fair they looked at us exactly the same way. My heart leapt. Could it be that F.A.T.E. had made a mistake? We were close. I could feel it. I could smell it. No really, the air was cleaner up here, fresher. There were doors to the outside somewhere close.

I heard yelling from behind us and turned. My heart sank. The female Hunter was closing fast.

"She can only follow one of us," was all Junie said before he took off to the left. I went right running as fast as I could, but stumbled every time I looked behind me. The Hunter went after Junie without hesitation. He was the bigger threat.

I ran and ran, trusting my gut, trusting my senses. Finally, I turned down a hallway, and my heart jumped. There were double doors at the end: thick, with two small, blacked-out windows.

If there had been a giant cliff through those doors I would have fallen to my death. I flew out of them without pausing and into the most beautiful thing I'd seen in weeks. The woods. The sky overhead, visible through the trees. Clouds. Sunlight.

This was no illusion. This was no room done up to look to it the part. No, this was real. I was really outside. To my left and right a sidewalk hugged the building's wall—vast, seemingly endless in both directions. I had grown up in the woods. This was home, this was my domain.

I took two deep breaths of fresh air before sprinting off into the trees. A couple hundred yards in I realized I was smiling. For the first time I began to think, to believe, I could do this. I'd be the first. I was careful where I ran, trying not to break twigs or leave an easy trail to follow. I started moving faster, slicker. I was water. I was free—

I jerked to a stop. A chain-link fence, a fifteen foot beast, suddenly appeared in front of me. I grabbed it and started climbing before I saw the massive coils of razor wire at the top. Climbing was not an option. My lungs heaved. I dropped to the ground and looked around, desperate. I was so close. If up was out, under was the only other option. I grabbed a stick and began to dig.

"Nearly there," came the familiar, soft, accented voice behind me.

Not thinking, I spun around to face my enemy, clutching the stick like a club.

Luka was leaning against a tree not ten feet away. He smiled kindly at me. "Fair enough. I'll play." He smoothly flipped up a fallen branch with his foot and snatched it out of the air with his hand. As he spoke he ripped off the smaller twigs, fashioning his own club. "No one's ever gotten this close. I'm honored to have found you Ms . . . ?" He lifted his eyebrows for help.

"Sharpe. Ren Sharpe."

"Beautiful. I'm honored, Ms. Sharpe, and thus compelled to offer you another chance at your freedom. Strike me cleanly and I will turn around and leave you be. Strike me cleanly and freedom is yours."

"And if I don't?" My mind was coming around to the situation. There was always a catch.

"Then you don't, and you will return with me. We both believe that is punishment enough, am I right?"

I nodded.

"Now, we haven't all day. You're freedom awaits, Ms. Sharpe." He bowed to me and I did the same. Bowing was a reflex now.

I went after him with all I had. I'd had no training in any weapons other than guns so I swung at him like I was trying to cut down a tree. He easily spun around my hacks, blocked a few others, and then rapped me on the knuckles with his stick. "Aggressive, but clumsy. Again."

The result was a harder crack to my knuckles that drew blood and made me drop my stick. I clutched my throbbing, bleeding hand to my chest. Continuing was pointless. I'd lost.

He sighed. He wasn't the slighted bit winded. "I was hoping for a different outcome," he murmured. "I mean that."

I honestly believed him.

"Alas, a deal's a deal. Come with me, Ms. Sharpe." He nodded for me to follow.

I hung my head, too tired to protest. But as we walked, he kept talking. "It really is impressive how far you got, Ms. Sharpe. Do please remember that as your studies continue."

It was hard not to like this guy. As we walked I noticed that his footsteps made no sound whatsoever. It was eerie. I watched him; his movements reminded me of a panther.

Something big was crashing through the woods to our right and instantly Luka was in front of me, as if protecting me. Tom, eyes wide with terror, came running at us.

"Help me," he choked out. Blood dripped from his lips. His face was ghostly white.

All at once, something shiny popped out of the middle of Tom's chest. I knew what it was, but I didn't want to believe it. The tip of a knife. He stumbled forward a few more feet before falling to his knees and revealing the smaller, shaved-headed hunter with the cold, grey eyes behind him. His body was still positioned in a throwing motion. He straightened up with a smug grin as he saw us.

"*No!*" I wanted to cry. No sound came. The word died in my throat.

I fell to my knees and caught Tom in my arms. He was so big and so heavy he knocked me onto my butt. I clutched at him as he began to cough, his eyes full of fear, staring up into mine.

"You're going to be okay," I lied.

"I want to go home," he managed, his mouth now full of blood. He began to cry. "I want my mom."

"Help!" I cried at Luka. He was gone. My head whirled.

And that's when I saw them: Luka and the stocky Hunter were locked in an all-out battle. It was a blur of action. Punches, kicks, throws. Watching them, a weird thought occurred to me: how fake combat was in every action movie I'd ever seen. This was moving death. But it was like ballet, in a way. I was mesmerized and frightened by it. Frightened for Luka and frightened by what might happen to me if he lost.

Tom's body gave a violent heave in my arms. I tore my eyes off the fight. When his body relaxed his eyes were blank. He was still. This was no fake death, like Katie. This was the real thing.

"No, no," I whispered furiously, shaking him. "Come on Tom, no."

"He's gone, Ren" came Luka's voice.

I looked up. He had wrestled the other Hunter to the ground and had him pinned.

"I'll kill you," gasped the other Hunter as he struggled, "and then I'll kill her."

With barely as much as a glance, Luka struck the man in the throat and he went limp. Then he stood, gracefully strode over to me, and gently pried my arms off of Tom's body. I allowed him to lift me to my feet. My arms and shirt were covered in Tom's blood. I couldn't stop shaking.

"I'm sorry for this," he murmured. Once I was steady, he let go and motioned toward the unconscious killer. "He will be dealt with accordingly, you have my word. You must go back now. Walk around the building until you find a door. Enter the code. 3904. They will come for you. Now please go."

"What about Tom?"

"Tom will be handled with honor."

He put his hands on my back and gave me soft push. At first my feet didn't seem to work, but they figured it out after a few steps.

"And Ren? Should you try to run you will find out what it truly means to be hunted."

I turned to him, and then turned back. I picked up my

pace. Once more I was flying through the woods—only this time, back to captivity. And strangely enough, as awful as it sounds, I no longer thought of Tom, even though I was soaked in his blood. My only thought was: They make mistakes here. They're human, just like me. Which means they have a weakness because there's always someone better to punish you for your mistakes. So that's who I had to become.

CHAPTER 10
SWEET-A MONTAGE

Okay, so let's imagine we're in a movie, and this is the sweet-a montage sequence in the middle of it. So flip through your music collection. Queue up your favorite *Eye of the Tiger*-esque, inspirational, I-am-becoming-a-badass song. Crank the volume and hit play.

Here I am getting my butt whooped all over the place by dozens of different kids and instructors in every form of martial art and fighting style on the planet. Cole, of course, is a reoccurring butt whooper with his smarmy grin. But wait; I've got this hard, determined look about me. A never say die, blow the bangs out of my face, get up, and keep fighting mug. And what's this? I'm doing push-ups and sit-ups in my room. I'm training harder in the gyms and dojos. I'm all sweaty and gross as I shadow box, perspiration dripping off my brow. But it's all paying off, as I get better, stronger, faster. Next image: I take out five masked attackers at once. Oh, and I just knocked out Cole with a spinning something or other kick.

Now I'm failing to put together a gun. Shameful. So I practice in the gun room. My hands and fingers are caked in black gun oil as I get better. Failed attempts turn into successes. I do it blindfolded in under five seconds . . . with one hand cuffed behind my back. Wassup.

I'm driving a car, backward, shooting at targets as I go. I jump out of perfectly good helicopters, airplanes, and hovercrafts. I slide a motorcycle under a moving semitruck and then keep moving. If it's got an engine, I can drive it, crash it, and escape from it.

Oh, and since this is a Hollywood movie montage, I'm getting better looking by the shot, naturally. I grow out of my awkward, gangly body and fill out as only a hot, Hollywood leading woman can. I can kick butt but still look good doing it. I'm totally smokin', kids.

Don't picture the countless nights I spend in the fetal position in absolute agony from the fire. Ignore the seven broken bones and over 300 stitches I get over four long years of my training. Don't squirm in your seat at the various forms of torture I suffer through. Ignore all of that and see me becoming an absolute beast.

This montage has officially concluded. Now's the time we test your memory and see how well you've paid attention.

Milkshake.

CHAPTER 11

OUR LITTLE GIRL'S ALL GROWN UP

I splashed warm water on my face and looked at myself in the mirror, the first I'd seen in four years. My own reflection was still a stranger to me. I hardly recognized the hard, emotionless face that stared back from the glass. It wasn't the same Hollywood hottie from my montage. It was just me, only older now. The short bangs sticking to my forehead were a surprise at first; then I remembered the decision to cut. It came about a month into my time here when they kept dangling in front of my eyes and screwing with my shooting. A pretty funny reason to cut your hair. I fingered the small scar under my left eye. Thanks for that one Cole. But other than that I looked like an older, thinner version of myself. No more baby pudge, but the freckles were still there. *Lord, had they gotten worse?*

I scratched against the hard shell bandage on my chest. Whenever you got badly hurt the hospital smeared this strange gel on the wound. The gel would seal up the skin and then harden into a protective shell. It allowed you to heal faster and let you keep training without worrying about the wound ripping back open. It didn't hurt, just itched like crazy.

When the most recent batch of kids had arrived, I was tasked with trying to make a run for it. The kid who had tried to do it in my year had given them the idea. It had worked so well on us that they did it every year now. But instead of giving me a beating they shot me. It served as part of my final mark of training, and it terrified the kids into obeying without question.

It was hard to not smile as the guards dragged my "dead" body past the kids in the hallway. I tried to find someone in the hospital to give some advice to like Katie had done for me, but there was no one. No regular like myself to give a good old pep talk too. Besides, I was only in the hospital for a day before I was brought here.

I still couldn't quite believe my new digs. To avoid complete culture shock when were unleashed into to the real world, we spent the time here before we got linked to our FIP. It was a regular apartment, complete with a TV and computer. I was surprised at how little I cared about the TV. I used to obsess over shows. What happened on TV just seemed silly and sad now.

But oh, how I'd missed music.

I walked over to the stereo and flipped on the radio. I didn't care what was on. I stopped at the first station I found. Classic rock. I sat on the couch, which was surprisingly comfy, and closed my eyes as the radio let the Led out. I zoned to the music; yeah, zoning out is still one of

my top five things I do. It was no longer accompanied
by texting, playing the cello, being annoying, and loving
horror movies (with an asterisk). No, its top five compan-
ions now included: killing, feeling no pain, the ability to
drive anything, and being really sneaky.

Alone in my new apartment, with no schedule to follow,
I stretched out on the couch and let the time pass. After
four long years it was a little disorienting to know I had
nowhere to be and nothing coming up. I could eat what
and when I wanted and sleep as long as I wished. I was
free until they assigned me my FIP. And that could take
months. Of course I would keep up my training, but for
now I could recharge my batteries.

Of the 313 kids who'd started with me, only 29 of us
had made it through to the end. Some had died in various accidents that occurred during training. Big Tom was
killed for reasons I'll probably never understand. Mary,
the gerbil-like girl, had crashed a motorcycle going about
180 miles per hour. Others had been shot, some stabbed,
and a few were blown up from faulty explosives. And sadly,
most had lost the battle with their sanity from the fire and
were never seen or heard from again. Of course, they were
studied and used in other ways. Waste not, want not, right?

It was never a pretty sight when someone "turned," as we
survivors called it. Something flipped in their heads. Some
kind of wild animal aggression took over and they blindly
attacked anyone and anything within reach. The younger
the kid, the less damage there was, but when someone older
and bigger turned, the damage could be awful.

I once saw a burly seventeen-year-old kill three guards

before being killed. After Tom, I'd been inconsolable. But eventually I became immune to it. It was just another part of training. Their deaths served to teach me how to be better, to be constantly in control. They had been foolish, or too risky. They were weak. But I only half-believed all of that to keep myself from falling apart.

And lying there on the couch, with the guitars blaring, something strange started to happen. I began to cry. I hadn't cried in years. Where had this blubbering girl come from? I was a hard-edged killing machine now. Tears were a waste of hydration.

Not here. Not anymore had been my mantra, carrying me through those endless days and nights. But why not *here?* I had made it, right? I'd defied the odds and done it so why not give the armor a true break? So here, finally at the end, I allowed myself to grieve properly. *All right, tears. Have at it.* And no, the classic rock didn't help.

My watery eyes found the large sliding door to the balcony. I could see buildings and a park outside. It had been four years since I'd seen the real world. Watching the trees, real ones, sway in the wind calmed me.

I got up, walked across the living room, but paused when I reached the sliding glass door. *What if the air isn't as sweet as I remembered it? What if the cool breeze doesn't feel right?* I'd lived on memories for four years, depended on them. What if the real thing couldn't compare?

Summoning my courage, I slid the door open. The wind hit my face and I took a deep, intoxicating breath. It tasted like a mixture of dirt and rain. It was *better* than I had remembered. They should bottle this stuff and sell it. I plopped down into one of the patio chairs. The wind played with my hair, gently tossing it around. I closed my eyes. I could get used to this.

After a couple hours of being a complete veg, I watched my first sunset in years. Then I got up and headed back inside. I still had goosebumps from the cold that had whipped across the patio as night had fallen.

Hungry, I went to the kitchen and made a big bowl of scrambled eggs for dinner. I didn't really have a craving for them, but when I looked in the fully stocked fridge, I realized that eggs were all I knew how to cook. Along with some toast it did the job, but I would definitely be picking up a cookbook when I got out of here.

I cleaned my plate and put it away. No maid service here. I poked around in the bedroom but found nothing of note. Inside the closet was an assortment of clothes and, no way, JEANS! And T-SHIRTS!!! I stripped off the blacks I was wearing—gone were the yellows; fourth years wore black tracksuits—and slid on the jeans and T-shirt. They were perfectly worn and felt like heaven.

I found a small library of books in the living room. I almost laughed when I spotted *Harry Potter*, comfort food for the head. I grabbed the first book in the series, curled up in my bed, and read the familiar words until I fell asleep.

I HAD PLANNED ON sleeping in, finally, but no dice. Training us to need only four hours of sleep a night was intentional. It was logical solution when your life revolved around the protection of another. You could fall asleep after they did and wake up before them. Because, aside from us, who in their right mind sleeps less than four hours a night? Crazy people and us, that's who. To be honest though, there's only a razor thin line between those two groups when I think about it.

It was before dawn, but I might as well have breakfast. Whoever had stocked my place knew me well. I found a giant box of Golden Grahams in a cupboard and went to town. As I drank my sugary milk it sent me back to my childhood. Delicious.

After yesterday's complete veg-a-thon, my body was itching for exercise. I hadn't punched anything, flipped anyone, or fired a weapon in way too long.

I went to my closet and, I know it sounds silly, got really excited again that I got to choose my own outfit. I began to grab stuff. The options were overwhelming. Keeping it simple, I pulled out a blue tank top and black jogging pants. Oh so much comfier than those damn tracksuits. I hurried to the elevator. In the briefing packet, I was told the gyms were on the third floor of the basement. I punched B3 a little too aggressively and slighty cracked the button.

"Sorry," I said toward the little camera in the top corner and gave a shrug. "I'm antsy."

As I expected, the gym had every kind of weightlifting and fitness machine imaginable. There were also boxing wrings, MMA cages, bamboo-floored dojos, weapons training areas, anything and everything you could want. I was a kid in a candy store.

There were maybe twenty or so people going about

their business. Some guy was absolutely demolishing a set of dummies with a wooden samurai sword. He was good, too good. His long brown hair swirled around his face as he moved obscuring me from a clean look at him, but he looked strangely familiar. If he was still there later I would try to work with him for a bit, but first I felt a good run would warm me up nicely.

The elevated track that wrapped around the gym was empty and calling my name. And then I saw him. Okay, I heard him first. I would know his laugh anywhere, so when I heard his deep giggle my stomach gave a little jump. *Junie!* I turned to see him picking himself up after being thrown down by a tiny woman I didn't recognize.

Interestingly, he was wearing a blue shirt and black pants like me. Fully upright he brushed his messy blonde hair out of his eyes and bowed to the little lady. He towered over her and his wide shoulders blocked her from my view entirely. He had the body of an elite athlete, perfectly chiseled.

The tiny lady saw me heading toward him, so I quickly raised my finger to my lips and mouthed a silent *shhh*. Playing along she pretended to show Junie a throw.

When I was directly behind him, I wrapped my arm around his neck and flipped him over my hip. I rolled with him onto the ground, landing on top of him, pinning his arms to the ground.

Our faces ended up inches from each other. He burst into a wide smile he tried to hide.

"Damnit, Ren." He struggled, but I kept him pinned easily. "Let me up," he said, doing his best to sound annoyed.

"Say it," I demanded, smiling.

He smirked and clenched his mouth shut. He struggled harder, but I kept him down easily. To add insult to injury, I lightly slapped his cheek and said again, "Say it."

He fought it for a bit more and then burst out laughing., "Please, go." He looked at me and added, "Happy?"

"That's it. That's your one time."

I relaxed—only slightly. It was enough, and with lightning quickness he flipped me over and pinned me to ground. Frustrated by my momentary lapse I struggled to get away but knew it was hopeless.

"Say it," he commanded with a grin.

Now it was my turn to shake my head and clench my mouth shut.

He grabbed my arm and slowly torqued it until we both knew it was dangerously close to breaking. It didn't hurt, of course; I'd been pain-free for months. But mentally we both knew how long a break would take to heal and that they wouldn't assign you a FIP with a broken bone. It was a pretty serious threat since no one wanted to spend any more time here than necessary.

"Say it," he said again and twisted a fraction more threateningly. I shook my head.

With a sigh he let my arm go and said, "You suck."

He helped me up. We shared a brief hug. As always, I fought the feelings that always appeared when that happened. He was warm and safe. Being with him felt right, but it was never to be. We both knew this. We were each other's family now, our only family. Neither of us wanted anything to change that. So all feelings were locked deep inside and any that escaped were hunted down and forced back in.

I hadn't seen him since the day before I was "shot."

He pointed at the bandage that was plainly obvious under my tank top and asked, "You okay?"

I nodded and said, "Yep. They put the gel on it so it's fine. Itches like crazy though. You?"

He turned around and pulled up his shirt showing me a huge two foot-long bandage across his muscled back.

"What the . . ." I said as I instinctively reached out. He put his shirt back down and turned back to me.

"I got to fight him," he said and pointed to the guy still destroying things with the wooden samurai sword. "He's even better with a real one. Sliced me across my back then stabbed me through. Didn't hit any major organs. Dude's a pro. Isn't he that Hunter who caught you in the woods on . . . wait, don't tell me, you reference that day all the time . . . day . . . thirty-fo . . .?"

Realizing we were watching him, the samurai guy paused and looked at us. It *was* him.

"Twenty-two," I muttered.

"Twenty-two! Was just about say that," he lied.

I hadn't really heard him, though. *Luka.* I'd relived the memory of him and Tom in the woods so many times I was numb to it. But I was no longer that scared little girl. All that memory did now was motivate me angry.

Completely unaware, Junie waved at Luka goofily. All he got in return was a slight nod of his head. Luka's eyes flickered back on me for a full three seconds before he went back to his training.

"Not much of a talker though," Junie whispered.

With the moment over, I asked, "Up for a run?"

Junie hated running and I knew it. Running for running's sake was way too boring to him. I agreed, but it was the easiest form of exercise.

He must have missed me as much as I missed him because he said, "Sure."

We ended up doing a little more than ten miles. It was a great warm-up. We followed that up with some grappling and fighting. I would miss this the most, this sparring with Junie. It was always an even fight, no matter what we did. Whatever edge Junie gained with his reach and superior power, I was able to cancel out with my quickness and speed. I picked him apart while he tossed me around like a doll. It was, as always, tons of fun.

Junie was itching to shoot something and wanted to go to the range, so we agreed to split up for an hour and meet in the building's deli for some lunch. I watched him leave and for the briefest moment wondered if I'd see him again. What if he was called for his link before lunch? What if I was?

I turned toward the far corner and the wall of knives. I understood Junie's itch. The blades were calling to me. Their high polish reflected rainbows of light across the training area. About six months into our training I fell in love with the things. They were so much more personal and frightening than guns. Don't get me wrong, I could hit you square between the eyes, dead to rights, from 500 yards with any gun on the planet, but I didn't enjoy it. If I was going to kill someone, I wanted them to know I had done it; Ren Sharpe had killed them. It was more than a formality thing in my eyes. It was courtesy. A matter of honor.

I grabbed a curved eight inch knife from the wall and begin to wield it. Playing with it in my hand, doing tricks to learn the weight of it. When you fought with a knife it was more dancing than fighting, and maybe that's why I enjoyed so much.

I spun, flipped, and rolled around the mat imagining the villains as they attacked me. After five straight minutes of practice I stopped to grab a second knife from the wall to practice my double attacks. Then I froze.

Luka was standing there, watching me.

"Hello, old friend. You've improved since we last met." For reasons I can't really explain, his soft strange voice comforted me. I was glad that he remembered me. "Simple and impressive movement. Do you have a secret?"

He still spoke with that stiff politeness. I figured why lie and smiled shyly as I said, "I imagine I'm dancing to music."

He glanced around, as if to see if anyone were listening, and added, "Me too."

I nodded, unsure of what to say.

"Care to spar?" he asked.

I gulped. I definitely wanted to spar, if only to show him I wasn't that skinny little girl with a stick he'd found in the woods. More than that, I wanted to see how I stacked up against a Hunter—correction, the *best* Hunter. But I didn't want to get hurt and have my assignment delayed. I had to get out of this place.

Reading me like a book he smiled and said, "I won't

hurt you, I promise. And if by some chance I do, I'll make sure they know it was my fault. You're departure won't be delayed by me."

"Okay then."

"Your weapon?" he asked, looking at the wall.

I held up the knives. "Got 'em."

"Excellent. Now, I want you to try as hard as you can. You will not hold back. Do you swear to this?" he asked.

"I do."

"Good." He put down the wooden sword he'd been using earlier and drew a metal sword from his belt. He held it beside him at the ready. We bowed to each other. I twirled the knives in my hands as I waited for him to make the first move.

In a flash he charged me. I rolled out of the way and sliced at his legs. He slid effortlessly out of the way, and I felt the razors edge of his sword stop at the base of my neck. *Holy hell.*

He allowed me to get up before attacking again. This time I lasted all of five seconds, which was still a good three seconds longer than the first time.

"You are not keeping your promise to me, Ren Sharpe. If you do not keep yours I will not keep mine not to hurt you." He said this so matter-of-factly I had to believe him. "Try your best, or else."

Fine. If he wanted my best shot he'd get it. He charged, and I dodged. I took a swipe at him and barely missed. I ducked, jumped, or blocked countless swings. He was unrelenting. After I blocked one aggressive swing, I took the offensive and began to weave and spin at him. He backpedaled, avoiding my swipes. I lunged with my right hand, knowing he'd dodge it, and used my momentum to do a spin kick that hit him square in the jaw. I kept spinning, cutting him across his chest with my left knife and swung my right at his neck.

I stopped with the dagger point on his neck. I smiled at him but couldn't understand why he was smiling back at me. A dribble of blood leaked out of his mouth as, a little out of breath, he said, "Well done, Ren. I knew you had it in you. But . . ."

His eyes flashed down. The point of his sword was millimeters away from my stomach ready to stab.

"Draw?" I asked with a smile.

"A very good one at that," he said. He slid his sword back into the sheath and extended a hand. I hurled the knife in my right hand into the forehead of a dummy about fifty feet way, then took his hand and shook it.

"Thank you for this. Best of luck, Ren. It was truly an honor."

"Thank you. And the honor was mine, Luka." I added.

His smile softened. "I hope I never see you again, Ms. Sharpe."

"Me too," I replied—maybe a bit too overdramatically.

And with that he walked away. I couldn't believe that I had just done that. I'd nearly beaten the unbeatable. If anything deserved a sinister evil laugh it was this. *Muhaha!* I couldn't wipe the stupid grin off my face as I took the knife in my left hand and tossed it at the same dummy as before. I had drawn with the guy who had beat up Junie. I couldn't wait to rub it in his face.

CHAPTER 12
WORST GOODBYE EVER

On my way to the deli I formulated what I considered to be an aggressive yet affective plan for giving Junie's ego a beating. Maybe secretly I hoped a good-natured ribbing would ease the pain of the inevitable: our time together was drawing to a close, and we'd never see each other again. So best to make the most of it with as many insults as possible. When I found him I was about to unleash the hounds—but he hugged me, grinning like an idiot. It caught me off guard and threw me off my game.

"It's happening," he whispered in my ear.

"Huh?" I stepped back.

He grabbed me by my shoulders. "I'm getting my FIP. I'm getting out of here."

My jaw dropped and my eyes widened. I managed a smile and attempted to recover. "That's awesome."

"I know, isn't it?"

Thank goodness Junie had never been good at reading

people, especially me, so the swirl of emotions was lost on him. I *was* excited for him, really I was. He was getting out of here and finally beginning his life. But I thought I'd go first and he'd be the one left all alone in this trash bin. Luka aside, I knew the truth. Junie was better, stronger, more confident—so they'd save him for somebody *really* important. Selfish, yes, but still it's what I had thought. I'd never considered it happening the other way around.

I played my part well as I transitioned from smiling-surprised Ren to head-shaking-can't-believe-it Ren. This would of course be followed up by totally-happy-for-you Ren. But the you're-leaving-me-all-alone Ren was always lurking underneath.

As head-shaking-can't-believe-it Ren I said, "It really is great."

Enter totally-happy-for-you Ren with a, "I'm so excited for you."

"Thanks," he said. When we sat down he asked me, "Are you okay?"

"I'm fine, really." I had given in momentarily to you're-leaving-me-all-alone Ren and somehow he'd noticed.

"You sure?"

"Yeah. Do you know where you'll be going?"

"No."

"When will it happen?" I asked.

He looked at a clock on the wall and said, "Fifteen minutes. I was supposed to go shower and change, but I had to say bye."

"I would have figured it out."

"It would have been rude."

And that was one of the many things about Junie I loved. He now knew a thousand different ways to kill a person but still kept his country boy manners. Here he was minutes from a moment four years in the making and all he could think about was not being rude to his old pal Ren.

Was this going to be the last time I'd ever see him? His hand was resting on the table. Reflexively I reached out and held it with my own.

I looked at him in the eye. "Good luck, Junie. Goodbye."

He swallowed but tried to smile. "That's it? That's all you got for me?"

"I was trying to say goodbye." I snapped my hand away. "I thought this was it. I didn't know if I'd ever see you again. I'm not good at this stuff."

"Obviously." He then looked at me in a way I'd never seen before. "Ren, you'll know when I'm saying goodbye to you." He stood up and said, "I'll come by after my link."

There he left me, sitting in that damn deli with nothing but my own stupid eighteen-year-old-thoughts to myself. The damn had burst and the feelings I'd held in check for so long were loose. It was a good thing he was getting his FIP. The quicker he was gone, the quicker I could start forgetting about him.

I WAS A ZOMBIE as I made my way back to my new apartment. Whether Junie had meant to or not his comment had infected my brain like a virus. What the hell had he meant by "you'll know when I'm saying goodbye to you?"

Before I knew it, I was standing there staring at my door not moving. Was this the moment he was finally going to say to hell with all the rules we'd set up and the sidestepping we'd done to avoid hurting the other? Should I let him?

In the shower the argument, privy only to myself, continued. *Maybe I should I initiate it. I don't want to live the rest of my life regretting I never did anything either. Besides, don't I owe it to myself to make sure I know how I really felt? Or better yet, I could treat it as a reward for making it through this place? Yeah, it would be my well-deserved reward kiss.*

While blow-drying my hair I got queasy. I'd never kissed anyone. Not for real anyway. Maybe I should suddenly become ill. No one wants to kiss a sickling. I put down the hair dryer and gave a weak cough.

I looked in the mirror and squeaked out, "I got the black lung, pop." I smiled at my own funny. No, pretending to be sick wouldn't work since I was a terrible actor. So it was back to the reward concept; best I had.

I felt like I was about to vomit.

Oooh, vomit breath. Now that would totally back him off. And we're back to the sick idea. Come on body, heave away. Alas, no heaving.

Tired of my own crazy, I sat down at the desk with a hmph. If Junie wanted to give it a shot when he got here, who was I to stop him? He'd put up with me for so long he earned the chance. But I wouldn't make it easy. I'd be sure to make it as awkward and embarrassing as possible for him. Heck, for both of us. *Boy thinks he can kiss me huh? Ha!*

THREE HOURS LATER AND still no Junie. Maybe once you got linked they shipped you out immediately? Poor planning on Junie's part if so.

While waiting for Prince Idiot I made the mistake of checking to see if my old email was active. It was. Most of it was junk. A lot of penis enlargements and Viagra ads. Know your audience, folks! Come on.

But then I saw it. An email from my mother. And then there was another. I did a quick search and it brought up more. She had sent a new one every week. The first few were begging me to come home, saying she was sorry for whatever had caused me to leave. They then transitioned to pleading for some kind of contact to let her know I was okay. After they identified my "body" and held my funeral, the emails stopped for a few months. But then they started up again, with a new tone. She'd accepted I wasn't coming back. Instead each email was an update on the family, and what was going on in their lives. I ate it up.

I got through about a quarter of them until I couldn't take it anymore. Tears streamed down my cheeks. I wanted to email her back. I even hit reply and typed out I'm alive. I even went so far as to hover the mouse over the send button before caving and deleting the response.

Had I gone through with it a visit from the Hunters was a guarantee. As much fun as my sparring with Luka had been I knew in the real world I was no match for him, let alone a group of five exactly like him. The secrecy of this program was bigger than any one of us. If I made any contact with my family they would be killed too, after me. Secrets must be kept.

My emailing trip down memory lane had been more of a plummet, and it put me in a funk. A bad one. The usual routines did nothing to get me out of either. Knife tricks.

Nothing. 500 push-ups. Nada. Harry Potter? Even my wizarding friend couldn't break this one. I was getting mad at myself the longer this took. If I was going to experience my first kiss I was going to enjoy it damnit!

When I was about to explode, there was a knock on the door.

Son of a! I was still funkified and not ready for this pivotal moment in my ever-so-eventful love life.

"It's open, come on in," I said loudly but with a touch of bitterness.

But no one did. "Come in, Junie," I said a bit louder.

Another knock. Finally I stormed to the door. "Jesus, Junie, just come in."

Before me stood a small girl dressed in an outfit similar to what a hotel staffer would wear. She held out a cardboard box. "I was asked to deliver this to you by Mr. Miller."

I took the box from her and asked, "Where's Junie?"

"He's been assigned and is being shipped out. Good day, ma'am." She turned on her heels and headed toward the elevator.

Huh? Seriously? My fingers felt clammy as I closed the door. The silence was suffocating. Reality set in. He was really gone and I'd never see him again. Ever.

How could he have not come to say goodbye? He said he would. Instead I get this stupid box? I was beyond angry. I was enraged about a kiss that never was. I had been nervous, yes, but I *had* wanted it. No Junie meant no kiss. I would be living that life of regret after all.

Funk on with a vengeance. I tossed the stupid box on the kitchen table and slumped down into a chair glaring at it. It wasn't even wrapped. On top was a sticky note with his sad little chicken scratch on it: *Sorry I couldn't do this in person. They were pretty adamant about it.*

Adamant?! I'd show him adamant. I tore the note off and tossed it on the floor. I ripped open the cardboard box and took out the ornately carved wooden chest from inside it. It had my initials, R.S., carved into the top. I unhinged the latch and flipped open the box. There were two nasty looking trench knives inside. Vicious little things they were, with brass knuckles around the handle, a blade on top, and a small point called a skull cracker on the bottom. If you couldn't stab your enemy, you could beat them to death. Trench knives were my favorite.

I picked one up. Even furious, I could appreciate how badass these were. It was practically weightless and perfectly balanced. My reflection shone back off of the blade. I looked how I felt: pitiful and angry. I put the knife back into the box and closed the lid. There was some small writing under my initials on the lid of the box that I had originally passed off as decorative swooshes. It read: *Remember when?*

The waterworks were hinting at an encore performance when there was a knock. But it didn't come from the door. It came from behind me.

Standing on my balcony was Junie Miller.

CHAPTER 13
BEST GOODBYE EVER

I barely managed a stuttered, "Wha . . ." and finished it off with an odd, "How?"

Anxiously he said through the glass, "I climbed."

"But—" I started to say but was cut off.

"Hurry up, they think I'm packing." He motioned for me to let him in.

I ran over to the door, unlocked it, and slid it open. He took one step inside and, without hesitating, took my head in his hands and kissed me. It was sweet, passionate, a little wet. It smelled like toothpaste. It was the most wonderful sensation I'd ever felt. It was the release of years of pent-up emotion. And it was over way too quick.

He pulled his head away, but kept my head cradled in his hands when he murmured "*That's* me saying goodbye."

He wrapped his arms around me and held me for a few seconds. He let go of me, backed through the patio door, and climbed over the edge of my balcony railing where a grappling hook sat firmly latched to a post. Upon grabbing the rope, he looked me in the eye. "I love you, Ren Sharpe," he said.

Then he jumped off and disappeared down the side of building.

Funk gone.

"I love you, too," I whispered.

I HONESTLY HAVE NO idea how long I stood there before the ringing of a phone snapped me out of my trance. *Would somebody answer that damn thing?* My body still tingled from the whole experience with Junie, and I wanted to cling to the euphoria because I knew as soon as it was over the cold truth of his goodbye would take over. The kiss made me feel alive again. But that stupid ringing was messing it all up. Finally it stopped.

Junie freakin Miller. I got to hand it to the simple-minded kid, I did not see *that* coming. What a way to go out. Something inside of me had been awakened. Was it love? Or just hormones? All I know was I wanted more.

RING!

God damnit! Answer your phone! Wait, is that my phone? I turned. There was a small screen on the wall by my front door that was flashing, ringing.

When I tapped it, a uniformed young man with a clean-shaven face stared back at me.

"Yeah?" I asked annoyed.

He cleared his throat and said, "Ms. Sharpe. Your assignment has been found."

Holy nut jobs.

"Your escort will direct you to your linking tomorrow at 6 A.M."

The screen went blank. Like a tidal wave, the excitement grew and grew until I could hardly contain it. It was official. I would be a Shadow.

The only problem was I had to wait until morning. This was downright mean, people. This was worse than any of the physical and psychological torments they had put me through here. Couldn't they have called me in the morning to tell me instead of putting me through this? Now, of all times? On the plus side, I knew that linking would accomplish something crucial. It would focus my mind on someone other than Junie Miller.

I GOT ZERO SLEEP. My imagination ran wild all night. But when I tried to picture my FIP, all I could picture was Junie. Six A.M. could not come fast enough. When there was a knock on the door I had it open before the second knock

It was the same small girl who'd given me Junie's gift. She seemed equally as bored to be doing this as delivering packages to me. Or maybe she was just annoyed that she had to be up this early and thus the sourpuss face and sulking demeanor.

I followed her to the elevators. Instead of pushing the down button, she walked right up to a solid wall and placed her palm on it. There was a ding, and the wall slid open to reveal a super-secret elevator. We stepped inside, and she pushed a button marked L2. But before the doors shut, she stepped out, leaving me alone on my trip.

CHAPTER 14
GETTING LINKED

I was antsy on my solo ride to Link-town. As much of a buzz-kill as that lame girl was, at least she was company. Was it me or had I been in here a while? Was it broken? I toyed with the idea of pressing a new button to check but thought better of it. Instead I did what I do best: zoned out.

Would it hurt? Would my person be cool? I pray they're not an infant. How boring would that be? Good lord, where is this thing taking me? What if I actually failed my training and they're taking me back for round two? I would be that older, stupid kid doing it all over again, the one that they all laugh at . . ..

I hadn't even realized the elevator had stopped until the doors slid open. Waiting for me was Not-Beth. We'd become as cordial as two people can be when one issued the other a dosage of liquid hell every night. I'm sure she's a really swell person with a pet puppy in real life, but to me she was and always will be the evil shot girl. Not-Beth equaled no sleep and pain.

Not-Beth smiled.

I returned it with a, "Hey."

She stood in a hallway that led into a spherical room. It reminded me of a planetarium only instead of a telescope in the middle there was a circle of light. My first day and my last day with these stupid lights. Seemed fitting.

"How are you?" she asked.

"Nervous," I said, eyeing the light.

"You don't need to be. You've got nothing to fear here," she said.

"Yeah, I've heard that one before," I said sarcastically.

"Touché. Well, come on." She motioned for me to follow her into the room.

She was about to speak again when I interrupted her. "I'm not an idiot."

"I never thought you were," she murmured.

I moved into the middle of the circle of light. Not-Beth pulled out a small shot from her pocket. I'd gotten so many of them they didn't even phase me any more.

"What's that for?"

"Helps with the link. Opens your mind and makes it more . . . permanent."

I rolled up my sleeve and said, "Let 'er rip."

She gave me the shot and left.

"Well, well, Ms. Sharpe. I knew you had it in you," came the friendly sound of my old buddy, Mr. Speakervoice. I smiled.

"Come to say goodbye?" I asked. I had begun speaking to him directly a few years back. It had been fun pretending he could hear me.

"I thought I would, yes." Only that last part didn't sound quite right. It hadn't come from a speaker above my head. No, it come from behind me *and* it had answered my question.

A very good-looking, kindly older man stood behind me. He had graying hair and green eyes, was maybe in his late forties. He wore a white lab coat and was leaning against the wall grinning widely like a proud parent.

"Mr. Speakervoice?"

He chuckled. "One of the best names I've ever been given that's for sure. You've certainly been a fun one, Ren."

I blushed at his compliment. I kind of wanted to hug him. Even in his lab coat, he looked so comfy—like a model dad in an Eddie Bauer magazine. He moved closer.

"I never do this, but since you've been such a hoot I had to come by and wish you luck. You were a joy to watch. I'm glad you made it."

He offered his hand for me to shake. Grinning like an idiot school girl, I stepped out of my circle and shook it. I kind of dead-fished him too, but I didn't care. It was Mr. S, he'd understand.

Up close, I saw that his eyes were super light green, almost white. I got a funny feeling in my gut from them, but pushed it aside. So he had creepy eyes; I bet there were some people who thought freckles were creepy. Who was I to judge, right?

We stopped shaking and Mr. S. motioned for me to return to my spot.

"We're not monsters, you know," he whispered. "It's

harder on us than you'll ever imagine." His voice rose. "Now relax and enjoy the show!"

I watched him walk away. "What's your name?" I blurted out.

He looked over his shoulder as he said, "Blake. But my friends call me Mr. S."

He left me alone, still grinning like a moron. I knew I shouldn't be happy, but I was. Why?

Not-Beth returned and said softly, "That was a first."

She held a black metal box. Inside was a pair of lighter-than-air glasses, similar to the kind that had given me my history lesson when I first got here. Only these looked different, sleeker. I started to grab them from the box but paused. I looked at Not-Beth, and she nodded encouragingly. I took a deep breath. This was it.

Not-Beth patted my shoulder. "Good luck out there, Ren Sharpe." She then left me alone in the room. Without warning, the circle of light turned off and the room went dark. But in my hand, the lighter-than-air glasses glowed light blue and hummed.

I put them on.

HIS NAME IS GARETH Young.

My life no longer matters. I only care about one thing: him. I have to see him. I have to make sure he's okay. As I remove the glasses I find I'm having difficulty breathing not being sure he's safe; not seeing so with my own eyes.

It isn't love, or a crush, it's more of an obsession. But for his safety only. It's hard to explain the feeling any more than that.

Regardless, I can't stand it here anymore. I have to get to him. I have to leave right now or I'll lose my mind. Everything else is inconsequential.

AS WITH ALL LINKS, I did not know what or who he would become. That way, I wouldn't try to influence him. All I knew was that my FIP, GarethYoung, was about to begin college and thus I was going as well. *College.* My parents would be so proud.

I could hear the conversations of the other students already.

Oh, I went to this high school, or *I got this on my SATs. What about you, Ren?*

Me? I can kill you with a Capri Sun straw.

Gareth had been identified for our program three days ago and had been assigned a temporary protective unit immediately. They would be officially handing him off to me in two days. I didn't want to wait that long to see him, but this was how it was. He had made it this far without me, so what was another couple of days? Thank God he wasn't a baby.

I got back to my apartment. No-Personality-Girl was waiting at the door. She gave me a box and told me I could put whatever I wanted in it. All the clothes had been packed up and taken away already, so there wasn't much left to snag. She waited while I packed.

I put the knives from Junie it first. It was all I had really that was truly my own. I then tossed in the Harry Potter books and a couple others for good measure. And the giant box of Golden Grahams. Unless I wanted to take the pictures off the walls, or keep the silverware, that's all I could really take from the place. I shrugged.

"That's it I guess." I told her.

"Your clothing and other necessary gear have been loaded and are already en route to your location. They will be waiting for you upon arrival. Proceed to the elevator and press D."

"The real one or the super secret one?"

"Real," she said in the same flat voice.

I grabbed my sad little box of items and started to leave but paused when I glimpsed the grappling hook still attached to the balcony. My mind went back to the kiss with Junie. Now that I was linked, nothing was going to get in my way, and yet Junie had fought that same overwhelming desire, been strong enough to push it aside to come see me. I didn't know if I'd have been able to do the same.

"You need to leave now, Ms. Sharpe," came the girl's stupid voice. I couldn't help but give her a little snarl as I left the room. I smirked as I heard her mutter to herself, ". . . don't need this crap . . ."

The 'D' stood for departure, because when the elevator doors opened I found myself facing a long hallway with an open end. They were oh-so-clever and original here. Sunlight streamed through from a vast open space. I was guided to a small jet.

The aircraft's interior was a huge disappointment. I'd seen enough movies growing up to expect nothing less than plush chairs and sofas on private planes. Not the case here. The plane had been stripped to its bare bones, the necessities. It, like me, had a job to do, so why waste any-thing on bells and whistles? Regulation jump seats lined the walls and nothing else. I took my seat halfway down the plane and buckled myself in.

The windows were blacked out, so when the cabin door was shut only a small reading light provided any illumina-tion. Even if I'd wanted to sleep I couldn't. The need to see Gareth was a burning fire inside of me. The longer this took, the hotter it burned.

THE LANDING WAS HARD. Who was this rookie at the wheel? Should have let me fly. My internal clock guessed we'd been flying for a little over three hours.

After a very brief taxi, the plane stopped. I was abso-lutely blinded by the bright sunlight when the cabin door opened, and hit by a wave of pure heat and humidity that nearly knocked the wind out of me. The air was heavy and hard to breath. Still half-blind I stood up and hopped off the plane onto the tarmac. With watering eyes, I got my first look at College Station, TX, the home of Texas A&M University.

CHAPTER 15

JUST LIKE EVERYBODY ELSE

If America had an armpit, it was College Station, TX in August. I instantly began to sweat the moment I got off the plane and cursed the stupid jeans I was wearing. I'd probably never be able to comfortably wear a pair of them in this place.

Ahead of me I saw a giant water tower that read, '*Welcome To Aggieland*', and beyond that, sitting in the middle of campus, stood the monster of a football stadium they called Kyle Field.

The campus was a few miles away from the airport with nothing but dead, summer-withered plants as far as I could see. I felt like I was about to go into Thunderdome from the Mad Max movies. Two men enter, one Ren leaves.

Behind me the door of the plane shut and the plane began its taxi for takeoff. Job done, get the hell out of here, crank up the AC. As it moved away, it revealed an old, beat-up green motorcycle with a sidecar sitting across the tarmac.

It looked like it'd seen better days, much better days. This must have been their idea of a gift. I'd always chosen a motorcycle over a car whenever I could in training. Would have liked something a bit newer, but this would do.

I watched the plane take off, bank away, and soar off into the horizon. Finally alone.

I then did what I hadn't done in a very, very long time: the happy dance. It must have been about 140 degrees on the asphalt so if anyone had been watching it probably looked like I was trying to avoid melting my shoes. But if they had really looked they'd have seen the telltale spins, hops, and claps of a genuine freedom dance. Yeah it was hot. Yeah it was humid, but I didn't care. I was out, suckas!

Upon completion of a very extended and in my mind very deserved dance, I jogged over to the motorcycle. In the sidecar was an envelope with two sets of keys. One was for the bike and other was for my dorm room. *Hot damn.*

I started the bike and it hummed like a kitten. It looked like hell, but it was all a ruse. This thing was a hoss and proved its derelict façade was just that as I tore off out of the airport and let the wind whip my hair and fly across my face. I had a lot to do before my FIP would arrive the next day, but I allowed myself an hour for a joy ride around town and down a few country roads.

The campus was a beehive of activity as everyone was moving into the dorms. There were sobbing mothers, hand-shaking dads, and jealous younger siblings surrounding the over-excited kids finally tasting true freedom. In that respect we were similar, these college freshman and I, but that was probably about the extent of it.

When I pulled up to my dorm, everyone took notice. Some stopped what they were doing altogether; others glanced sideways at me. I saw my reflection in a mirror and realized why. First of all, I had no helmet. Second, I had no makeup. Third, I was wearing a beat-up pair of jeans, tight T-shirt, and old school classic grey New Balances. Combine that with pulling up on old Hank— yes, I named my bike Hank—and I got it. So much for blending in. I looked like the dangerous badass I was.

A group of Abercrombie girls gave me the stink eye. *Bitches.* I stared back until they scampered off.

I turned off Hank, hopped off, and made my way inside, keeping my face cold and emotionless so no one would bother me. I snaked my way through the students and their over-protective parents. Seeing this made a small part of me miss my family. Not so much for their company, but because I knew it would have meant a lot to them to be here with me. Okay, fine, everyone seemed to have someone besides me and it sucked.

I found my room at the far end of the building on the corner and slipped inside. Boxes. Cases. More boxes. The place was packed floor to ceiling. They had finagled me my own room somehow, which was good because the very numerous and very obvious cases of guns would probably have been a little awkward to explain to a roomie. One was even marked *C-4*. Real subtle, guys. Anyone who'd seen a decent action movie knew what that was.

I found an inventory list by the door and took stock of

what I had, making sure it was all here. It was the basic package given to each Shadow. I could list everything that came with it by heart, but I still wanted to be sure.

An hour later I had successfully accounted for all 532 items included in my slightly non-traditional welcome baskets. Enough dillydallying, time to go to work.

Gareth's room was right next to mine. *Coed dorms, heyo!* With all of the activity going on, no one noticed as I slipped in and out of his room, setting up equipment. I hid eighteen pin-sized cameras in the walls, lights, and bathroom so that there were no blind spots. I placed seven microphones in strategic places. And to finish off the job I installed infrared motion detectors at his door, inside his room, and outside his window. I then spent some time in my room fiddling with the various feeds. I was done by four o'clock.

I looked at the train wreck that was my room but wanted no part of unpacking anything else at the moment. I needed to get out. I needed to stretch my legs. I needed to keep myself occupied as the excruciating wait for Gareth dragged on and on.

Okay, I needed to hit something.

I found workout gear in one of the clothing boxes. Walking to the rec gave me my first good look at the campus. They're all pretty much the same though, you know? A library. A quad. Old buildings. Juvenile idiots running around. Hippies tossing Frisbees. There was far too much here to annoy a trained killer.

As if on cue, I ducked under a rogue Frisbee before it could hit me in the head. As he passed me, a long-haired, bearded, cut-offs-wearing dude said, "Nice duckage."

I watched him go. Protecting Gareth was going to be easy. Protecting these idiots from me was going to be the real challenge.

By the time I reached the rec center and received directions to the punching bags, my fists were already clenched, If I heard one more excited sorority girl scream, frat boy "bro," or unnecessarily loud laugh, I would rip someone's heart out through their belly button.

Solace came in a fifty-pound bag. I didn't even bother to wrap my knuckles or put on gloves before unleashing hell on that poor thing. After fifteen minutes I was beginning to wear a small hole in it. I was just starting to feel better when a deep, cocky voice interrupted me with a, "You know, your form's off."

I dropped my hands and turned. A had-to-be-frat-guy was about ten feet away. You know the type: short spiky hair that takes hours to look perfectly messy and tiny stick legs because all he works out are his chest and arms. He instantly reminded me of Trey, the boy I'd crushed hard on back in Amherst, two lifetimes ago. He was the spitting image of the person I imagined Trey had become. Not good for this guy.

I raised my eyebrows at his comment.

"Yeah. You need to rotate your hips more." He then demonstrated for me slowly, showing the "hip" rotation.

I kept forgetting that if you didn't know me, I might actually be attractive. In my mind I was, well, *me*, so those thoughts didn't exist. That was why I tried not to sound too annoyed when I said, "Thanks," and went back to my business.

I only got in about five hits before he walked over and said, "Still wrong. Like this." He then grabbed my hips and began to twist them for me. That's what you would call the final straw.

I was about to break his thumbs, but luckily he spoke up again first. "You know, I could maybe show you a thing or two if you wanna spar."

Funny: all at once I remembered that beating the hell out of Trey was something I'd once dreamed about, after "the splash zone." I still owed him for ruining the only day of high school I ever got to experience. The similarities between Trey and this idiot were too close for me to pass this up.

I smiled. "Now that's a great idea."

We walked over to the mini-ring that was set up.

"So my name's—"

"Yeah, yeah," I said cutting him off.

He grinned as if he liked whatever game I was playing. Poor thing. We climbed into the ring and put on gloves. Lame.

"You see, it's all in the hi—"

"I learn a lot better by doing, actually."

"Cool."

We touched gloves. I allowed him to circle me once. He feinted a few times, but I didn't even flinch. He took one half-hearted swing at me which I easily ducked, and in quick succession I hit him with a right cross to the chin, a left hook to the ribs, and then finished him off with a spin kick to the temple.

Kid was out like a sack of potatoes. I crouched down

next to him and lightly slapped him on the cheek until he came too.

"You all right?" he asked me.

"Fine. Thanks for the lesson."

"No problem," he said groggily. As I walked away he called out after me, "Wanna go out sometime?"

"How bout Nevuary," I said over my shoulder.

"Cool," he said. Then I'm pretty sure he passed back out.

I caught a nerdy, runt of a kid staring openmouthed at me. I smiled awkwardly and waved. No response. I still had energy to burn but sticking around here seemed like a silly idea after what I had done to stick-legs.

So now what? Treadmills? No, overcrowded with girls "running" at speed two while reading magazines. I hadn't brought a suit, so swimming was out. With no real options, and the fear of being ratted out by the runt, I decided a simple run around the massive campus, like any normal student, would do the trick. A normal student who had just assaulted and knocked out another one. Who hasn't done that, right? Totally normal.

AFTER A QUICK SHOWER and a check that all of my surveillance equipment was still working, I made my way to one of the cafeterias. I found a table off in the corner and sat down ready to do work on a big bowl of mac and cheese. Before I could raise the fork to my mouth, a tray slapped down across from me.

It was the runt from the gym.

"That was the coolest thing I've ever seen," he said breathlessly. "You were like wham, hack, walloo, and he

was all uhhh, budoooo, out." He of course had punctuated every odd sound he made with finger and hand
movements. "You should be in movies. Or have your own
TV show." He stuffed a massive spoonful of mashed potatoes into his mouth and then added, "I'd watch."

I was frozen, my first bite of mac still on the fork inches
from my lips. He sat there beaming as he worked the potatoes around his mouth and swallowed.

"I'm Lloyd," he said right before popping in a whole
chicken finger. He reached across the table to shake my
hand.

I forced myself to be polite. I shook it. "Nice to meet
you, Lloyd."

"You gotta name? Cause if you don't I'm gonna call you
Kung Fu."

I kind of liked the name, I admit. "Julia," I said.

Julia Roth was my F.A.T.E.-given alias. Better to use
a phony name than your real one in case you ran into
someone from your old life. Weirder things could happen.

"Cool name. Like Julia Gulia."

This kid—and he was a kid, he looked about twelve-
years-old, max—was ridiculous. I didn't want to like him.
I didn't want to be his friend. But come on. Coke bottle
glasses, short hair, and clothes that had obviously been
passed down from an older brother. Not to mention the
random The *Wedding Singer* reference.

"How old are you?" I asked.

"Just turned eighteen," he said. I raised my eyebrows
and he quickly said, "Okay sixteen . . . fifteen."

"You're not fifteen," I said loudly.

"Shhhh. Yes, I am." He paused and then added, "Why, do I look older?"

I snorted. "No. You look like you're twelve."

"Well keep it on the low-low." He looked around. "Don't wanna ruin my rep."

"It'll be our secret." This kid was awesome. He was the little brother your friend hated but who cracked you up. I nibbled on my food a bit before asking, "So are you some professor's son or something?"

He shook his head.

"Visiting your brother?"

He shook his head and looked a little confused. That made two of us.

"I'm sorry, I don't get it," I said. "Why are you here?"

"Because I'm a student." Then, speaking to me like I was an idiot, he added: "I graduated early. Real early."

"So you're like Doogie Howser smart."

"Wow," he said dully. "Never heard that one before." He gave me a look that said, *You completely unoriginal horseface.*

"Hey, that show was awesome and being Doogie smart is a compliment."

"That show sucked."

"You know the guy that played Doogie's best friend?" I asked. Lloyd nodded so I continued, "That's my uncle. So if you think the show sucked, you think he sucks and by indirect correlation, me."

Total lie. All of it. But it was too good of a lie not to run with. The mac was okay, but watching Lloyd struggle with how to respond was pure entertainment. I could see his puzzled face form questions, then shake them off. After a minute or so he gave up. His head dropped and he began chewing on another chicken finger.

It was so pathetic that I caved. "Kid, totally kidding."

He stopped chewing. His face reddened "I knew it. I knew you were joking. But man . . . that was good."

As we finished up, I learned that Lloyd had been home-schooled, shocker, and didn't have many (code for any) friends, double shocker. Until now, I supposed. He kept me laughing. It felt good to talk with someone who wasn't like me. Someone who would lead a normal life. At one point he asked me what my major was and what I wanted to be. I didn't have an answer for either.

"Well, if I were you, I'd major in takin' ass with a minor in kickin names."

I stared at him, waiting for him to realize what he'd said. It took a few long seconds but when he did we both cracked up.

He insisted on walking me back to my dorm for my protection, cute, and refused to leave until I took a sheet of paper with his email, cell phone, Facebook, and Twitter information on it. (That way, I couldn't fake entering it into my phone. You couldn't delete a hard copy.) It was for, as he put it, "If you ever, you know, wanna hang, study. . . or make out."

I spent the rest of the night unpacking and making my room look like a normal freshman's. I'd been given classes on how to do it. No, really, actual classes. You ever try hiding a grenade launcher in *your* room?

Some things were easy. Clothes went in the closet. Posters, provided for me, went on the walls. Other things, like the aforementioned grenade launcher, were difficult even with the classes. At one point a couple of girls knocked on my door. I had been inspecting my blocks of C-4 at the time and hurriedly tossed them under my bed before opening up a crack. They invited me to a little party down the hall. I politely thanked them but said I had a lot of unpacking to do first and that maybe I'd make it down later.

I didn't.

When I was finally done no one would ever guess this room was anything but normal; boring even. And that was the point. Be boring, be ignored, and don't draw attention to yourself. Speaking of which, I'd get a motorcycle helmet first thing tomorrow. If someone were to walk in they'd never think the room housed a small arsenal, or that the person that lived there could kill them with anything, like a sticky note. No, the person who lives here is a sad girl who only likes to study. And sure, ride her sad little motorcycle. A loner. Awwww.

I SLEPT POORLY, AND by poorly, I mean an hour at most. What little sleep I did get was filled with weird dreams. In one I watched Gareth arrive at campus, and when he opened his door he was run over by a bus. In another he never showed up at all and I was told to watch over Lloyd instead.

Luckily, I had stayed up until nearly dawn unpacking. That and checking the Web. I decided to look up my old pal Mr. S.by name-searching "Blake+MIT." I'd noticed the MIT class ring, the Grad Rat, on his finger when I'd met him. His image popped up almost immediately; he was an MIT grad, younger than I thought. So he existed in the real world, too, just like me. Interesting. I memorized his CV and shut down the computer. When I finally decided to get up and get dressed it was a respectable 8 A.M. Yeah, it was early for a youth, but not so early it would draw suspicion. Besides, if someone saw me awake, it would only enhance the loner image I was going for.

I had access to any funds I needed—basically unlimited cash—and I could have eaten breakfast anywhere. But I wanted to stay on campus, close to where I needed to be. I chose a new cafeteria this time. I did this partly to try something different, but mainly to avoid running into Lloyd. He was a sweet kid, but I couldn't have him tagging along.

There were maybe thirty students, older grad-looking types, in the cafeteria. It wasn't hard to find a table off on my own. I grabbed a copy of the student paper and sat down with a big plate of bacon and eggs. Student papers are hilarious. It's funny what the top story of the day in college is versus the rest of the world. For example the day's top story was how the star quarterback was going to miss the first game due to a concussion. For real? Top story?

I unfolded the paper, and it showed a picture of the poor sap. I dropped my fork on my plate. It was stick legs from the gym. I quickly skimmed the article, fearing they'd give some kind of physical description of his attacker. I scanned for words like gorgeous, and angelic-looking. You know, words that described me . . . To be safe I also looked for words like homely and bitter shrew. Just in case, mind you. But there was nothing about an attack of any kind. He said he'd hit his head while getting out of his car, which apparently this entire campus was ready to believe.

I guess between admitting you got your ass handed to you by a 115 pound girl, or looking like an idiot, he chose idiot. I still felt kind of bad when I read that apparently the team had title hopes this year or something. Oops.

When I finished my breakfast and had read the paper front to back I checked my watch. 9:12.

My FIP was to arrive at approximately 10:15, according to intel. I was to wait at the clock tower, and once his car drove by, the temporary team would leave and he would be all mine. With nothing better to do I figured to hell with it and headed to clock tower early.

I was about halfway there when I heard a confused, soft voice. "Ren? Ren . . . Sharpe?"

I froze in mid-stride and turned. She was older, but I recognized her instantly. Crap. The girl's name was . . .

"It's me, Becky. Becky Dooley. Is it really you?"

They had trained us for this moment, but all the training in the world didn't prepare me for the rush of emotions that came at this sudden contact with my old world. Beating up Not-Trey was one thing. And it wasn't like we were friends. But she was real, and she still represented a part of me that I had buried. It was a part of me I never wanted or needed to creep back up. Yet here it came and I was fighting to control it.

I had to act quickly.

"I'm sorry, are you talking to me?" I asked her.

"Ren, it's me. How . . . how are you here? They told us

you were . . . dead. That you died. My little brother went to the funeral."

It was hard, but I played my part well. "I'm sorry, I have no idea what you're talking about. My name's Julia."

She stared at me for a moment. I could tell she was contemplating whether to believe me or her memory. Luckily, she shook her head and said, "Sorry, you look like someone I knew. But of course it couldn't be you. She, um . . ."

"Died" I finished gently. "You said."

Becky nodded, troubled.

I gave her a sympathetic smile, and then for good measure added, "Sorry about your friend. That sucks."

"It's okay. But, wow, you really look a lot like her. See you around." Still not sure about what had happened, she walked off taking a few extra glances as she went.

"Yeah, see you around," I said after her.

My heart was pounding in my chest. I was happy she had relented because if she had kept going and called my bluff I would have had to kill her. No, really I would have. *Whew.* Rattled, I continued my trek toward the clock tower. It was one of the tallest buildings on campus and right by my dorm so it was easy to find. I parked myself right under it and waited with my hands in my pockets. I pulled my hoodie over my head though in case someone else out there felt like recognizing me. I had grown up thousands of miles from here and hadn't even heard of this place. What the hell was Becky Dooley doing here?

I swear time was moving backward, or really slow on purpose. The ten o'clock chime even seemed to take longer than it should. Felt more like the nooner. But when it finished a new wave of excitement rushed through me. Fifteen minutes to go!

I was looking for a silver Honda SUV. I never noticed how many damn silver cars there were in the world until now, not to mention how many of them were freakin' Hondas. Was there a convention or something?! I was sure I spotted Gareth about a dozen times before I started to get frustrated and angry. With my background, angry was not something you wanted me to be.

And here comes another one . . . wait . . . license plate T9L-ZZR?

HOLY S***!!!!!!!!!!!!

CHAPTER 16
STRANGE NEW WORLD

I snaked my way through the heavy traffic, following the car. It slid into an impromptu unloading zone. After an interminable moment, he stepped out.

Time froze. Everything went silent and there was only Gareth. He was beautiful. No not looking. In fact, he was average looking at best. He looked shorter than he really was because he slouched. His brown hair sat in a curly mess on his head. His face was wide, his green eyes set far apart. No, he was beautiful to me because I was now complete. I had been uncomfortable since my link. No, *hollow*. Yeah, that's a much better way to describe it and I had never really been able to pinpoint why. Now I knew. He made me whole. I never wanted to take my eyes off of him. His folks got out of the car with him. They seemed more excited and curious than their son.

I watched Gareth. Studied him. Tried to pick up on any mannerisms not covered in his bio. His clothes were just clothes. They were nothing trendy, nothing name brand. It was as if they served the purpose of him not being naked and aside from that what was the point? He reminded me of Junie in that way. But that was where the comparison ended. Junie was a huge, intimidating guy and Gareth was the exact opposite. Gareth was wicked smart; Junie, not even close. They actually could have been cast in a modern remake of *Twins*, only Gareth was much better looking and not as short as Danny DeVito. Sorry Danny, low blow I know.

Gareth looked uncomfortable, not sure what to make of the scene. His parents must have said something annoying to him because he snapped his head around and said, "Sure."

I was within about twenty feet of him at that point. His voice was, like the rest of him, a big old stick of average. Not too high, not too low. But to me it was like a singing bird. I got goosebumps from it.

They grabbed boxes from the car and headed inside. With that came my first real choice. One of many I would make every day from now on. Should I stay put, or follow? At some point if they didn't notice me lurking behind them someone else would. I'd scouted out the dorm. It had been secure enough. And with my added improvements I had no doubt he was as safe as he could be while in there. So I stayed where I was.

The moment he was out of my site, however, I regretted my decision. That hollow feeling roared back to life inside me. I considered chasing after him and his parents but instead imagined them walking up the stairs and down the hall. I reached the corner of the building and looked up at his window at same time they entered his dorm room. Thankfully, none of them noticed a pasty, black-haired girl creepily staring up at them from the ground—because, well, let's be honest, that's what I was. A thought crossed my mind as I stood. *Wasn't this occupation more like a glorified stalker than anything else?* Seemed like it to me. I guess Shadow sounded cooler. Yeah, saying I was part of the Stalker Program didn't have that cool ring to it.

I watched them drop their first load and briefly take in the room before they came down for another. This process was repeated four more times. I finally followed them up on the last trip, passing the open door as I shut my own door behind me.

I watched and listened to them on my monitors. It was like reality TV, only right next door and a lot more important-feeling. His mom wanted to help him unpack, but he just wanted her to leave. She was embarrassing him. With no one in the room with them it was hard to understand how she was doing this, but you know how kids are.

Gareth's roommate hadn't moved in yet, so Gareth took the bed by the window, which bugged me. Snipers love it when you stand by a window. He told his folks he wanted that bed because of some crap about leaves and birds. *Huh?* Okay, the rational part of me wanted to wait a bit longer to pass judgment on the kid who made me whole, but I couldn't. It was official. Gareth was a nerd. A mega one. There were hints, of course. His clothes. His grades. The fact that he and his roommate knew each other from, and I'm not making this up, computer camp. All of this could have been brushed aside, ignored even. You know, he's just one of those really smart, cool kids who gets good grades and doesn't even try. But the "leaves" comment really sealed things. No huge parties for me. No late night concerts. No real college experience. On the other hand, this would make my job easier. He wouldn't be hitting on any female that moved, driving drunk, or trying to show off to anyone. Even Lloyd, while also a nerd, had some charm and self-confidence. I doubt Gareth would sit at my table unless invited. No, nerds like Gareth shied from danger, at least the real kind. Video games and lab experiments do not a tough man make. I suddenly began to appreciate him a bit more for what he would be. A loner. Like me.

I followed him and his parents to some place that served giant (and I mean GIANT) burritos. I ate mine in the corner across from them pretending to read the paper but really watched them through the reflection in the window.

After the meal, the three of them took a stroll around campus before going back to the dorm to bid adieu and good luck. His mom cried. His dad started with a hand-shake, but crumbled and went in for the real deal bear hug. Then they climbed into their car and drove off. He watched them go and went upstairs to his room.

LIKE A GOOD LITTLE dweeb he stayed inside and unpacked for the rest of the day. Even after his roommate, Law-rence by the way (I know, *Lawrence*), moved in they hung out and played video games. They even ordered pizza so they wouldn't have to leave. This job was cake. I was also happy that my little FIP nerd didn't have a car. It's tough

to protect someone when they're driving. Yeah, he had a
bike, but nerds wore helmets and used hand signals.

I toggled the camera controller and zoomed in on his
phone as he set his alarm for 8:30 A.M. He, well I guess technically *we*, had an engineering class at 9:15 A.M. I was in all
of his classes so I'd have an actual reason to be around him
all of the time without causing suspicion. It helped that he
was an engineering major, too. Engineering majors had
block schedules, which meant you took all of your classes
with the same 200 people. It wouldn't be easy to avoid
direct contact, but it wouldn't be too hard, either.

The lights in his room went off, and my cameras
instantly switched to night vision. Even with all the security I still couldn't go to sleep. Every glance away from the
screens seemed to bring back the hollow feeling from
before. I had to keep my eyes on him. We were told these
feelings would be very intense at first but over time they
would lessen and just become a part of who we were—like
any true emotional attachment. But now that I was here I
wasn't sure I believed them.

At about 5 A.M. I decided not even to pretend to try to
sleep anymore. Instead I flipped on my real computer to
see if my mother had sent her long-dead daughter anything new. Nope. But my heart jumped and I grinned.
There was an email from Junie.

We had talked about our old email addresses years ago.
I had forgotten his but instantly remembered it when I saw
the message from *sexpistol_danceman* in my inbox. For a guy
who numerous times forgot if the grenade he was about to
throw had a three or five second fuse, remembering my

email was impressive. I blushed, thankful no one, especially Junie, was around to see it. Never would have heard the end of it from him.

Ren! What's up, hooker?! I'm pretty sure this is your email, but if it's not, my apologies, sir or madam, for calling you a hooker. I'm sure you're a lovely person and not a prostitute. But assuming it is you, Ren, hey! Where are you? I'm in Austin, TX. My FIP's four years old! Four! I live next door to her and tell everyone I'm a writer (I know, all it takes is speaking to me for ten seconds to know I'm no writer). It's so no one thinks it's strange I stay home all day in such a big house. Not working, though. I think all the neighborhood kids call me "that creepy dude." I bet if I showed them my gas-powered machine gun they'd like me more. I'd also probably get arrested shortly thereafter, but I'd go out as "cool" which would be awesome. It's so boring here. Nothing happens. All this training and I'm really a glorified babysitter. I don't miss being there but I do miss you. Way too much. Let me know how you are. Oh, her name is Emily.

–Junie.

P.S. Remember when balconies were for views?

I blushed again at his mention of balconies. I missed him too and instantly hit reply. I didn't know what to say though; I was never good at this stuff. I missed my friend but there was definitely something else there, too. I wanted to do more than just see and talk with him. That moment on the balcony had flipped a switch, and I still wasn't sure how to deal with what it had turned on. Yeah, yeah, insert dirty joke here.

I was about to write, but I paused. While contact between Shadows had never been forbidden—many FIPs might one day meet and even work together on some Future Important Event—was this okay? Revealing who we are to the outside word meant certain death at the hands of a Hunter. But it was assumed a Shadow could encounter another Shadow out there. Would I get a phone call about this later warning me not to do it ever again? *Better to ask forgiveness than permission, right?*

BUZZ! *Movement in Gareth's room.* I cursed myself for being distracted.

My right hand instinctively reached for a gun I had hidden under the desk. Gareth was groggily stumbling toward the door. Was he leaving? Crap! I wasn't ready. Not even dressed. I turned and grabbed a pair of jeans to throw on over my pjs and bolted out of the door, but paused as the telltale sound of a guy peeing came through my speakers. Disgusting. Half asleep Gareth dropped back into bed. I dropped my jeans, slumped back into my chair, and went back to my email to Junie.

Here I was unable to take my eyes off one guy and longing to see the other. On the other hand, Junie had reached out. I wanted to respond. I needed to respond.

So this is what I wrote him:

Junie. My dearest love. Every fiber of my being aches for your touch . . .

Seriously, folks? Like I would, ever. For real this time:

Junie! It is me! Which you probably have figured out by now since I've responded. I wish I was a hooker, more freedom, better tips! I miss you too. Sorry to hear about your FIP. But at least you get a yard. I'm stuck in a dorm room next to a mega-nerd. Did I say I miss you too? I'm in College Station, TX. I think that's close, no? Maybe one day my FIP will go to Austin. I would have no hesitation knocking him out and tying him up for a few hours so that we could hang out. Just kidding. Kinda . . . not really. ByEEEE!

I pressed send before I could reconsider. *Ugh.* Being a girl is exhausting.

With Gareth sleeping soundly, and me unable to sleep, I worked out in my room for an hour. I kept it silent for the folks below me. 6 A.M. is too late for parties and too early to be up. I spent another hour double-checking all of my weapons' hiding places. The guns were all still loaded, the knives were still sharp, and they were all still very well hidden.

I took a shower (I had installed a waterproof monitor in there, too, to keep an eye on Gareth) and got ready to leave. It was already 82 degrees outside and humid as hell. I began to sweat just thinking about it. I opted to wear the least amount of clothing as possible and thus put on a worn, light shirt and my first pair of non-gym shorts since my abduction. They were cut-off jean shorts, and they felt strange. I looked like some kind of retro-hippie-surfer girl. Was this even in? Had it ever been? I didn't care about fashion any more, I really didn't, but I also didn't want to look so ridiculous that people stared. Then again, the people who had supplied my wardrobe would not have bought me anything that would stick out.

Gareth's alarm went off at 7:30 A.M. Good morning, Nerdville! I strapped on a pair of sneaks and sat on my bed, fiddling with a butterfly knife until he was ready to leave. I waited for him to be about halfway down the hall before grabbing my backpack and following him. The bag had a false bottom where I'd hid a pistol. The gun lightly bounced against the small of my back. Though I preferred knives, it was oddly comforting to me. Sometimes guns are all you need.

CHAPTER 17
POISON CONTROL

The engineering class was held in one of those classic giant auditoriums you see in teen movies. The last time I had been in a room this size I'd been learning how to build explosives using basic household items. I assumed this would be a tad different, but if not, I'd get an easy A.

Gareth took a seat up front. I could tell he had wanted to front-row-Joe it, but they were all taken. He was forced to sit in the third row with all the other got-here-too-late-for-suck-up-seats-geeks. With the only exits in the back of the class, I was happily a back row Betty, sandwiched between two kids who looked too sleepy for a first-period class this early.

There was a closed laptop on the table in front of each of us. No one had opened theirs. Wanting and needing to be a lemming, I waited.

A quiet, yet noticeable "Hey, Julia!" came from a few rows in front of me. Took me a sec to remember that was my name. It was coming from Lloyd. Great. The world is annoyingly too small sometimes—and I imagine that's especially true at college. He gave me a grin and a head bob. I gave him a wave. Thankfully the seats on either side of me were filled so he turned back around and annoyed the guy sitting next to him instead of me.

The Prof came in and motored his way down the stairs. He looked irritated, like he had something really important to be doing but was forced to be here instead with the peons. He flipped on a projector showing a Power-Point slide, and in true, don't-give-a-damn fashion, began to read it verbatim. It was all that crap about what the class was about: exam schedules, skills we'd learn, yada, yada, yada.

Of course the final slide read: "You will all do great things."

I snorted. *Nope, only one of you will.*

It took me a second to notice that the room had gone dead silent and people had turned toward me. Apparently my snort had been a loud one. The Prof removed his glasses and stared in my direction. The rest of the class, who weren't already doing so, followed suit. 200 pairs of eyes on the one person whose job was to be invisible. My face became the same color as my freckles.

What made it worse was that I knew Gareth was looking at me, too. Like everyone else, he was wondering *who is this girl?* It was not something he should be doing. I wasn't supposed to exist to him.

"What's your name?" the Prof asked.

I thought about lying. I thought about running. I even

considered pretending to pass out, you know, go dead fish on them. But instead, "Julia Roth," came out of my mouth.

The Prof smiled, and said, "And you thought my comment was funny, why?"

I quickly answered with something my mother always said to me, "World needs ditch diggers too."

There were a few chuckles—the loudest from Lloyd. Prof wrote something down on a piece of paper. He looked up with a sinister grin that was reminiscent of Cole. "Well, my money's on you, Ms. Roth. Failing this class will be an excellent first step."

I kept my face emotionless as I stared back at him. When he turned around to write something on the whiteboard, the eyes of the class turned with him. The tips of my fingers tickled the handle of a folded knife I had in my pocket. I could have it out and in the back of his head in half a second. He'd never know what happened.

Of course, I remembered something then that made me smile and relax. Little did he know that all my grades would be fixed. I could get zeros on everything, fail every course I took (and probably would anyway), but all of my records would show B's. *So threaten all you want sucker. Ren Sharpe, aka Julia Roth, owns you.*

He had finished writing whatever on the board and turned. His eyes flashed to me. Everyone around me was hurriedly copying what he'd written down. I didn't want to give him the satisfaction, so I looked right at him and gave a big yawn. I knew it was a childish and stupid thing to do, but if felt good. I quickly went through scenarios in which I could justify killing him. Unfortunately, the only real justification I had would be if he ever threatened Gareth. Who knows? Maybe he would. A girl can hope, right?

As the Prof dug into his boring lecture I wondered what Gareth thought of me now. That was not the best first impression. I know it sounds weird, but I wanted him to like me. Of course I did.

I also realized the flaw in the plans of those who'd assigned him to me. Who the hell thought all of this was a good idea? The same people who'd left that stairwell door open and almost allowed me to escape, twenty-two days in? How the heck was I supposed to avoid direct contact with him? He was my neighbor, and we were in all of the same classes. Yes, the idea of it all was convenient, but was it practical? I could not talk to him, easy enough, but what if we were placed in the same study group together? O   r how was I to stop him from approaching me and talking to me? What if he ran out of printer ink and knocked on my door to borrow some?

Class ended with my thoughts racing. Just my luck: Prof asked for me to come down for a quick word. I panicked, realizing if I was forced to stay here, Gareth would leave without me. Luckily, like the rest of the front rowers, he wanted to introduce himself to the professor. I wouldn't take the good fortune for granted. I needed to keep my mouth shut from here on out and at least pretend to take notes in classes from now on.

Again, all eyes were on me as I strode down the stairs. I passed right by the line of do-gooders waiting to speak with him, Gareth included. I didn't want this. I didn't need this. I was tired and this cocky bastard was rubbing me the wrong way. Something nasty was a-brewin'. And that's when the idea hit me.

Gareth wanted this guy to like him, the same way I wanted Gareth to like *me*. He aimed to be the student who asked questions, took copious notes, and laughed at all the stupid jokes Prof told. Above all, he did not want to be associated with anyone the Prof didn't like. I needed to show Gareth that I was that smart-ass lazy back rower he'd do well to steer well clear of. I had to become poison. It would sting, but it would work.

So while I had originally planned on apologizing, I had something a little different in mind.

"I noticed you didn't take any notes during my class," Prof stated.

I pointed at my head. "Keep it all up here."

He grinned without humor. "Ah, right. So you wouldn't mind telling me what I said about the volatility of benzene with regards to petroleum refineries?"

"Just cause I keep it up there, doesn't mean I can access it whenever I want. I gotta let it digest for a bit first. Can I get back to you on that?"

He nodded without missing a beat. "An excellent idea. How about we say in ten pages by tomorrow at 9 A.M. or you don't bother to come back on Wednesday."

I pretended to think about it for a moment before cockily saying, "Let's make it fifteen. I wanna really explore this one; dig into it."

And that's what we in the biz call shock and awe. I left them all wide-eyed and speechless, and in the case of the Prof, angry. Job done. Poison.

While waiting on a bench for Gareth to finish his schmoozing I sent a text to the homework number I had been given telling them what I needed. They instantly texted back: *Ready in an hour.*

When Gareth came out of the auditorium I took my customary place thirty paces behind him. We still had two more classes that day: Calculus and our Chem lab. Funny how I could have the lab for a class before I even had the actual class.

In Calculus we both stayed true to form. He sat up front, me in the back. I kept my head down and occasionally caught myself actually taking notes, which made me laugh at myself. *You ain't no real student, Julia Roth.*

I was briefly worried in our lab because when we got there I realized it was only a thirty-person class. Luckily, my plan to be poison worked, and Gareth sat as far away from me as possible; everyone did. You know when you're on a plane and the seat next to you is empty and you fantasize about curling up for a nap? About rubbing your luxury in the faces of all the sardines around you, but then that hurried last passenger arrives and steals your dreams? Enter Lloyd. Out of breath, sweaty, and embarrassed he came flying into the room. His eyes lit up when he spotted the one available seat.

"Hey," he said, dropping his bag on the table and hopping up on the stool.

"Hey, Lloyd."

"I got lost."

"It happens," I said.

He looked at me in awe for a moment before saying

so loud that everyone in the room heard, "You are the ballsiest person I've ever known!"

I grit my teeth. "Thanks, Lloyd."

He then recounted the other ballsiest people he'd known, how they'd gotten to be on such a prestigious list, and why I was ballsier. This went on until the lab teacher came in and shushed him.

I almost groaned when the teacher explained that whoever was next to you would be your lab partner in class all year. Lloyd beamed. But then I beamed, too, because as annoying as Lloyd was, I would be more than dead weight to him in this class, and thus punishment enough.

We had a "simple assignment" (the teacher's words) to do that first day. Lloyd had to show me how to do the entire thing since I didn't understand any of it. It was cute watching him try to explain things to me. The little squirt was so proud when *we* finished *our* assignment and the TA gave *us* an A.

I gave him my biggest, flirtiest grin and a pat on the back. "Thanks, you're the best." He ate it up. I should probably go easy on him. He had no idea what he was dealing with. So before he could ask me to marry him I quickly gathered my stuff to chase after Gareth.

My wonderful nerd boy stayed in that night playing video games, just as I'd anticipated. So with the night off I did something I hadn't done in while. I looked in a mirror. Really looked.

All I had on were a sports bra and shorts. I had gotten a good number of glances today (aside from the bewildered and irritated kind)—even caught some guys turning, their gazes lingering. I had never been attractive before, and I didn't think I was now. I mean, yeah, I was thin and in shape from years of training. I had boobs. I guess those two things were all that really mattered to guys in college anyway. But the level of attention seemed to go beyond that. Why? Yup, I had hair. Oh, and I had freckles too. I could, at most, safely say I was a decent seven-on-a-scale-of-ten. Was that all it took to make a boy's head turn? Maybe in college, the answer was yes. Which was probably a bad thing for a Shadow.

CHAPTER 18
JUMP, JUMP AROUND

Okay, let's move ahead. Three months since school started. Yeah, I'm fast forwarding a bit. I mean, it's not much of a story, or at least a good one, if nothing is happening, right? No one wants to read about the mundane monotony of life. We all go through it every day so why be reminded, you know? So. Deal with it. Seriously, nothing really good happened. Fine, want the highlights? Here they are:

- I lose Gareth a few times, totally panic, and imagine he's rotting in a ditch somewhere, or floating upside down in a creek. But I always end up finding him in his room or a lab.

- I start to agree with Junie. All of that training. All of the mental anguish, the kidnapping, the torture, and I'm just a glorified babysitter which is more acceptable then say, a stalker.

- Lloyd asks me out almost every day, and he tries

to kiss me once. I slam his head into a table and feel terrible about it. It was a reflex.

- A while later he decides to tell me he's feeling guilty about something bad he did. I take the bait and ask him what. He tells me he's thought about me a few times, alone in his room. Ew is right. Who tells a person that? Hey, you said you wanted the highlights.

- Lloyd catches me following Gareth and asks me what I'm doing. I lie and say it's a new social media game I'm helping a friend research. He buys it. My explanation was pretty convincing, but he really only buys it cause my bra strap is showing. Either way? Crisis averted. I didn't want to have to kill him.

- Junie and I continue our emails to each other. As boring as my life is his is excruciatingly so. You know what four-year-olds do? Nothing. Junie goes full weeks without leaving his house sometimes. So I tell him about the classes I'm taking, about what college is really like, anything and everything I can to keep his mind off of his own boring situation. He eats it up. And since he's now living vicariously through me he always wants to know more.

EVERY NIGHT, I CAN'T wait for Gareth to be asleep so I can email Junie. We have each other's cell numbers, but neither of us ever call. I tell myself it's because I'm sure we're being monitored and that would bring in the hounds, so to speak. But part of me isn't sure I can talk to him. Our emails are so perfect, and I know that the moment I actually speak to him I'll screw it all up.

And them's the highlights—or lowlights, if you prefer.

AS USUAL, IT WAS late Saturday night and I was waiting in the lobby of the engineering building for Gareth to emerge from the lab. He had been spending almost all of his spare time there now, and the couch I'd been sitting on for the past month was beginning to remember the shape of my butt far too well.

I was minding my own business when an older security guard walked over to me and sat in a chair across from me. I wasn't sure what was happening. My first instinct was the knife in my boot.

He looked sweetly at me as he said, "Now, I know I should mind my own business, but just go for it, honey."

I raised my eyebrows, confused.

He continued, "You're here every night waiting for that boy. He doesn't get it. My wife was the one who approached me and," he snapped his fingers, "forty-five years later we're still happy. So go ahead and ask him out. You're a pretty girl, he'll say yes."

I smiled at him. "Maybe I will."

He returned as he stood up. "Now I'll go back to minding my own business."

I let out a cursory laugh. "Don't worry about it."

Gareth exited the lab door across the lobby a few minutes later and the guard gave me a not-so-subtle thumbs-up.

Gareth looked extra happy this evening. He was

grinning from ear to ear. I guess one of his gizmos was doing what it was supposed to.

It was late, about 1 A.M. when most college kids were either at parties or bars, so the campus was pretty much deserted. The weather was beginning to turn. A brisk early winter breeze whipped through campus. It never gets freezing cold in Texas, nothing even close to Amherst. I wondered if I'd ever see snow again.

There was a sidewalk between the library and the math department that Gareth always took. It was more of an alley, but I guess when you line a walkway with bushes you get to call it something better.

Right before he was about to take the shortcut Gareth paused, mumbled something to himself, and quickly did a one-eighty. The sudden turn caught me off guard and in the open. Deer in the headlights sort of thing.

For the briefest of moments our eyes locked. I froze. He shook his head, then turned again and hurried toward the alley

I had become too lax in my attention here. Too comfortable. I'd been caught following him red-handed, and instead of at least trying to hide, or coming up with an excuse, I had froze. It was official. I was horrible at my job.

CHAPTER 19

AN EXPLOSION OF VIOLENCE

Embarrassed by what had happened, I hung back extra far, cursing myself.

When Gareth reached the halfway point down the side-walk-alley, a large figure leapt from behind the bushes to the left, blocking his path. Another smaller figure popped up from behind him and shoved him to the ground at the feet of the larger one. Before Gareth could get up the larger guy punched him in the face and hissed, "Stay down."

I saw this. I felt it when he punched Gareth. I wanted to rip their heads off, skin them alive, but I couldn't. The only time a Shadow could intervene was when the possibility of death was certain. For all I knew, this mugging was the catalyst for everything Gareth would become.

So instead of doing what my instincts screamed for, what I had been trained to do, I ducked behind a bush and observed, enduring it. It was torture. I flinched in rage with every kick. One in the ribs. One in the back. Two on the hips. I bit my lip to keep from screaming and tasted my own blood. *Just stay down, you idiot! Don't try to get up!*

The larger of the two ripped the backpack from his shoulders and swung it over his shoulder.

"Got it, let's go," the larger one said.

"I want his wallet," said the smaller one.

"We don't need that, come on," bellowed the larger one, but his partner ignored him. He bent over Gareth. In a bit of bravery I would never have guessed he was capable of, Gareth blindly kicked and caught him in square in the face.

The smaller guy didn't go down, but stumbled backward grabbing his nose and yelling in pain. The larger attacker clocked Gareth on the side of the head. Gareth grabbed his face and slumped to his knees.

Gripping his bloody nose with his left hand, the smaller one lurched back over to Gareth. "Now you die." With his right hand, he reached behind his back, his fingers wrapping around the handle of a pistol.

The blade of my knife punctured his hand an instant later. And I was not much farther behind it. I covered the distance between us before the gun clanged onto the ground. I'd never moved so fast.

I jumped and caught the smaller one in the face with my foot, feeling the satisfying crunch of his cheekbone breaking. He tumbled into the bushes. I landed next to the larger one in a crouch, spun around, and elbowed the side of his knee. As he buckled I continued my spin and cracked him across the jaw with my foot. He was out cold before he hit the ground.

The smaller one was trying to extricate himself from the brush. It took every fiber of my being not to kill him where he stood. Instead, I kicked out his legs, and he fell to the ground. Taking a page out of Cole's book, I wrenched his arm around to its breaking point and placed my knee across his throat. Except I made sure to break his arm before he passed out. I wanted him to feel it.

After the crack, there was silence.

The incident had lasted mere seconds. Neither of them would be getting up any time soon. Neither would ever fully recover, either. I turned to find Gareth, his nose and lip bleeding, staring up at me in a combination of fear and shock. My stomach turned. I felt that same blazing connection I'd felt first time months ago under the clock tower. Only better. I would have enjoyed it more if the circumstances had been a little different.

"Are you okay?" I asked him.

He nodded, unable or unwilling to speak to me.

Voices floated down from the far end of the alley. A group of kids, some unsteady and probably drunk, were lurching toward us. There was blood everywhere. Two unconscious and battered bodies, and a gun. This was not good.

I gathered Gareth's backpack and papers as fast as I could and tossed it back to him. Then I grabbed my bag from where I had dropped it in the bushes and slid the bloody knife and gun into it. I quickly worked up some tears, good ones. Lastly, I helped Gareth stand up and put my arm around him to hold him up. He was wobbly, but I had him. Energy coursed through my skin wherever I was touching him. The sensation was so sudden and so intense I got a head rush, stumbled, and almost dropped him. Almost.

I dragged him down the sidewalk-alley toward the group of kids. I could see them clearly now: four guys and four girls. Gareth found his feet and was able to help carry himself as he we exited onto a large square with a fountain. I gave a strangled, "Help!"

They were goofing off before, but came running toward us at my call. I pretended to be in near hysterics when they reached us.

"Call the police. These guys tried to rob us back there. Some . . . guy saved us, and then took off chasing one." The tears were streaming down my face. *Oscar, anyone?* I even did the wobbly lip bit as I pointed toward the alley. "There are two back in there, I think they're, like knocked out, or something."

The guys took off to check it out. The girls stayed with us.

Gareth started to say something, but I quickly covered his mouth with my hand and gave him a cold, hard glance. It was long enough for him to get my meaning. The girls had been too busy watching their men take off down the alley to notice. I quickly returned to the scared freshman routine.

One girl asked, "Are you okay? Do you need us to call an ambulance?"

I shook my head. "We're fine. Just scared." I hoisted Gareth up. "He rolled his ankle and hit his head. Our dorm's right there, and I've got ice." I pointed toward a building that was most definitely not our dorm.

Gareth didn't try to speak up this time. In fact, when I started to drag him away, he played the part and conjured an exaggerated limp.

The moment we were out of sight, I picked up the pace. Each step made Gareth wince, so I gripped his belt and half-carried him. About halfway to our dorm, I heard the telltale scream of a girl who had chosen to be brave and seen two unconscious bodies and blood. Neither Gareth nor I spoke the whole way back to the dorm. Sirens wailed in the distance.

I dragged him up the stairs and down a thankfully empty hallway. He didn't fight me as I opened the door of my room and took him inside.

"Sit."

He did so without question, perching on the edge of my bed. He watched me go over to my closet where I took out a first aid kit. I placed the kit next to him.

"Please stop staring at me." I muttered.

"What . . . who are you?" he asked.

"Nobody. Now shut up and stay still."

I proceeded to check him out for any major injuries. I started with his arms and back. Each time I touched him that same tingly feeling of warmth flowed through me. Everything I checked was fine until I got to his right knee. He winced.

"That hurt?"

He nodded. I rubbed my hands over his jeans around his knee. It was swollen, but nothing felt broken. Then I bent it a few times, testing it.

"It's just a sprain. You're fine."

His lip and nose had stopped bleeding. But the gash over his left eye was still slowly leaking. I gently grabbed his face so I could look at it. His skin was smooth and soft. His eyes, green with blue speckles, were slightly dilated. *Concussion.* I didn't want to let go, but any longer and it would get awkward. I dropped my hands, opened the medical kit, took out a cotton swab, and doused it with hydrogen peroxide. Then I gently dabbed the cut over his eye.

"Ow!" he yelled pulling his head away.

I rolled my eyes and sat there, swab at the ready. "Whenever you're ready, champ." I said flatly.

Hesitantly, he leaned back toward me. I cleaned the wound and then handed him a fresh swab, "You can do the rest of your face yourself."

While he dabbed his nose and lip, I took out some butterfly bandages and put them on the cut over his eye. He never took his eyes off of me.

"Thanks," he murmured.

I looked at him, our faces inches from each other, our eyes locked. His breathing was slow and intoxicating.

He continued, "For, you know, helping me."

"Forget about it." *No really, forget about it. Forget the whole thing. Never happened.* I closed up the med kit and put it back into the closet.

"How'd you do it?"

I looked at the med kit and said, "Discovery Channel?"

He was acting a bit loopy as he smiled and laughed. It was half giggle, half laugh, 100% adorable. "No, how'd you, like absolutely destroy those guys?"

"Oh, that. My dad owns a Muay Thai gym. Guess I just

picked it up." One of the many well rehearsed lies they'd trained us to tell if we were ever caught in combat in the open.

"Just picked it up?" he said raising his eyebrows. "That was the craziest thing I've ever seen." There was a pause before he added, "And it was sort of hot."

Awkward. Must be the concussion talking.

Having had plenty of concussions I knew what they were like. You act kind of drunk, and don't have full control of your inner monologue. Stuff tends to slip out and you say stupid things. They're usually true, would-never-normally-say-out-loud things. He wouldn't remember he had said it in the morning. It wasn't his fault, but it was still embarrassing.

I cleared my throat. "Well. You have a concussion, for sure, so you shouldn't fall asleep for a while. Go play video games with your roommate and tell him you have to stay awake for a few hours. Tell him you could die if you don't."

He looked at the wall between our rooms as he said, "That would suck . . . wait. How do you know I play video games?"

Because I know everything you do and have cameras in your room. "Can hear it through the wall," I said, which wasn't a total lie.

"Oh, sorry." He got up gingerly, keeping his weight on his good leg. "I'll keep it down."

"Doesn't bother me. Really."

"Well, anyway, my roommate's not here. Went home to Dallas." He yawned as he started to limp toward the door.

"It's cool. I'll drink some Dew, eat a candy bar or something. I'll be okay."

When he reached the door he turned and asked, "Can you check on me in the morning and make sure I'm alive?" He finished off the question with a crooked smile.

CHAPTER 20
BESTEST BUDDIES

It felt like a dream. A good one. Except I was doing something really, really bad in it. Something that, dream or not, could have world changing consequences.

I had no business whatsoever being in his room and sitting on his roommate's bed. But what choice did I have when he'd started to leave? Wasn't the threat of dying from a concussion equally as viable as the threat of a gun? I guess I could have stayed in my room, watching him through the monitors and banging on the wall whenever he dozed off. *Yeah, that wouldn't have seemed strange at all.* Couldn't risk it. Once he fell asleep there was always the risk he couldn't wake back up again. I had to be with him; it was the only way to ensure his survival.

So here I sat. I think I had officially broken every rule (of a pretty short and simple list mind you) there was to break. Direct contact? Check. Dialogue? Check. Physical contact? More please, and check. Allowed into living quarters? Check. I hadn't let him die, which *was* rule number one, but about everything else on the list was a goner at this point. Had I screwed up the future beyond repair now? Were the future human beings now living in a *Waterworld*, or a *Back to the Future Two* one with cool floating skateboards? And was it all my fault?

What was done was done. How would, or could, this make it any worse? That's what I was telling myself. Deep down though, I also knew I was here because I liked being this close to him. I was the junkie and he was the drug.

He sat on his bed across from me. The thump of music from down the hall tried to disrupt the silence, but it wasn't doing the good job. I knew every poster, note, and lost hair in the room—but it was still weird to see it all in living color. The roommate's comforter was exactly like the one I had back at the F.A.T.E. center, and surprisingly I felt a twang of homesickness. Hey, go through what I did and see if you don't come out a bit messed up too.

"Would you like a drink?" he asked me.

"No, thanks."

He stood up and walked over to the mini fridge in the corner of the room that was full of soda. Mine was full of reserve blood packs, vials of poison antidotes, and adrenaline shots. He took out a Mountain Dew.

"You sure? They're delicious."

"Yeah, I'm sure."

"Well, they're in here if you want one."

He had barely sat down on his bed when he cracked open the soda and asked me, "Wanna play a video game?"

To be honest, the answer was no. Hell no, actually. I

was terrible at them, for one thing. They looked stupid, and when you played them, you did too. Your eyes glazed over; your mouth drooped open; it wasn't exactly a turn-on. But compared to sitting on his roommate's bed doing nothing, even playing a video game seemed like a good idea. Plus, I was here to keep him awake, so if this is what it took, so be it. I would die for the kid, but I wouldn't play a video game with him?

I shrugged. "Sure."

"All right!" he said, full of nerdy excitement. He slumped to the floor and crawled over to the entertainment system to flip it on. "Coming at ya." Blindly, he tossed a controller at me over his head. It was nowhere close but I snagged it out of the air before it could go straight through the open window. (You know, the one with the birds and leaves? *Sigh*). He held up two games.

"Which one?" he asked.

"Which one is better? Wait, no, which one is easier?"

I had apparently posed a pretty complicated question because he furrowed his brow and studied both of the games while having a quick conversation with himself. He then looked up at me and then down at the controller in my hand, which I was pretty sure I held both upside down and backward. He gave me a pitying smile before dropping both of the games and gently taking the controller out of my hands.

"How about this?" He held up a new game. "No controllers. It's all motion sensors."

"I've never played one of these."

"It's easy, all you have to do is stand up." He said. He

pointed out the motion camera sitting on top of the TV and said, "This will do the rest. Just, you know, be normal."

Ha! Normal. Would he have still wanted to hang out with me had he known that my idea of "normal" was what had happened back in that alley?

He navigated through the video menu with hand gestures and before I knew it we were playing ping pong. I felt silly swinging my hand through the air at a ball on TV, but before I knew it I was actually having fun and laughing. I lost spectacularly, but wanted to play again and again.

And so it went for the next few hours. I, who had previously hated video games with a deep passion, not only played, but actually liked it. He beat me most of the time, but I demolished him in all of the fighting games. We laughed, drank Mountain Dew, I clobbered him virtually. It was the closest to fun I'd had since I'd sparred with Junie.

When Gareth got tired, I told him I was going to stay just in case, even though he was safe to sleep now. He grinned and said, "Awesome."

I prayed he wasn't reading it the wrong way.

I curled up in the other bed as Gareth flipped off the light. The sun was coming up. The movie *Gladiator* was on TV, but the volume was practically on mute. He lay down in his bed on his back. His breathing was deep and tired. I wanted go over there and curl up next to him. Again, the drug and addict. I had a pretty good feeling he'd be totally okay with it too, but for entirely different reasons.

"You still awake?" he asked quietly.

"Yeah."

He rolled over on his side and faced me.

"You feeling okay?" I asked with a smile.

He nodded. "Yeah."

"Good."

"Are we still going to be friends tomorrow? Or will you go back to being a ghost?"

The question took me off guard so I didn't really have a good answer. "What do you think?"

"What do I want or what do I think?" he asked.

"Both."

He looked away, avoiding eye contact as he said, "I *want* to be friends, but I *think* you'll be a ghost."

And with that he rolled over and turned his back to me. "Good night, Julia," he said.

"Good night, Gareth. And my friends call me Ren." The moment I said it, I knew I'd messed up—for more reasons then he could ever know. He'd given me an out, a way to end this quickly, and I'd passed on it. He slowly rolled over to look at me. I smiled at him, and he smiled back. I felt warm inside; his happiness meant my happiness. I didn't care if I'd violated the rules. He could never know what Ren meant, other than it was a nickname only my closest friends knew—and now he was one of them. In a way, that was true.

"Now shut up and go sleep," I added.

I rolled over, my back to him. I could feel his bliss. It seemed to radiate from him and roll over me in waves. I waited for him to fall asleep before rolling back over to keep an eye on him.

I DIDN'T SLEEP MORE than an hour, so when Gareth's alarm went off I made a good show of waking up. You know, the big yawn, the arm stretch.

"You stayed," he said to me as he swung his legs over the side of the bed.

"Good morning to you too," I said with another fake yawn.

"No, I just figured you would have left."

While stretching I asked him, "How do you feel?"

"Okay. Last night's kinda fuzzy though."

"That's a concussion for ya." I stood up.

He giggled.

"What?" I asked. Self consciously checking to make sure I hadn't taken off my clothes or something. No nippage either, phew.

"Nothing," he added, but was still smiling.

"What?" I said again.

"Nothing, really" he replied again.

I hate it when people do this. HATE IT. Maybe because nobody ever did it during training. It reminds me of the life I had when I was fourteen. *There was something; or you wouldn't have giggled.*

I asked once more, "Seriously, what?"

He gave me a look of like "fine" and said, "I was thinking that when my roommate finds out you slept in his bed he'll never wash his sheets again. Happy?"

I winced, the blood rushing to my face "Ew."

"You asked."

Again, this whole suddenly-good-looking thing had reared its ugly head. It was a factor I'd really have to start being more aware of. I had to break the mood, so I clapped my hands and said, "Well, I'm gonna go, you know, shower and stuff."

I slipped off the bed and grabbed my shoes and socks off of the ground. When I reached the door he called out, "Hey."

He was looking at me in a way I wished he wouldn't. I could tell his mind was thinking, hoping, this could someday go somewhere. It wouldn't. It couldn't. He gave a sad, little half-smile and quietly said, "Thanks again for everything. And for staying."

"Sure thing."

IN CASE THERE WAS a police APB out for a small, black-haired ninja with freckles wanted for snapping bones and slicing people open, I put on some baggy clothes. I even added a hat and some sunnies too. With the ensemble I pretty much looked like a fifteen-year-old boy. This new "look" would not only protect me from the swarms of police I was sure were combing the campus, but it could also put an end to this now-attractive nonsense.

Dressed and ready I took my seat on my bed waiting for Gareth to be ready. As was his usual routine, Gareth got dressed, ate a Pop Tart, and hiked his backpack on before leaving his room. Now, usually he heads right, and once he starts down the stairs I follow. But this time he turned left.

KNOCK, KNOCK went the door and so too my heart. What the hell was this?

"Yeah?" I said a little more harshly than I meant as I opened the door.

His eyes widened a bit before he got all flustered. "Oh, uh, sorry. I just, you know, we're in the same classes and I figured we could, you know, walk together or something," he stammered. He dropped his head. "Stupid, stupid idea. Sorry." He turned to walk down the hallway.

I wanted to yell at him to keep going. Yeah, go all *White Fang* on him. *Go! Get! Can't you see I don't want you? You're not welcome here.* And then I'd throw a rock at him for good measure. But I was fresh out of rocks, and the moment I opened the door and saw him I didn't want to be anywhere but next to him. So when he started to walk away, and even though I knew I should let him go, I started to get that empty feeling again.

Out of pure selfishness, I called out, "Wait up."

I grabbed my bag and bolted out of the door after him. He looked like a fat kid who'd won an eight-foot donut. He had done it. He'd won. We had become friendly, if not friends. Oh if Mr. S.could see me now, side by side and talking to my FIP.

"Nice look you got going there," he commented. "That so the fuzz can't recognize you?"

I nodded.

"I was gonna suggest something like that to you but forgot. The hat helps. You sorta look like a dude, though. Just FYI."

"Kind of what I was going for," I said flatly

When we reached our dorm exit he put his arm in front of me, stopping me from leaving.

"Wait here. I'll go check it out."

As sneakily as he could, and I use the term loosely since

he looked like cartoon character, he crept outside and looked around. "All clear. Let's go."

It was cute. Even with the irony. In fact, the irony made it cuter.

We made our way down the all too familiar paths toward the engineering area, only this time together. Yes, I liked having the company. I was all too happy to let Gareth jabber on about how awesome last night was and how he'd like me to teach him how to (and I quote), "deliver ass-kickery." All I had to do was occasionally nod to keep him thinking I was listening.

". . . I mean, can you believe this, Julie, I mean, Ren? It's like a real-life comic book or something. A hot, quiet girl who lives next door. Kind of nerdy. Big loner. You know, the girl you dream about hanging out with but since it's been so long since you became neighbors it would be weird to introduce yourself now, so you fantasize about some exotic moment that finally brings you together. And then BAM! Suddenly it happens. *This* doesn't happen in the real world." He finished by gesturing toward me.

He was rambling on so excitedly I was having Lloyd flashbacks.

The momentary pause cued me that it was time for my line. "Uh-huh."

"I know, right . . ." And so he continued. Past the clock tower. Across drill field. Around the library.

There was police tape blocking the alley shortcut where the "incident" had taken place. So we went around it. A small part of me got scared a cop would stop us for questioning and recognize me from a security camera or something, but the few who were there drank their coffee and ignored us.

Either my disguise worked, or, as was more likely, they had no idea who had done it.

Safely past the crime scene I toyed with the idea of what I would have done had the police seen me and shouted, "There she is!" I could easily have taken them all out, but then what? Could I return to the F.A.T.E. Center? What would happen if the police caught me? Well, I knew that one. Actually, I think I knew the answer to both. The Hunters would come for me. I would eventually be found and killed, maybe even by Luka himself. And if the police caught me alive, well, I'm sure my first meal would be my last, laced with F.A.T.E.-supplied poison.

There was another pause in the jabber coming from Gareth. I had totally zoned out and had absolutely no idea what he had said.

"So do you?" he repeated.

"Do I what?" I asked.

"Do you want to see that movie I was talking about tonight?" he asked.

"Oh, uh . . . well. I kind of have a . . ."

"You have a boyfriend," he interrupted quietly.

I was actually going to say "project to finish" and was about to correct him on the boyfriend comment but stopped. *Did I? Didn't I?* This was another opportunity to fix the mess I'd created. Besides, what exactly was Junie to me if not that? There was the balcony, the emails every night. On the other hand, if odds were a million-to-one you'd never see the other person again, could you really consider him to be your boyfriend? I think I *wanted* Junie to be my boyfriend, but logically speaking how could he be? But he definitely was more than a friend, so I finally nodded. "Yeah, I do have a boyfriend."

While the look on Gareth's face made me want to take it back, I didn't. It was true, at least as far I figured it, and it would be better if Gareth didn't fantasize about something that would never happen. We were friends. That was it. And if I could somehow tone it down, not even very close friends. Acquaintances perhaps.

"Well, that sucks," he said before continuing, "Lemme guess. Tall. Good-looking. Athletic?"

That was Junie. "Pretty much spot-on."

"Shocker."

"What?" I asked defensively.

"Well, I mean, it's almost cliché, isn't it?"

And maybe it was. But I think if given the circumstances we'd met under, you could look past that.

As if grasping, Gareth asked, "Is he smart?"

I kind of cringed and lightly said, "He thinks he is?"

Gareth nodded at the small victory, but it didn't seem to help much. We walked the final few blocks to class in silence. I expected Grumpy Pants to take his seat at the front of the class as always, so I was surprised to see him sit next to me.

"What are you doing?" I asked. "You don't sit back here."

"I only sat up front because my folks told me too. Said it would be good for the professor to get to know me, recognize me." He took a breath before adding, "Didn't work.

I ran into him a few weeks ago by the quad and he called me Walker. It's not even close."

I gave a snort, and he laughed too. The classroom quickly began to fill up around us as we talked crap about the Prof. Gareth was taking the news of Junie like a challenge it had spurred him to lighten up and try to be cooler.

Lloyd took his customary seat on my other side and was a little annoyed at the level of attention I was paying to Gareth instead of him. Look at me: queen of the nerds! Not to be cast aside so easily, Lloyd joined in on the spirited Prof bashing until Prof showed up—reminding me just how much I hated this class

As was my usual routine, the moment he started to lecture I made a big production of pulling out a newspaper and reading it instead of hanging on his every word. We seemed to have an unspoken agreement. I would ignore him all together and he would do his best to flunk me. I would win this battle no matter how hard he tried. It was kind of sad if you were on his side, but a lot of fun if you were on mine.

"Do you do this every class?" Gareth asked me out of the corner of his mouth.

"Pretty much," I said casually as I folded the paper.

"You are an impressive girl."

I shrugged and gave him a wink. He went back to taking more than copious notes, literally writing down everything the Prof said or wrote on the board.

I went to back my paper and almost started laughing out loud when I read the front-page headline: *Police Searching for Superhero.*

Apparently, my story about the random person coming to save us and chasing after the imaginary third attacker had stuck. The group of kids from the fountain had eaten it up and told anyone who would listen. One of the girls even "swore" she saw a cloaked figure scale one of the campus buildings. Right. The cloaked figure of embellishment, maybe. But the police had bought it, every word. They and the school were convinced that it was all the work of some local vigilante. They wanted to bring him in for questioning. The Editorial Board on the Opinion Page wanted to give him a medal. Shocking how it's always a *him*, huh?

The police were also looking for the girl and boy who were *saved* by the amazing superhero. But all that witnesses were able to tell the police about the victims were that they were college age and wearing jeans. So it was more of a plea by the police for the two victims to come forward. Like your little brother begging for you to let them play with you. *Come on, pleeeease. Pleeease come in for questioning?* Not gonna happen. I looked at my outfit and the absurdity of it. I was more than in the clear, yet here I was dressed like a fifteen-year-old white rapper.

I finished the crossword as class ended. I would normally leave and wait for Gareth to make his way out, so I'd never seen what exactly he did between the moment I boogied out of class and the moment he followed. It was one of the only parts of day I didn't have my eyes on him. I could finally put this mystery to bed.

He had taken about eight full pages of notes, front and back. Page by page he read them to himself. *So this is why it takes him so long to get outside.* Finished, he folded them up, picked up his bag, and stood up.

"Ready?"

I nodded. We moved down the row toward the door. When we reached the exit he dropped his folded-up notes into the trash.

"What are you doing?" I asked.

"What do you mean?"

I took the papers out of the trash. "You don't have to try and impress me or anything, Gareth. Here, keep your notes."

I handed the pages back to him and he grinned. "I never keep notes. Ever." And he tossed the pages right back in the garbage. He gave a wry smile, pointed to his forehead and said, "I keep it all up here."

"Don't let me be a bad influence on you, please don't do this." I said seriously.

"I have photographic memory, Ren. Once I read it, I have it forever." He laughed to himself. "You thought I did that to impress you? Man, you and your ego. Think all three of us can fit through the door at once?" Still grinning, he left me to follow.

I was stunned. More than that, I was impressed. "You really have a photographic memory?" I asked as I caught up.

"Yup."

"Cool. What's it like?"

"You mean to remember everything?"

I nodded.

He shrugged. "Handy."

CHAPTER 21
BREAK THROUGHS AND BREAK UPS

Over the next few weeks I spent more time with Gareth, in spite of my daily resolution to cool off toward him. We developed what he called our fake relationship with me being his fake girlfriend. As he said, oozing with sarcasm: "You know, the one you buy dinner and gifts for, and spill your guts to, but never sleep with. Love it."

Hey, it gave me more reasons to be with him, which I wasn't going to turn down. Was I worried about getting in the way of what he did or became? Kind of, but judging by his attitude, and the fact that he still spent most of his waking hours in a lab, it was pretty easy to guess he became some kind of great scientist or something. So with that in mind, I figured as long as I never kept him from his work, how bad could hanging out with him be? He even told me that spending time with me cleared his mind. His words, I swear: he was able to get more work done knowing he'd get to see me after. So really, by breaking the rules I was actually helping, you know? Convinced yet? Me neither.

Was this better than obeying orders and leaving him alone? Hell, no. But who's perfect, right? After what I'd gone through I could be a little selfish for a bit.

As it turned out Gareth wasn't so much a nerd by choice but by circumstance. It was something he felt obligated to be. As I got to know him more, he told me that he understood that the gift he had came with a responsibility to do something with it. He wanted to spend all day at the pool goofing off. He wished he was good at sports. But he wouldn't and he wasn't. While it seemed like everyone else our age was trying their best to be on a reality show or score a touchdown or make crappy pop music, he was trying to do something good, something that could change the world. Or at the very least provide the stepping stone for someone else to do it. And there was something honorable in that. Attractive, even.

IT HAD BEEN ABOUT three weeks since the back alley slice-and-stomp, and not so surprisingly three weeks since the "superhero" was last spotted.

I'd lied when he'd called. I'd said I was working on a project too and would meet him outside the labs after for a burger. He asked when, all weirdly out of breath. Per my rule not to get in the way of his work, I told him whenever he was done because I had more than enough work to keep me busy. He'd bought it. It's great how infatuation can blind someone. Or maybe I'm really good at lying. Probably a good mix of both.

Anyway, here I was, waiting as always on a sofa. I had been given a wide smile and thumbs up from the old security guard.

Now Gareth was late. A text had come a little over ten minutes ago saying he'd be done in a few minutes, so now I was anxious. I was watching the elevator waiting for him. When the doors slid open, the anxiety evaporated. He jog-walked over to me, beyond giddy, and grabbed my hand as he said, "Come on!"

I let him pull me from the building and outside, all to the security guard's amusement, of course. When he tried to drag me down the stairs I pulled my arm away and stopped.

"What's going on?"

He kept grinning stupidly. "I did it."

"Did what?" I responded.

He looked around as if looking for spies before saying, "Not here. Come on."

He reached for my hand.

"I'm not holding your hand," I said flatly. "Where are we going?"

"Back to the dorm."

He slowly started to leave but kept looking at me, making sure I was going to follow him. Little did he know.

Lawrence was home and preoccupied with some video game in Gareth's room, so we went into mine instead. (I always kept the weapons hidden in case of just such a surprise visit.) Once the door was closed Gareth dropped his bag and uttered, "I did it. I actually did it."

And then he did his own version of a happy dance. It

was a bit more macho then mine, more fist pumps, a few awkward leg kicks, some victorious arm raises too, and a pelvic thrust, of course. I sat on the edge of my bed and waited for him to be done. Obviously, since he was this excited, that connection we shared made me feel overly so as well. I wanted to do a happy dance too but instead held it in. This was his moment.

A little out of breath and with his hair a mess he stopped, turned toward me, and said, "Sorry."

"Enlighten me."

"I did it," he said again.

"We've covered that part. What have you done?"

"I figured it out. Broke the code so to speak. It's not done and I'll need who knows how long to perfect it, but I *should* be able to do it. Exciting, right?" When I didn't answer he continued, "Oh, right, sorry. Okay, Ren, I think I've created a wheat seed that can grow without water."

And. . .. was my first reaction. *Big deal*. . . was my second. Then I thought about it. *Holy hell!* My eyes widened with recognition, as I fully understood the implications of it.

"It could grow anywhere," I said. He nodded as I continued my out-loud thinking, "Deserts, droughts, wouldn't matter." I looked right at him as I said, "This could cure hunger. This will change the world."

He nodded as our eyes locked. And then he did something I should have expected. He leaned in quickly and kissed me.

If the feeling I got being around him was a ten, then this was a gajillion. I felt like every nerve ending in my body was alive, exploding with pleasure. I wanted to live in that feeling for the rest of my life. But then my stupid brain got in the way.

What the hell are you doing?

Before I could stop it, Old Brain took over. It was like an out-of-body experience. I watched my hands shove him backward, hard. His back and head slammed into the wall at the foot of my bed, and he rolled onto the floor.

He got up quickly, his face a fiery red. "I'm sorry. Oh, God, I'm so sorry. It was . . . I was excited, and you looked so . . ."

Little did he know I was currently in an end-all-be-all-battle-royale with myself. I wanted nothing more than to grab him, slam him onto the bed, and get me a little more of whatever I had felt when he kissed me. But my brain, the one that calls the shots, was putting the kibosh on it. So I sat there staring at him, frozen like a broken-down robot. He grabbed his bag and when he reached the door said, "Really. I'm sorry. Say something. Oh, jeez. Please don't . . . please don't." With no reaction or acknowledgment from me he slammed the door behind him, defeated, head down.

Only then did my brain give up the fight and allow me to slump backward onto my bed eyes closed, grinning like an idiot, like the way he'd been grinning when he told me what he'd done. I heard him go inside his room, and Lawrence's muffled greeting. I lay there, trying to hold onto that feeling for as long as I could. This junkie was officially hooked.

After a good fifteen minutes, it had worn off enough for me to get up. I had some business to take care of before I could become officially worthless.

I pulled from my pocket a small, clear glass tablet that I kept on me at all times. At my touch it turned on and connected me directly to the F.A.T.E. Center. If there was a situation, or update on our FIP that merited a question or response, we were supposed to let them know through this number There was a *beep*. I stated my name and voice recognition software cleared me through. As was protocol, I left a message describing what I had learned about Gareth's creation. Said I "overheard him talking to a classmate." I left out the parts about the mugging, our "fake" relationship, and the kiss. Was I covering my own ass? Yup. But logically speaking it was unnecessary information.

Satisfied with my report, I hung up.

THE NEXT MORNING, WHEN Gareth left his room he knocked on my door—as per our usual routine. Only I didn't answer it this time. He probably saw it as rightful punishment for what in his mind was a huge mistake; the lapse in judgment that had officially ended both the real and the fake relationship. But even though he did technically deserve it, I kept quiet for a different reason: to protect him from me. I hadn't slept a wink. I'd been up all night thinking about him. Fantasizing about him. Okay, not so much about *him*, but how he had made me feel. It was like some kind of animalistic lust that I wasn't sure I could control. So I didn't answer the door because I was afraid of what I'd do to him if I did.

I knew the truth then. It was for this reason we had been told, repeatedly, never to make direct contact. Whatever

F.A.T.E. had done to us during our link had some pretty intense side effects.

He finally slunk off.

Even as I followed Gareth to class from about fifty yards, it took every bit of will not to sprint the distance between the two of us, grab him, and do something dirty in the bushes. No joking. It was the greatest self-control I've ever had to exert.

SURE ENOUGH, MY SANITY improved as the week went on. Either I got stronger, or the feelings got weaker. It didn't matter. Either way, by the time he left the lab at the end of that week I felt fine again. I finally felt confident I could resist whatever voodoo magic was going on inside me.

When Gareth knocked on my door that night—he hadn't since that first morning when I didn't answer—I figured he'd overcome his embarrassment, too. We could go back to being friends. It was time to let him in. I took a deep breath and slowly opened the door, making sure to keep both eyes on the floor. To him it probably looked like I was still angry about what had happened.

The proximity of being that close to him again hit me like a truck. Deep breaths, steady breaths.

"I'm so sorry," he said for the thousandth time. "Are you okay?"

His voice rang in my ears, and when I finally looked at him, I gripped the door handle and my face flushed. I fought for control. As quickly as the beast rose up, threatening to take over and make me do unspeakably naughty things, I squashed it back down. Victory. For now.

I gave a small smile and said, "I am."

I invited him in, and we spent the next hour talking about his work and what he had done while we'd avoided each other. Whenever he recounted what he'd done in a day it was always tough to pay attention since I already knew. It was even tougher not to call him out when he lied—about going to the gym, for example. (Really? Did he think I'd be impressed?) Alas, the life of a Shadow is a tough one . . .

I asked him for more information about the seed. I regretted it as he rattled off some mumbo jumbo about nutrient enrichment, hybrid species, encapsulating, super seeds, blah, blah, blah. It was so beyond me he could have been speaking in binary code and I probably would have understood about the same amount. Good thing I could zone out. I was too busy taking solace in the fact that our relationship could go back to being normal, or as normal as it could be.

The problem was, *I* was lying. To myself. And I knew it. I couldn't keep my distance. Not anymore. But wouldn't it be easier to protect someone from the dangers of the world by their side instead of thirty yards away? Not to mention, this idea of his was the type of discovery that landed someone on the must-be-protected-for-the-future-of-mankind list so really what damage had I done? None, the way I saw it. After swearing over and over we were good and that we could hang out like before, he left to go to bed. I watched him get ready and go to sleep as always before turning toward my computer.

There was something I'd been avoiding lately.

Gareth had asked if I'd told my boyfriend about what happened. I had lied and said yes and that he wasn't happy. *Don't go to Austin for a while,* I'd told him as a warning. But the truth was since the kiss, I hadn't emailed Junie at all. Plus, how could I tell him about it, since that would mean admitting to breaking the rules and hanging out with my FIP? He didn't even know about the mugging. I had kept him in the dark, pretending all was still boring as usual. I was terrified that if he found out his reaction would only reinforce my deepest of fears; I'd really screwed up.

The emails from him had piled up, unread and waiting. The subject lines getting bolder the longer I let them sit. The last one read simply: "You still alive?"

He didn't deserve to be ignored. This was all on me and yet I was punishing him for it. After all that had happened to us, all we'd been through and everything he meant to me, this wasn't fair. Every part of me wanted Junie. Every part but one. And that part wasn't natural, wasn't normal. This part needed Gareth, craved him in an unnatural way that wasn't right no matter how amazing it felt. There was something manufactured, chemical, about it—and it left a bitter taste in my mouth.

That was the difference. What I felt with Junie was real. What I felt with Gareth was not, and it made me feel dirty, used. And yet I still wanted it. It was that old saying about how being bad never felt so good. It scared me, which is not easy to do when you don't feel pain or fear death. I desperately wanted to reply to Junie's last email, but how could I explain how I was feeling when I could hardly make sense of it myself?

I decided continuing the lie was best. I told myself that if I ever saw him in person again, I'd come clean. It was a cop out, I knew, since that would never happen. I can kill someone with an eraser, but I'm still a coward when it comes to feelings. Feelings suck. Why couldn't they have taken those away from me too?

Hey, sucker. Sorry, been crazy busy. My FIP has me hoofing it all over campus and haven't had much time to sit down. Oh, yeah, still alive and kickin'. Cold, dead hands ain't writing this stuff. Oh, I think he's got a girlfriend or something. Gonna be really weird if they hook up in his room. Think I have to watch that too? Ew. Anyway, gotta run. Nerd boy's heading back to the lab. Dude's got issues.

Sent. I reread it after I sent it. It didn't sound like me. Or, it did, but it sounded fake, like I was trying too hard to be upbeat and cool. It felt forced. Lying to Junie felt like I'd kicked myself in the gut. And making fun of Gareth wasn't much better. I deserved every bit of misery I was feeling. This was my bed, I would lie in it.

CHAPTER 22

COMETH THE MOMENT, COMETH THE (WO)MAN

It was Tuesday, which meant pepperoni rolls were two for the price of one. Really makes you wonder what's in the things if the company can still generate a profit selling them for $1 each. Try not to think about it. But while Gareth and myself were not typical college kids, we did partake in this weekly ritual like everybody else.

"Do you have any family?" Gareth asked with a mouthful of pizza. It caught me off guard. "You never really talk about them."

I swallowed and lied, "I grew up with my grandparents."

"Why? I mean, do you mind me asking?"

I shook my head. I'd rehearsed this speech a long time ago. "My parents and brother died when I was ten in a car crash."

"Oh, sorry."

"It's okay. It was a long time ago."

I had always imagined this conversation ending at this

point and hadn't prepared for more questions, so I was surprised when he asked, "What was he like? Your brother?"

Thinking about my brother, a kid I had fought, argued with, and hated for the bulk of my childhood overwhelmed me and a tear rolled down my cheek.

"I'm sorry," Gareth said, "Forget about it."

I shook my head, "No, it's okay. He was a blast," I said truthfully. "He made me laugh all the time. I miss him," I said softly. And I did. I missed them all.

"I'm an only child. Always wanted a little brother or sister," Gareth said. "Always seemed like it'd be fun."

"They are. But they suck too," I said as I cleared my throat. I was back in control as I reminisced. "He gave me a spider in a box for my seventh birthday. I hated spiders, but he was only three and thought I'd like it since it was fuzzy." It was one my favorite memories of my brother.

"You miss him, don't you?" he said.

I nodded.

"Sorry I brought it up. Buzzkill" he added.

"No. Feels good to talk about it. Makes him feel closer, you know?"

Gareth nodded, but then changed to shaking his head. "I don't actually. Everyone in my family's still alive." His voice softened. "I'm really sorry, Ren."

I'd kept my family locked up in a box in my heart, afraid of what might happen if I'd let them out long enough. Yeah, it was sad, but it was great to be able to talk about them. Gareth would listen for as long as I wanted to talk, I knew that. I could rely on him, as I'd relied on them

"Appreciate them while you can," I finished. "You never know what might happen."

After stuffing our faces for under $5 it was back to the lab for Gareth to work on a presentation for grant money, and back to the couch for me. Killing time while I waited for Gareth was usually difficult and boring, but recently I had found a series of books that (to my shocked surprise) hadn't been made into a TV show or movie yet. It was about a girl who finds out she's actually part leprechaun. The first book had kept me entertained for about a week, and I'd gotten the second book in the mail that morning—in which it was rumored she learned how to ride rainbows across water. For once, I was actually looking *forward* to some good couch time.

But I barely got ten pages in before I was interrupted by a "What are you doing?"

Gareth, bag in hand, was looking down at me. Usually he texts before he leaves the lab and I lie to say I'm done with whatever project I was lying about working on in the first place. Then I meet him. We had a system. He had messed with protocol. Not cool, dude.

"What are *you* doing?" I asked right back. "I'm not the one saving the world here."

"I'm not good at presentations. I'm fried. Can't think straight." He raised his eyes as if asking me: *And you?*

"I turned on the computer in the lab and stared at it for a few minutes. Figured I'd just read out here and wait for you instead of going home."

The idea that I chose to wait for him had the effect I'd hoped for. He was so tickled that any and all suspicion was forgotten. Again, thank God for the blindness of infatuation.

Winter, or what they call winter in Texas, was now in full swing. I actually shivered as we walked back to our dorm. It felt great to wear a hoodie and jeans and not be sweating in them from the heat. About halfway home I thought about his comment and asked, "How's the presentation?"

"Not ready for the dean next week if that's what you mean. It's got to be good so he'll help me get published so I can get a grant and do real work. Finger's crossed I'll finish it tomorrow."

"Cool, yeah, crossed." I said, more enjoying watching my breath fog then listening to him. I'd forgotten I could do that. "Anything I can help with?"

"Kiss for good luck?" he said with a playful grin.

Okay, that was funny. I gave him a loud, "Ha!" Then I shoved him into a bush for good measure. I put on a quick jog to put some distance between us. Laughing, he picked himself up, dusted off some leaves from his jacket, and jogged to catch up to me.

"Sorry," he said. "I had to. You set it up so nicely."

"Well played, sir. Oh, and the answer is no," I added as I gave him another playful shove. For the next few minutes we walked in silence, or almost silence since Gareth kept quietly giggling to himself over his funny. His giggling in turn made me start giggling. It was a vicious cycle. Before we turned the corner for the homestretch back to the dorm I said, "Make you a deal. You win the Nobel Prize, we'll put that kiss back on the table."

"Well, that should be easy," he said with a sarcastic

smile. "But I'll take it." We shook on it, making it official. The demon inside of me hoped he'd win it soon.

"But for real. You want help with the presentation?" I asked.

"I won't say no, but it's pretty sciency."

"Well, you can handle all that stuff, I'll make sure it all looks slick."

"Deal *numero dos*," he said.

Gareth and his roommate spent the night playing a new game while I hung out reading my book. After Gareth was in bed, I emailed Junie a boring update of the day. Since nothing had happened, it was easy to be honest this time. I even made the extra point of rubbing in the delicious pizza rolls since I knew he loved them. But I still felt guilty as I hit send because while I'd been honest, I'd still lied. If I didn't come clean soon I'd explode, but I had no idea how to do it. Something had to give.

Before I went to bed I had one more item of business to take care of. I called the update hotline number and left a message about Gareth's upcoming meeting with the dean. I told them he would hopefully get published if it went well. If this really was what had made him so damn important, it would be good information to add to his file for the archives. Better documentation of what he did, how he did it, and when. I also figured, why not, right? I had some new information, and this was the information number. It was one part of my job I could get right

GARETH AND I HAD agreed that we'd work on the presentation Saturday morning. But first, the rest of the week had to happen. Luckily, it flew by as everyone was preparing for finals or had end-of-semester projects due.

Earlier in the month, I had convinced Lloyd that Gareth wasn't my boyfriend (it wasn't easy), and with that cleared up Gareth and I had teamed up with him and another classmate for our own big lab project. With Lloyd, Gareth, and the other super nerd I did very little. It was great. I might actually get an A on this thing without the assistance of my grade changers. Maw and Paw would be so proud of me.

I'd insert some happy montage here, but there would be no point. The horrible feeling inside of me I had from lying to Junie was grotesquely large now. It kept me up most nights. What little dreams I'd been having weren't helping either. I had one where I told Junie I had kissed a guy (played by Will Ferrell in my dream). Junie gave Will a high five and said, *Me too!* They then talked about what a horrible kisser I was while arguing over who would have to date me. Neither really wanted anything to do with me, so they went out for yogurt together and left me by myself. And in another, when I came clean to Junie, completely clean, he walked away and I never heard from him again.

That dream sucked the most. It also had the best chance of coming true.

CAMPUS ON AN EARLY Saturday morning was one of my favorite times. It feels like you have the place all to yourself. Combine that with the brisk winter air, and today it almost felt like home. Today was looking like it would be aces.

Now, as we all know the mugging was the root cause of me being neck deep in the no-no's of my profession. But as Gareth and I left our dorm together at around 7 A.M., I was actually thankful it had happened. No, not because I had gotten to stretch my legs and hurt people, although that part was nice. You see, I was thankful because I had become complacent here and it had served as a reminder that I could never let my guard down, ever. It was because of that day that I saw it.

Across the street and down the block from our dorm was a plain brown delivery truck. Usually nothing to worry about, there are tons of them around campus all the time. But this was the fourth time in twenty-four hours I'd seen this exact one. I knew because it had a dent on the side that resembled the state of California. It had been parked outside our dorm yesterday morning, slowly cruised down the street by the cafeteria during lunch, and had idled in the loading zone of the Ag building next to the labs last night. Now it was here.

The driver's seat was empty, but exhaust curled up from the tail pipe. Someone was inside, watching us. I was certain of it.

When we rounded the corner I made a show of having to tie the laces of my New Balances so that I could determine if the truck was following us. It wasn't, but that meant nothing. I told Gareth I was cold and wrapped my arm around his. He assumed it was for warmth, on the off chance I was giving into my love for him, so he didn't fight it at all. The truth? It was so I could be as close as possible to him, ready for anything that might happen.

An attacker would literally have to go through my body to get to him.

For the briefest of moments I thought I was making it all up. Just being paranoid. I hoped I was. But when we reached the courtyard behind the Academic building I knew I wasn't. It was eerily silent and empty. No birds singing the sun up. Nothing. Predators were here. The flutter of a coat out of the corner of my eye gave me a start, but when I turned to look I saw nobody. It would happen and it would happen soon.

So this was it. Muggers schmuggers. This would be serious. This would be coordinated and the stakes would be real. I, or they, would be dead when it was over.

Then I heard it: the soft pitter-patter of running feet, flying up behind us. I spun around and tossed my backpack at the attacker. He caught it out of instinct as my foot connected with his jaw. He crumbled and rolled to a stop at the bottom of a staircase. But he was groaning, and still moving. He would recover soon.

I grabbed Gareth by the collar and dragged him to the doorway of the Academic building. The arched stone entry provided a good safe nook for him to duck into and wait, and the locked door meant no one could sneak up behind him. It wasn't ideal, but it was good enough for the moment.

"Stay here and don't move!" I yelled at him. "Promise me you won't move!" I barely saw him nod before a shin slammed into my chest Time slowed with the impact, watching him get further away from me, his eyes widening. I slammed into the ground, hard on my butt—and rolled backward, popping up almost instantly. But in that same moment a different foot, from the first attacker, connected with the side of my head. I cartwheeled, absorbing the force of the blow. *At least two of them*, I thought.

I found my footing in time to see both of them coming after me. Only two of them, at least for now. For clarity's sake, we'll call the smaller one Tom and the bigger one Jerry. Both looked to be about my age. I blocked a punch from Tom with my forearm but took a kick from Jerry to the hip. And so it went. I would block an attack from one only to get punished by the other. Don't get me wrong; I got in a few good hits myself, but I was losing the battle and couldn't hold out much longer. They were good. Well- trained, young, fast, strong, and fearless. But not invincible. Their overconfidence would be their downfall.

I let loose a stomp to Jerry's knee that buckled him to the ground. I took the moment to somersault away from the two of them. The trench knives that Junie had given me were strapped to my back, and in one fluid motion, I gripped the handles, pulled out the blades, and flung the coat I was wearing in the air behind me. *Now let's play.*

But instead of attacking, they kept their distance as if waiting for something. Tom almost had a smile. *Oh Crap!*

I spun to my left as the whisper of silenced automatic fire echoed off of the walls. The ground directly behind where I had been exploded with dirt as the bullets hit. More bullets whizzed all around me, barely missing me and hitting branches and bushes as I ran.

When I made it back to Gareth the shooting stopped. I nodded at him; it was all I had time to do before I poked my head out from the edge of the building to check on Tom and Jerry. I was ready to pull back, sure that bullets would be coming right at me, but there weren't any. No shooting. Instead I saw Tom holding his hand to his ear, listening and then nodding. He and Jerry both pulled out expanding metal batons and whipped them out. Their eyes met mine they slowly began making their way toward me.

"Are you okay?" I whispered to Gareth.

He nodded. "Are you?" he asked. His voice cracked. His eyes were still wide and his breathing quick and shallow. "What's happening?!"

"Do you trust me?" I asked. He nodded again, without hesitation "Then stay here, and keep your head low."

I took a deep breath and spun around the corner of the building. The move did what I had hoped and caught Tom and Jerry off guard. They had probably assumed they would have to drag me out of there. I dodged a swing by Jerry, sliced him across the stomach and drove my other knife through his neck. Tom swung his baton at me, but I ducked the swing and it cracked into Jerry's lifeless, still upright body instead.

Jerry's death clouded Tom's concentration and fueled both fear and anger. Now I had another advantage. He picked up Jerry's baton; so he had two. It took every ounce of training and focus to deflect his attacks. Boy, he was strong. But he wasn't thinking. Every time he swung, I blocked and cut him with one of my knives. I sliced and stabbed his arms, legs, shoulders. After one final weary swing I spotted a lethal opening: his neck.

His mouth was still trying to take tired breaths as I slit his throat. I didn't bother watching him fall. Before the gunman (gunmen?) could open fire again I sprinted back to Gareth. My battle with Tom had taken me all over the Academic building grounds and I was now some thirty yards way from Gareth's hiding place. I swiped my discarded backpack up off the ground on my way to him.

Dirty, covered with Tom and Jerry's blood and a little of my own, I slid into the hiding place and asked, "You okay?"

No answer. I looked behind me. Gareth wasn't there. A muffled yell was all I got and all I needed.

I jumped out of the archway and saw Gareth being dragged away by a third attacker. A *she*. I'd wondered why the gunman hadn't tried to shoot me after I had killed Tom. I had been in open space, an easy target. Now I knew. Tom was the distraction so this girl could grab Gareth. She, too, looked no older than any of my classmates. She kept one hand over Gareth's mouth and the other around his waist as she dragged him away. A large automatic rifle hung by her side from a shoulder strap. She was stronger than he was and was opening up the distance between us. As she got closer to the road, the dented brown van appeared.

I pulled the 9mm pistol I kept in my backpack and ran after them firing. I flattened the vans's tires, then shot at the woman. But she was clearly trained well, evading as she ran. Only one shot conntected, nicking her shoulder. She hurled Gareth into a large bush, pulled up her rifle, and opened fire on me.

I barely had time to dive behind a concrete bench before it started being destroyed by her high caliber bullets. I counted. I knew her gun. I knew how many bullets it held. Could the bench make it that long? It was getting blown to bits all around me. When I counted twenty-four shots I sprang up and fired again. She rolled to her right behind a tree, then popped out from behind it, firing a pistol of her own.

I rolled and sprinted between trees. But every time I did, she mirrored my movement to keep the distance. It was beginning to be a stalemate. I took deep, calm breaths, thinking of a way to end this. That's when I saw him. Crouched behind a stone wall at the top of a set of stairs was Lloyd. He looked both terrified and excited. The scariest, greatest day of his life I bet. Our eyes met. He waved and he moved his other hand toward me. He was holding something. *A phone.* He was filming the whole thing. *How long had he been there? What had he seen?*

I shook my head and mouthed *Go.* He shook his head right back and looked at me like I was crazy for even thinking it. Idiot. He would die here. If he didn't, I'd deal with him later. If there was a later.

I was about thirty feet from Gareth. When he caught my eyes, he nodded. I didn't understand what he meant until he jumped out of the bushes and took off—running away from the van, away from me, away from her.

It only took a second before the girl started chasing after him. She might have had no idea where I was. Either that or losing Gareth wasn't an option. Maybe both. When she passed me I shot her directly in the head and she crumbled to the ground like a rag doll. Before she even finished rolling, the brown van spun out and came bouncing toward us on its deflated tires, screeching and shaking, But it still had speed.

"RUN!" I shouted.

He didn't need the encouragement. But I had to slow my pace so I wouldn't leave him behind. The van was struggling now, trying to maneuver through and around the stairs, benches, and fountains on campus. It sideswiped a fountain, and nearly tipped over. I pulled out my phone and hit the emergency beacon that was programmed into it. Five minutes and the cavalry would be here. But we had to keep moving until then.

Within seconds, we were back at the dorm. Gareth bolted for the doors, but I grabbed his jacket and steered him around the building toward the back where Old Hank sat quietly waiting. Maybe this was why they'd given me the motorcycle with the sidecar. Maybe they'd knew this time would come. There could have been more attackers inside waiting for us. We weren't safe here. It was time to go and time to go fast.

I shoved Gareth into the sidecar and hopped on the bike. The engine purred to life, eager to prove itself, ready for the challenge. The van lumbered into parking lot as I tore out of it. Once I hit the open road it had no chance. I opened the throttle, kicked Hank into fourth gear, and opened up a massive space between us. I watched through my mirror as the van's headlights slowly got smaller and smaller. I looked down at Gareth, huddled in the sidecar, arms over his head for protection. I pulled the helmet off of the back seat where I kept it and handed it to him. He put it on and pulled the goggles down over his eyes. I took a second set of goggles out of a saddlebag and put them on myself.

All at once, I was punched in the small of the back by something. I lurched forward and nearly lost control of the bike. Warmth began spreading across my lower body. I looked down, trying to catch my breath. A bullet had gone through my back and out my side, thankfully missing any vital organs. I turned to look behind me and found a black town car right on my ass. A man was hanging out the window aiming a second shot. They had snuck up on us while I was dealing with the helmets and goggles. Stupid safety

I swerved the bike as the man fired off another round. He missed wide.

At the sudden movement Gareth spun around to see what was going on. I smacked the top of his helmet with my hand and yelled, "STAY DOWN!"

I opened up the throttle on Hank and tore around a semitruck like it was standing still. But still the car kept pace. A normal motorcycle could have gotten away easily, but with the added weight of the sidecar and two riders, 100 mph was about all I could expect.

After the semi, there was nothing but open highway. Breathing was becoming difficult. I had to do something. The town car was easily matching our speed so I continued to swerve across the lanes to keep from giving the man a clean shot. He was aiming high, only at me, even to the left to ensure he didn't accidentally hit Gareth. Whoever it was wanted him alive, needed him alive, and I could use that against them.

I screamed over the engine, "GARETH!"

I pointed at the back of his seat. Keeping his head safely behind the back rest, he crammed himself in to the foot of the side car and rolled over to look. There was a brass loop in the middle of the seat cushion. He pointed at it and I nodded. He looped his finger through it and pulled it off.

It was a fake cushion. Behind it was a metal lock box. He looked up at me.

I yelled, "3-1-3-9!"

He spun the lock and opened the door. Inside were four grenades and a pistol with extra ammo. Looking at him, I mimed grabbing a grenade, pulling the pin, and throwing it behind us. He nodded. He'd played enough video games to understand this.

With trembling, nervous fingers, he took out the first grenade, pulled the pin, and threw it. An athlete he is not. He missed well wide before it exploded harmlessly on the shoulder one hundred yards behind the town car.

He looked up at me for advice, but I had none. It was pretty self-explanatory how these things worked. Their only flaw was that a human had to provide the accuracy. Unfortunately, this human had none. His third attempt did hit the car, but with the five-second fuse, it bounced off the windshield and rolled into the grass median before detonating like the other.

Well, we've definitly called attention to ourselves, I thought, fighting to ignore the cold numbness overtaking me, my struggling lungs. There would be witnesses and cops and questions. Could F.A.T.E. really handle it all? I guess if anyone could it would be them. But a terrorist attack on a college campus in broad daylight? That's what this was, for all intents and purposes . . .

One grenade left. This had to work or we were dead. I watched Gareth out of the corner of my eye. He was looking around, working something out in his mind, biting his lip as he concentrated. I watched him pull the pin and let the clip fly. My eyes widened when he didn't throw it. He was going to kill us. He held the grenade for three full seconds then casually dropped it over the side of the sidecar onto the road.

He had timed it perfectly. The town car drove right over the grenade as it detonated. I watched in my mirror as the the blast lifted up the town car and tossed like a child's toy off the road, landing as a crumpled inferno.

Gareth didn't look back. Maybe he was too horrified at what he'd done. I could relate.

"Where do we go now?" I barely heard him scream over the engine.

"Some place safe." I yelled back down at him. He nodded and looked ahead at the open road ahead of us.

I looked down at the left side of my belly. The blood had soaked through my shirt and was beginning to drip off my jeans onto the road. But it was on the side facing away from Gareth, so he had no clue. I kept Hank running at full tilt. I was getting weaker, but I could make it. I knew it. I was going to get Gareth some place safe. I was going to get him to Austin. I was going to get to Junie.

CHAPTER 23
WORLDS COLLIDE

While driving down the desolate highway I replayed the events in my head over and over. First of all, where were the cops? Where was the National Guard? I hadn't heard a single helicopter or siren. Not one. Nothing made sense. I couldn't make heads or tails of any of it. There were too many questions and no answers. I, no, *we* had been attacked. That was all I had to go on. Why the hell hadn't anyone shown up yet to help us? Had the message not gone through?

Just do your job, Ren Sharpe. You're not paid to think.

Gareth was safe though. In the end, that was all that mattered. I checked the mirrors for the billionth time, assuring myself we were not being followed. I had no need for a map to Junie's. I had memorized the route long ago while fantasizing about the day I would travel it. I already knew the name of every farm road I passed. Each one represented one step closer to safety, to him.

The Austin city limits sign brought about the first butterflies in my stomach. Or maybe it was the gunshot wound. At least I wasn't dizzy anymore. But I was freezing, and I didn't know if that was because of the blood loss or the winter wind. It lashed my chapped face. Each passing mile now coaxed forth more queasiness. Of course I'd imagined our reunion under much different circumstances. In the dream reunion, there was lots of laughing, me actually looking cute, maybe a chocolate fountain— your typical girl who isn't a machine-like-killer stuff. In our real reunion, I would be on the lam, beat to hell, my face wind-whipped, near dead from blood loss. But since I had honestly thought we'd never see each other again, this was better than never. If he could love me looking like this . . .

When I finally turned onto his street, my damaged stomach did a jump. I counted the addresses on the mailboxes. Excitement grew as I got closer to his house. Gareth turned to me, looking bewildered. I'd explain everything. I would.

Made it. Managed to park. The world was fuzzy, closing in around me fast. Everything was a struggle now. I stumbled up the sidewalk toward his front door, clutching my stomach. Fortunately, no one was doing yard work. There were no witnesses to my labored, blood-soaked march up the well-manicured lawn. Try explaining that one at the summer block party.

I knocked. Heard feet approaching.

The door opened.

"Junie."

And everything went black.

I FLUTTERED IN AND out of consciousness only catching glimpses of what was going on.

-*Junie and Gareth carrying me.*

-*The feeling of hard wood on my back. A table?*

-*Junie cutting off my shirt with scissors. Dangit! I liked this shirt.*

-*Gareth cleaning my face. Are you crying?!*

I came to, albeit briefly, because of hushed voices that were trying not to be loud but failing miserably at it.

"We have to get to her a hospital," Gareth hissed.

"No, we don't, and for the hundredth time, we can't. Trust me, I can do this," Junie replied calmly.

"You're not a doctor. I'm taking her." Gareth stated.

"You can't take her to a doctor. Too many questions," Junie said a bit more sternly.

"Well, there will be a lot more of them when she dies."

"She won't die. I won't let her. We've been trained for this. If you let me get to work, it's nothing I can't handle. The longer we wait, the worse it gets. Please trust me."

"Sorry but no, I'm calling for an ambulance. She's too important to me."

"And what do you think she is to me? If any part of me thought a hospital would be better for her, do you think I'd be standing here right now? You have no idea what you're dealing with here. It's nothing you could understand."

I heard movement, footsteps, and some scuffling.

Then Junie said, "If you get in the way of me saving

her one more time, I'll kill you where you stand. Do you understand me?"

There was silence. I tried to speak, tried to tell them to stop, but nothing seemed to be working. My brain was telling my lips to move, but they wouldn't cooperate.

"I'm Type O negative. I'm a universal blood donor." Gareth said quietly.

"Good. Now we're talking. Roll up your sleeve." Junie replied.

I heard cabinets opening and dishes being collected before passing out once again.

Gareth, holding my hand and watching Junie work.

Junie, hands bloody, checking my breathing.

Rolled onto my stomach looking down. What an odd pattern for a dining room rug.

I HAD DREAMS ABOUT the attack. But instead of fighting the attackers I was fighting *me*. Like clones or something. It was a weird sensation to be fighting mirror images, punching my own face to a bloody mess. Truly strange. But something had irked me about the attack. The age of the attackers, their movements, fighting styles . . . it all had felt too familiar. Thus the odd dream about fighting myself. And like dreams seem to do, when I began to wake up, it slipped away a dim mist. Almost Forgotten. Gone but for the faintest trace.

I WOKE UP IN a dark room on a couch. Junie was sitting next to me, holding my hand and smiling down at me.

"Morning, sunshine," he said.

My face flushed red. I wanted so badly to jump up and hug him, kiss him, lose myself in his arms. I couldn't move. I weakly gave him a "Junie." I could feel the all-too-familiar sensation of the hard gel bandage over my stomach and back wounds.

"Put a scare in me there for a bit," he said softly.

I itched my stomach, and Junie gently lifted my hand away.

"Let it be," he said sweetly.

"Where's Gareth?"

"Asleep. Or passed out to be more exact," he added with a sly grin. I gave him a look he knew all too well. "I *may* have taken a little more blood then was needed so he'd pass out and shut up for a while." He raised his eyebrows and grinned guiltily. I glared at him. "I'll apologize when he wakes up."

My glare melted into a smile

"I've missed that," he said grinning back. I realized he was lightly stroking my hand. I liked it. It felt right in every way that Gareth's touch didn't. I squeezed his hand in mine.

"You feeling okay?" I nodded and he continued, "Because you look awesome."

"That good, huh?" I grunted, struggling to sit up. He moved to stop me, but knew better and helped me instead. I caught my reflection in a mirror across the room. *Wow.* One black eye, cut over my other eye, a badly bruised jaw, and who knows what was going on beneath my clothes. *My clothes . . .*

"Who put me in these?" I asked staring down at the

extra large gym shorts and old T-shirt I was wearing. Junie's silence told me all I needed to know. Angrily I started with, "Junie Miller . . ."

"I didn't peek when I was doing it I swear," he said holding up his hands.

"Oh, really, how'd you do it then?"

"Not easily."

I guess they were more hygienic than the filthy rags I had been wearing. I took a deep breath to calm down and caught a whiff of something. Something clean and flowery. *Was that me?* I smelled my arm. Soap. *I was clean!* I looked up.

Junie smiled and raised his hands up even more, "Okay, the bath was a little harder and I *may* have seen some stuff." He started to laugh a little.

Of course I wasn't mad; how could I be? My anger was less at him and more about how crappy the circumstances had been that had led to it. There was nothing attractive about cleaning an unconscious, limp, bloody body in a tub. He'd done what was right, but that didn't mean I couldn't have a little fun with him.

"Stand up," I said flatly.

Still grinning, he hopped up from the chair beside me, even stood at attention to be an ass about it.

"Now take off your clothes." I commanded. "It's only fair. You saw me, now I see you."

He started to smile, thinking it was a joke, but when I didn't return it, he got straight-faced again. I glanced at the stereo in the corner and added, "You can put on some music if it makes you feel better."

He took a deep breath. His shoulders dropped, and he lowered his head a bit. He grabbed the bottom of his baby blue T-shirt and raised it over his head. The moment it blocked me from his eyes I forced myself to my feet and stood directly in front of him. The good thing about not feeling any pain is that you can ignore injuries. When he got his shirt off I was right there, my face inches from his.

"Hi," I said softly.

"Hi."

"Thanks."

He shrugged and said, "It's you. I'd do—"

But that's all he got out before I kissed him.

I WOKE UP WRAPPED in Junie's arms, curled up on the couch. He was warm and smelled like summer. I wished we could stay that way forever. It felt right.

I pushed the blanket aside and wafted some air into my shirt to cool off a little. Yeah, I was still clothed, not naked. Get your mind out of the gutter. What we did or didn't do last night is our business. Stop prying.

Yes, this was good, this was real, but it wasn't everything I needed. I needed something else, something I couldn't control, and fighting it any longer wasn't an option. By my count it had been over twelve hours since I'd last seen Gareth and that equaled the longest I'd gone without seeing him since that first day on campus. It was too long. Painfully so. I needed to see him. As great as being with Junie was at that moment, I had to see Gareth with my own eyes to believe he was safe. The beast inside had to be satisfied. It's like when you're in the backyard and you know you blew out the candle in your room, but that little voice inside you nags and nags until finally you cave and you go to check on it even though you know the answer. I tried to fight it but I couldn't. I had to check on my candle.

As gently as I could, I lifted Junie's arms off of me and rolled off the couch. He gave a quiet, sweet mumble of something and wrapped his arms around a pillow, still asleep. I kissed him gently on the forehead and stood up. I crept upstairs to Gareth.

When I cracked open the door at the end of the hall, that unnatural sensation of pleasure flooded me. He was fast asleep, comfortably nestled in the blankets. Having not had my fix for so long, the jolt was more powerful than usual. I could only imagine how great it would feel to curl up next to him. Would it feel like it did with Junie? Could it? Or were those feelings still a lie, a sham? I wasn't so sure anymore.

I shut the door. As I walked back down the hallway the rush of seeing Gareth faded and left me light-headed and woozy. Side effects from massive blood loss no doubt. I wall-walked my way back to the stairs, prepared to lie back down with Junie on the couch.

When I got back to the living room, he was gone.

He wasn't upstairs; I knew that. A quick search of the ground floor led me to the basement door. It had been left slightly cracked open, like an invitation, and there was a faint bluish glow creeping out. I silently padded down the stairs. Walls hid my descent on both sides and opened up at a landing where the stairs turned. I stopped there.

Junie was sitting on a couch in the middle of room

facing the video feed of a small child sleeping. Emily, of course. To the left of the huge image were many smaller feeds showing other places in the house: a dark, empty kitchen, a hallway lit by a single night light. But Junie was transfixed on the sleeping child and nothing else.

Junie looked so at home, so at peace watching her. I knew that peace. I did the same thing for hours on end each night with Gareth. It was a feeling unlike any other. I held my breath. I didn't want him to know I'd invaded. This was his space, his moment, and I wanted to let him keep it.

Emily gave the cutest little sigh and rolled over. A fatherly grin slid across Junie's face. She was as much a part of him as Gareth was of me.

"You gonna stand there all night?" he asked without so much as a backward glance. He motioned with his head to come join him.

I slid into the couch, brought my knees up to my chest, and rested my head on his shoulder. He reached over and wrapped his arm around me. We sat there together in silence staring at the screen. Strange—having just gotten my Gareth fix, and now snuggling with Junie—for the first time ever I felt truly and fully complete.

"Gareth okay?" he asked.

"Yeah. Sorry I got up. I had to." I looked up at him. His face was a mixture of understanding, and pain. I understood. It hurt me, too.

He squeezed me tighter. "It nags on you, I know."

"It does. How's Emily?"

"Fine. It's funny . . ." but he didn't finish his thought.

"What?"

"Nothing. It's stupid."

"I like stupid." I lifted my head off of his shoulder and stretched on the couch with my legs across his lap.

"I know you do." He took a deep breath. "Tonight was the first night I've missed her being tucked-in. Every single night since I was linked, I've been there to tuck her in. I know not physically there, but . . . it's hard to explain. It's dumb, forget it."

"It's not dumb, Junie, not to me." I reached over and grabbed his hand.

"It was like the moment I missed it, I knew it in my gut. I got nervous. When I woke up and you were gone, part of me was glad. It made me feel better to know that you have the same sort of . . . sickness. That you have to know . . ."

". . . that they're safe," we said together.

He absentmindedly began to pet my left calf with his free hand while his eyes went back to the screen. I closed my eyes, ready to fall back asleep. But my brain, doing what it does best, annoyingly reminded me of a promise I made to myself a long time ago. A promise to come clean, about everything, if I ever saw Junie again. One of these days me and my brain are gonna have it out. It ain't gonna be pretty, either.

Who knew how much longer we had here. The F.A.T.E. team could arrive at any minute, or more attackers could bust in on us. Good timing or not, it was now or never. I took a deep breath, opened my eyes, and sat up.

"We need to talk."

"Like, really talk?"

I nodded.

"Coffee?"

"Absolutely." I said, grateful for the postponement. .

He got up from the couch and walked over to a coffee machine in a small kitchenette in the corner. He pushed a few buttons and it filled two mugs. He carried them over to a small table and sat down. I sat down across from him.

I cupped my hands around the steaming mug, staring into the dark liquid. "If you could just let me say it all without interrupting, it'd be easier."

"Sure."

I took a sip of the too hot coffee and before I lost my nerve let it all out. A rush, a jumble. I started from the very beginning, from the moment he jumped off of the balcony and left me alone in my room. I told him about the first time I'd seen Gareth and the feelings that came with it. He nodded, having felt something similar with Emily, though obviously not in the same way—his devotion was paternal. I told him about the mugging and the unbelievably amazing, almost indescribable sensation I felt from Gareth's touch. Our fake relationship and subsequent break up from the kiss were covered too. Then to Gareth's wheat breakthrough, and finally to the attack that had brought us here.

Jumie kept a poker face throughout, but his eyes gave him away. The kiss bothered him a lot. It pained him, which pained me. It was a hurt I never want to be responsible for. Only the anger from the attack made it go away.

When I finished I took a big drink of coffee, which was much cooler now, and looked at him. It felt like the weight

of the world had been lifted off of my shoulders. I felt free.
I felt great. Except for one thing.

"Sorry about the kiss," I finished.

"Nothing to be sorry about. *You* didn't kiss *him*, right?"
he asked.

I aggressively shook my head.

"And you didn't enjoy it, right?"

I looked at him. My non-reply was confirmation enough.
"Oh."

I scrambled to explain it to him. "No, not like that. Not
like *that*. It's just, you know that feeling when you see your
FIP?"

He nodded.

"Times a thousand. I'm programmed to like it. We both
are," I then added, with a smile, "I pushed him into a wall
after he did it. He won't do it again."

He turned back to the Emily screens. "I know it wasn't
your idea, Ren, and I get it. I do."

He leaned across the table and kissed me. It was genuine and gentle and said everything Junie couldn't say in
words. And I knew what I felt was real and not fabricated.
That was all that mattered.

When he leaned back into his seat he looked troubled.

"What?" I asked.

"I took a lot of blood from that kid yesterday. Let's just
say he'll wake up with one hell of a headache." He smirked
impishly. "I don't feel bad about it now."

"Fair enough," I said.

He blinked and then started talking. The next part
tumbled out with the right amount of guilt and with a

pinch of it being something he'd been dying to say, "I've been babysitting Emily for over month now. Like, *really* babysitting. As in spending time with her and playing with her and—"

"Seriously?" I interrupted. And I had to admit, I felt pretty freaking awesome. I always assumed I was the only idiot. The only one who had broken the rules. But Junie too? Follow-the-rules, top-of-the-class Junie? How many more Shadows were out there like us?

He smiled. "It all started a couple months ago. I was in my front yard working on my flowerbeds. My boxwoods weren't rooting."

I shot him a look. He flushed.

"Shut up. So I'm gardening when I feel a tiny little tap on my shoulder. It was Emily. The feeling was, like you said, indescribable. I nearly passed out right then and there. Anyway, Chris and Michelle, her parents, were nowhere to be seen, so I took her hand and walked her back to her house. As we were going up the stairs her mother came running out scared out of her mind. We laughed and, well, one thing led to another . . . and I'm now their go-to sitter for Thursday date night."

"You, the stay-at-home writer?"

He laughed. "We read! She's really smart, and loves to cook so . . ."

At that moment the fourteen-year-old kid I fell in love with so long ago was gone. That kid was replaced by the adult sitting across from me. As he spoke, I began to see him doing all of these things. I saw him reading her stories, baking cakes, being, well, a father. He loved this kid like she was his own flesh and blood. She was more than a link to him now. The glow in his eyes, the enthusiasm—it was love, real love. But if his feelings for Emily ran deeper than the link, could my feelings for Gareth be that deep as well? Could I honestly brush them off as nothing more than side effects?

"We dress up and have tea parties. She calls me Miss Pippy Bottoms . . ."

I started laughing. The image of a Junie sitting in a tiny chair, wearing a dress, speaking with a high-pitched English accent and sipping a tiny tea cup popped into my head, and soon I was in hysterics. "Miss Pippy Bottoms!" I was crying it was so bad.

I wiped the tears from eyes and nodded. "Oh, wow," I said slightly out breath. "That was a good one."

"Finished?"

"Oh, I'll revisit that one later for sure, but yeah, for now . . . Miss Pippy Bottoms."

"Hardy har. It reminds me of babysitting my little sister. Of being home. So make fun of me all you want I don't care. It's the best part of my week." He paused. "Well, that, and when you email."

There were footsteps upstairs. Gareth was awake and heading our way.

I then realized this could be the last time we were together, alone, for, well . . . ever. "Quick," I said and leaned in for one last kiss. We stopped as Gareth came walking down the stairs.

His hair was messed, and he was holding his head. "Got any Advil in this place?" he croaked.

We shared a look before Junie said, "Far right, top shelf," and pointed at a cabinet.

"Morning?" I said with a smile. My voice had the tone of *hello, I'm here and alive.*

Gareth stopped halfway to the cabinet and came stumbling over to me. He hugged me from over the back of the chair. Junie sighed and nodded.

"I'm so sorry," Gareth said to me. "Rude. I'm only . . . my head hurts so bad. Are you okay?"

"I'm fine. Go get your drugs."

"Thank you," he said as if I'd released him from prison. He popped a few pills in his mouth and grabbed a cup of coffee to wash them down. Then he joined us at the table and slumped into the chair. The triumvirate. Too awkward. Too quiet. Somebody had to break the tension. I opened my mouth, but Gareth beat me to it.

"So, I've been a pretty good sport about all of this, right?"

"You've been great," I said, exhaling.

"You have," Junie added sincerely.

"So then when do I get to know what the hell is going on?"

Junie and I exchanged a glance. He'd been through everything and had no clue why. Went with the flow when he had no idea where it was taking him. He'd earned the right to know; I owed him that. He was injured, filthy, far from home, and still covered in what had to be my dried blood.

I took the cup of coffee from him and said, "After you take a shower. Open book. Deal?"

"Open book? You mean that? I can ask anything, and you'll tell me?"

I nodded.

He looked at himself. "Shower's probably a good idea."

"Linen closet is at the end of the upstairs hall. Blue towels are for company, so grab one of them," Junie told him. I gave a snort of laughter and he added, "Shut up, Ren."

"Blue towels, got it."

As Gareth reached the top of the stairs, he called down, "You realize you're both staring at a sleeping child. Add that to the list of creepy things that need explaining."

Once Gareth was upstairs, Junie looked at me. "Did you ever hit the beacon to alert F.A.T.E.?"

I nodded. "While we were running."

"And nobody came?" he asked.

"Nope."

"Weird."

"I know."

It had been something that bothered me—or didn't, depending on how you saw it. But it was new information to Junie, so I let it sit before asking, "Be straight with me, Slick. How bad is this?"

"Slick?"

"It just came out, no idea why." I said honestly. Total brain fart. "But come on. How bad?"

"On a scale of one to ten?" he asked.

I nodded.

"Twelve . . . no, thirty."

"Twelve jumps to thirty just like that?" I said with a snap of my fingers. But my smile faltered.

"I'm not very good at math," he said. He tried to smile, too, with equal lack of success. This wasn't good. "I mean, you've pretty much broken every rule we have, Ren, and there aren't that many. But you broke them doing what you were supposed to do, so I wouldn't worry about it. You can explain everything to them when they get here. I'm sure they'll understand. It'll be fine."

I nearly spit out my coffee. "When *who* gets here?"

"Them," he said as if needed no more explanation. "They called while you were asleep. Said you'd gone missing and they couldn't find you. I told them you were here."

"Junie, no." I said, my pulse picking up a notch. I guess I wasn't entirely fearless. I could feel no pain, but I knew what certain death meant.

"What do you mean, no?"

"The attack on me. Us. Was too . . ." I struggled for the words, ". . . I *recognized* it. It was them. F.A.T.E." And there it was. Once I'd said it out loud I knew it was true. "It's been them this whole time."

The mugging had been sloppily executed but well coordinated. They knew Gareth used that short cut. .Someone had sent them there. They knew if Gareth wasn't in mortal danger I'd stay out of it, and I did until they drew the gun. Had they left with his backpack as planned I'd never have intervened.

The attack yesterday had felt too familiar because it was exactly how I would have planned the execution. (Of the plan, not of Gareth.) A team of four. Two killers, one shooter, and a driver. Spotty images from my dream hovered at the edge of my consciousness. I was fighting versions of myself on campus because they *were* just like me. They'd come to kill me and to kidnap Gareth. If they'd wanted him dead he would be. Killing was easy. They wanted him alive and there was only one reason for that. The same reason he was a FIP, the same reason we'd been linked.

"I have to go," I said. "Now." But as I stood up a metal canister shot down the stairs, clanked off the wall, and landed on the floor. I knew what it was before the gas began steaming out of it. This was the end.

The effect was almost instant. I became groggy, and my movement clumsy and slow. I had to get to Gareth but couldn't move.

All I could muster was turning my head toward Junie. My eyes were teary as I pleaded, "Junie, what did you do?"

He opened his mouth in horror and confusion, but I never heard what he said.

The floor came crashing toward me, as did the dark. My last thought was of Gareth and how I'd failed him.

CHAPTER 24
NO PLACE LIKE HOME

So here I sit, in a grassy meadow overlooking a breathtaking valley below. It's complete with a running river, a small village, and the last strips of late spring snow. It's absolutely beautiful.

"Ren, we're all waiting for you!"

It's my father's voice. I spin around and see him standing at the crest of a hill waving me over. He looks like I remember him, maybe a little younger and a bit more handsome, but he's still my dad.

I get up and walk through the knee-high grass over to him. He puts his arm around me and steers me over the crest of the hill. Everyone is there. It's a picnic. My mother and little brother are having a watermelon eating contest with my grandparents. Junie and Gareth are playing catch with a football. All of my old friends are there too. What the hell, is that Will Ferrell again?! They all drop what they're doing and yell, "Hey, Ren!"

I wave back shyly.

So this is death, huh? Well, it ain't half bad then. No pitchforks or hellfire. No elegant clou- living either. No, only this. Simple, peaceful, and exactly what perfection is to me.

I make my way down the slope of the hill toward all of the people I love or have loved. All of them are waiting for me to reach them.

The blue sky looks like the ocean and a cool breeze is blowing through the trees. I take a deep breath. But there's something off. The air carries a scent that makes my skin crawl. I will never, can never, forget it. It's a mixture of stale, recycled oxygen mixed with bleach and cleaning products. It's purely antiseptic; it reeks of a place that's too clean, of the place where I was kept prisoner for years.

The woods around me erupt into loud wails of pain and misery. The sounds of suffering. The sounds of broken minds.

No, this was not death and this was no dream. I'm back.

I REGAINED CONSCIOUSNESS STRAPPED into a chair in an all-too-familiar medical room. Good old déjà vu. I struggled against the binds, but unlike before, I recognized there was no chance of escape. I stopped to conserve my energy. I did some deep breathing to calm down, to prepare myself for whatever was about to happen. Was there anything in here to give me a clue?

I had never been in this room before but I could tell from the white subway tile and the surround-sound of agony that I was somewhere in the hospital wing. The room looked a bit older than the others. The door must have been behind me because there wasn't one anywhere I could see.

The hairs on my neck stood up. Maybe I was just cold?

There was a sudden stabbing sensation in my stomach.

I hadn't felt pain in so long I had forgotten what it was like. It overwhelmed me. I vomited on the floor to my right. The strange pain lessened but didn't go away. With that, a door hissed opened behind me. I assumed it was a doctor, nurse, or even a Hunter here to put me down. But if they wanted me dead, they could have easily done so by now. Would have been much easier while I was out. No, someone wanted me alive, someone wanted me here. But who?

Mr. S. slowly appeared in front of me, holding a steaming up of tea.

"Ren Sharpe. I'm so glad you're still alive. You were always one of my favorites." He smiled.

CHAPTER 25

PLAYING ALONG

He took a sip of from his mug. Funny: I thought he'd brought it for me.

After his sip he nodded knowingly as he said, "I know, I know. I've got some explaining to do. And some apologizing. The muggers were an insult and the attack on campus was so ill-conceived I'm ashamed to have sanctioned it. Please forgive me."

"Where's Gareth?" I demanded. "Is he safe?" He could explain later.

"He's here."

It was not the response I was looking for. The tea was annoying me. "Is he safe?" I repeated.

Mr. S. toyed with the thoughts in his head, rocking his noggin' back and forth, but still wouldn't answer me.

"I have to see him. Please, let me see him."

Mr. S. pursed his lips. "I'm sorry. I can't let you do that."

He lowered his eyes to look as sad as possible while he said, "He's being broken, Ren."

Gareth was in agony, so as a result, I was too. There was only one solution. I had to save him and punish those responsible, starting with the man in front of me. I could think of nothing else. I struggled stupidly against the binds again, screaming as I strained every muscle in my body to free myself.

"Ren, please calm down," Mr. S. said

He was right. Struggling was pointless. Whatever he was going to do, I couldn't physically stop from happening. I had to calm down. I had to try something different.

"Let me talk to him," I pleaded. "He'll listen to me. I'll get him to tell you whatever you want."

"Not necessary. He'll break soon enough and we'll get everything we need from him then. Your voice could prove a setback. There's no need to risk it. He's put up a hell of a fight for a civilian though. I'll give him that much."

The pain in my stomach grew worse. I was shaking. Gareth was being hurt, and I could do nothing to stop it. I nearly vomited again.

"Ren . . . I wanted to come down and say thank you. To tell you what a great job you did and that I'm proud of you. I see now it was a mistake and it would have been kinder to have done this while you were unconscious."

"Wait," I was able to blurt out. I had to keep him talking. I had to buy more time. For what, I didn't know, but I couldn't give up, not yet. I stopped struggling and clenched my jaw. I tasted the blood in my mouth. "I'm okay."

"Good. I would have hated for it to end like that," he said. "So quick, so cold. You've performed admirably and I thought you deserved to know it before we unlink you and forget it all. You earned the praise."

I couldn't think straight. "Unlink me?"

"Yes, why do you think you're alive? Killing is easy."

My words. No, not mine: the words of the F.A.T.E. Center. He drained the last of his tea, put the cup down on a counter, grabbed a stool, and sat right in front of me.

"Like a Band-Aid, here it goes, Ren. In the very near future your link will be broken and then Gareth will be dead shortly thereafter. There's nothing you can do to stop it, so the sooner you accept it the better off you'll be."

My eyes teared up. Unable to wipe them, they softly flowed down my cheeks, off my chin and onto my clothes.

"Do you know what happens to a Shadow when their Link dies?"

I couldn't shake my head. My body was wracked with sobs.

"Of course you don't because we never told you. It's a terrible thing, losing yours. I don't have to tell you how strong the connection is between a Shadow and Link; you've had enough experience with it already. More so than others if the reports I've read are correct." He flashed a sly smile. "When your link dies there is . . ."

"Gareth," I choked out, interrupting him. "His name is Gareth." He could at least call him by his name, show a smidgen of respect.

"Of course, sorry. Gareth. When *Gareth* dies there is only one outcome for you. You will lose all sense of yourself, all sense of purpose, all sense of right and wrong. That pain you are feeling right now will turn to uncontrollable aggression and your thirst for revenge will be unstoppable. Everyone becomes a foe. And blinded by rage, you'd be a highly trained, fearless, killing machine. No one would be safe anywhere near you."

The only person who's not safe right now is you. Pray I don't get loose.

The pain had become a sharp stabbing pain. Gareth was getting worse.

"Unfortunately, once this happens, once your mind has abandoned you, there's no getting you back. It's similar to what happens when someone succumbs to the fire treatments. We send that sort to a second home where their aggression can be put to good use. But I digress and am off point. You're too talented to allow this to happen. Far too skilled and valuable to us. So the decision has been made to unlink you and then reassign you."

"I won't be reassigned to anyone else," I wept. "I can't do it"

"Yes, you can actually. If we unlink you before he dies, you'll be free and your mind will be fine. You don't honestly care about him. It's only a byproduct of what we've done to you."

"No, it isn't," I fought back.

"No, it is," he said sadly. "But don't worry. When it's done you'll wake up and think it's your last day of training. You'll have no recollection of the past six months, or of any of this. You'll be a blank slate again. But this time we'll make you a Hunter, what we should have done the first time around. Gareth will be gone and you'll be none-the-wiser."

All gone? All of it? If he could take away the past six months, could he go farther? Could he erase all of it and send me home? My mother and father's faces flashed in my mind. Even my brother's. Then Junie's. And then Gareth's.

"It only goes back to your link, a sort of reset button," he said, as if reading my mind.

From somewhere an old obnoxious rap song blared. Mr. S. got excited and blurted out, "Ooh!"

He pulled out a small glass tablet from his pocket. There was a flashing message on the screen. He tapped it and his lips curled into a smile. "He's broken. We're extracting the information we need as we speak. It's over." He tapped the screen again and the message disappeared. "Time's up."

He opened a small black box sitting on a surgical tray next to him and took out a pair of the same lighter-than-air glasses I'd worn for my linking with Gareth.

"Upload Project *Sharpe* Reversal," he said toward the tablet. "Get it?" he asked me with a smile.

A tiny light on the side of the glasses began to flash red. A few seconds later, red turned to steady green. He gently placed the glasses on my head. They carried a heavy weight of foreboding. He checked to make sure they were securely behind my ears.

"Snug as a bug," he said.

A small red button was now pulsed at the center of the tablet screen.

"All I have to do is push this and it all goes bye bye."

"Wait. Let us go. You have what you want. Just let us

leave. You'll never see us again. I can make us disappear; you know I can."

"True," he toyed with the idea for a moment then finished with, "but then I'd lose you."

I'd failed. Gareth would die and I would never remember him. I'd rather die than be unlinked to Gareth. I *would* die, rather than be unlinked. Mr. S.'s mind was made up and now so was mine. I had one hand left to play and it was time to play it. If you're gonna go out, go out with a bang.

"Let's cut the bullshit shall we, Blake?" I spat.

The use of his real name caught him off guard.

"How much faith do you have that this," I nodded toward the tablet, "will work?"

"Absolute. Why do you ask?"

"Blake Alexander Adams. Parents Charlie and Samantha. Little sister Megan, sophomore at Boston College. Parents address 23015 West Ogletree."

Hearing his full name, and those of his family, did the trick. The cool, commanding demeanor vanished. His jaw flickered. "How . . . ?" He shook off the shock.

"I was well trained," I said coolly. "And *you* screwed up. Brass rat."

He instinctively touched the school ring on his finger.

"You have no idea how many people I told this too." I hadn't told a soul, but *he* didn't know that.

"I . . . had not expected this . . ." Glassy-eyed he pulled out a gun from his belt, cocked it, and pointed it at me. "No one threatens my family."

I closed my eyes. *Gareth, I'm sorry.*

BANG!

CHAPTER 26

THE CHARGE

Pain. Indescribable pain.

It felt like my memories were being ripped from mind with razor blades. At first it was the little stuff. Following Gareth around campus. Taking fake notes in class. But then bigger, more intense, more personal moments. And the more powerful the memory, the more difficult and painful it was to lose.

I think I was screaming, but was it all in my head? And then the glasses were ripped off my head and it stopped. It was screaming.

"Ren! Ren!" came the sweetest voice I knew. "Ren, are you okay?"

I opened my eyes, the tears still streaming out of them.

Junie?

"Are you okay?" he repeated.

I nodded. "Think so." I jogged my memory. There were definite holes, but most of it was still there. The important stuff anyway. "Yeah, I'm good." I looked up at him. "Junie?"

There was a groan behind him and Junie's face contorted with rage. Over his shoulder I could see Mr. S. leaning against a counter clutching his bloodied right hand to chest. On the ground sat his tablet. The red button now green. Junie thundered toward him and slammed the butt of his machine gun into his stomach. Mr. S. crumbled like a sack of potatoes.

I'd never seen Junie *truly* angry. It was terrifying. This was not my Junie, my best friend, my soul mate. This was a giant, hellhound of a man. He had grenades, pistols, knives, and other weapons tactically strapped to every part of his body. A nightmarish war machine to anyone but me.

"How'd you . . . ?" I asked.

"I took a page out of your book. I was sneaky."

He dropped the large black bag he'd been carrying and sliced the binds off of me. I quickly wrapped my arms around him, but there wasn't time for crap like that now. I leapt out of the chair and crushed Mr. S. in the face with my fist. God it felt good. Then I hauled him up against a cabinet and crushed his windpipe with my knee. "Where is Gareth?" I asked.

Mr. S. didn't answer. I pushed harder, putting all my weight behind it. Anymore and I'd kill him. We both knew it.

"Ren, hurry. We need to get moving," Junie grunted, dragging two unconscious guards into the room.

He was right, we didn't have time for this. The gunshot would not go unnoticed and soon enough the beehive would wake up all around us. I stopped choking Mr. S. and stood over him.

I recited, "23015 West Ogletree . . ."

He looked up at me, terrified. "Floor R1, room 3907."

Liar. "Parents: Charlie and Samantha—"

"Okay, okay." He reached past me, trying to get to his tablet. I swiped it off the ground and handed it to him.

"Status," he croaked into it. He held it up for me to hear.

A voice, Cole's, responded. "Extraction finished; we've got it. Project Midas complete. Subject is alive, moving to garage C3 for removal to the nest. Will you meet us there?"

I grabbed the tablet and said, "On my way."

Cole had unknowingly given me my answer. Gareth was alive. I would find him. I put the tablet into my pocket, spun the pistol around in my hand, and cracked Mr. S. in the temple with it. It might have finished the job Junie had started with his gunshot. I didn't care.

"Ready?" Junie asked behind me.

I turned to see him kick the black bag toward me. It slid across the floor and stopped at my feet. I unzipped it and grinned: a fully loaded kit. Everything I would or could want was in there. Bulletproof vest, grenades, guns, and best of all, knives, my knives.

I strapped on the gear. With guns in their holsters and knives and grenades in their places, I was ready. And not a moment too soon.

Sirens began to wail from all over and emergency lights began to flash.

There was gunfire behind me as Junie shot at someone

through one of the small windows in the doors. He repositioned himself by the door, popping up to fire off more rounds through the now bullet-riddled window.

"How many?" I asked as I positioned myself on the other side of door to fire the opposite direction.

"Eleven," he said and then fired off a quick burst before saying, "now ten. But more keep showing up and this is our only way out."

"Won't be easy," I said.

He flashed a faint smile and said, "Never is with you, Ren."

A sudden barrage of gunfire ripped into the door and into the room. We were well protected by the thick cement walls. Voices could be heard giving orders. They were organizing. Not a good thing. I looked around and had an idea. I took a block of C-4 that my lovely Junie had brought me and slapped it on the opposite wall. Then I set the detonator.

"What are you doing?" he asked.

"Making a door."

His eyes widened. "Christ."

"Flash," I yelled, but he was already ahead of me. He took a flash bomb from his vest and tossed it through a door window. It went off in the hallway seconds later, and the moment it did, I flipped the trigger and the C-4 detonated, slamming me back into the wall. My ears were ringing. Two strong hands grabbed my vest and yanked me to my feet. *When had I hit the ground?* A bit dazed, I was about to hit whoever it was, but at the last moment realized it was Junie.

"We're gonna have a little chat about this later," he yelled.

The room was full of smoke. The sprinklers kicked on, but the small bomb had done the trick. There was a good size hole in the wall we could climb through.

I popped my head out. The hallway was clear. I hopped through the hole and covered Junie who was barely small enough to get through.

My heart jumped. I knew this hallway. I'd spent enough time going to and from the hospital wing here to recognize it. We were a long, long way from the garages. For good measure, Junie tossed a grenade through the makeshift door I'd just created and came jogging toward me. It exploded, the ceiling collapsing and blocking the way behind us.

We moved like cats through the halls, a pack of two working together as one. Anything that moved went down. We made sure to go up and down stairs whenever it didn't take us too far out of the way. We kept them from pinpointing us. The sirens, flashing lights, and sprinklers only added to the confusion. Nobody came close enough to stop us.

We were about halfway to the garage when Junie stopped me from turning right down a long hallway.

"What?" I asked.

"Need ammo," he said gesturing to his gun.

I checked mine. I was running low, too.

He pointed to the right and said, "Gun ranges."

I nodded my agreement and said, "Go."

It was strange: Not only had we avoided any large

groups, we'd come across no Hunters. Were they not here? Were we really that lucky? Or were they biding their time, planning an attack that would easily snuff us out? *Too many questions and no answers. Stop thinking, Ren Sharpe, and get to Gareth.*

We barged into one of the gun ranges and found it empty. It took seconds to find the right caliber bullets for our guns in the ammo lockers. Maybe it was the situation, but I was loading clips faster than he could. He gave up and took position by the door to cover us.

He stood like a statue facing the door, ready to kill anyone that came through it. He had come for me. He couldn't have thought he'd ever actually get to me, let alone that we'd even make it this far. But he had fully been prepared to die today trying to reach me. I hadn't realized I had stopped working until Junie's head turned slightly.

"You okay? You done?" he asked.

I quickly went back to reloading. "I can't believe you came."

His eyes still on the door he said, "You're my Ren. I'd do anything for you.

Just don't die. Would really suck."

"I'll try, and ditto."

A few seconds later I was ready to rock. We slipped a small wire camera under the door. The hallway was empty, or at least appeared that way. Junie reached to open the door, but I stopped him. There was something I had to do. I was afraid of his reaction, but I had to say it. Junie had risked everything for me, I had to give him this.

"You should go."

"What?" he asked confused.

"To Emily. You should go to her, now while you still can."

"Ren—"

"They know. They know you're here. They know you're helping me. They'll go after her to get back at you. How did you get out of that basement, anyway?"

He looked at the door, but I knew he wasn't seeing it. He was seeing Emily, seeing her safe. When he turned back to me, his face had hardened, his mind was set. I prepared myself for his decision.

"After," he insisted.

That was not the response I had been expecting. Hoping for? Yes. But not expecting. And it caught me off guard. I opened my mouth to speak, but nothing came out.

"After," he repeated. "The only person who knows I'm here is still extremely unconscious. Trust me. Once we get Gareth, we go straight for Emily."

"I can't let you do that. If anything happens to her—"

"If anything happens to you, Ren," he snapped, both worried and annoyed. "Don't you get it? The conversation's over. We get Gareth. Then we get Emily. Together. In that order. Or are you gonna *White Fang* me here in the gun range?"

"I don't have any rocks," I said as I squeezed him tighter, my Junie. Somehow Junie had said no. He had said no to Emily and yes to me. Had the situation been reversed I don't know if I could have made the same decision. In fact, I know I couldn't have. I would have gone. I would have left him. Seconds later we rushed out of the range into the hallway, guns primed. Within thirty feet all hell broke loose as soldiers flooded around the corners in front of us and behind. They'd been waiting. A door to the stairs was ten feet away but it could have been ten miles for all it mattered with the bullets flying.

I flipped my gun to fully automatic and let the bullets fly as we inched toward our only way out. I felt a bullet graze my thigh and a few more slammed into my vest. The force knocked me into Junie.

"You okay?!" he yelled.

"Yeah, you?" I yelled back catching my breath.

A few more steps, and I kicked the door open and leapt inside the stairwell. I reached back into the hallway and yanked Junie along with me, slamming the door shut behind us.

After a quick check of our persons we found nothing too terribly bad. A few grazes here and there, but nothing major. Junie rigged a makeshift booby trap on the door, and then we were off. We hustled down five levels before getting to our door. We were on the Garage Level now but still a few good twists and turns of hallway away from C3.

Again, there was no resistance as we opened the door, exiting the stairwell into the hallway. But our footsteps echoed off of the floor no matter how lightly we stepped. There was an explosion from the stairwell. The building shook. Someone had been brave and stupid enough to test Junie's booby trap.

We rounded a corner and found ourselves face-to-face with two gun barrels. A girl with deep red hair in a ponytail opened fire on us. Her accuracy was only matched by her quickness. She sprayed her fire right across the two of us. Our vests each caught three perfect shots to the heart. She was back behind the wall before either of us could fire off a round. I had no doubt the next time I saw her she'd be aiming for, and hitting, our heads. She was no ordinary soldier. She was a Hunter.

"What do we do?" Junie asked, but I was well ahead of him.

All at once, I noticed he was bleeding. From his legs, his calves, his forearm. That girl had gotten off more rounds than I'd realized. She had all the advantages and we had none. Know when to hold'em, know when to fold'em.

"Run," I said and spun him around.

CHAPTER 27
IF YOU WANT BLOOD . . .

I ran, full sprint toward Gareth, full sprint toward anyone who got in my way. Junie stayed behind me, leaving a trail of blood as we went. He occasionally popped off rounds over my shoulders, but nobody was really chasing us. That couldn't be good.

I was shaking with adrenaline when we reached the doors of C3. I holstered my knives and drew out two pistols as I burst through the doors. Junie limped behind me. I had fully expected there to be an army inside, guns at the ready, waiting for me. I had been looking forward to the bloodbath.

As usual though, I was wrong. I found nothing but cars, trucks, motorcycles, the usual garage stuff. No army. No hit squad. Not even any mechanics.

This was very bad.

A quick scan of the room took my eyes to the silhouette of a figure standing one hundred yards away. The one figure who could stop me dead in my tracks. The one figure I honestly feared.

Standing in the middle of an open, empty space of concrete, smack in between two Humvees with twin .50 caliber gun mounts, was Luka. I should have known it.

While I had been running, it had felt like we were being corralled, guided through the halls. I had passed it off as overanalyzing everything. Why guide us to our destination? In reality, it had been that. The attacks had been coordinated so that if we did make it out alive, we would be left to face an opponent we could not beat. They had played a game with us and the end result, no matter how we played, had already been determined. I would lose. No, we would lose.

Suddenly I understood why we'd made it so deep into the facility with so little resistance. This place houses an army of the best killers on the planet, and we'd hardly run into anyone except for outside the armory No, the moment Junie had rescued me they'd arranged this moment with exquisite precision, like a chess game. It had all been orchestrated for this one confrontation. The silence was absolute as Luka and I stared at each other. The laser site from Junie's automatic was dead center on Luka's chest. In each of my hands I held two pistols. I cocked them and took a cautious step forward. Luka simply sighed, as if the threat was laughable. It was.

Hesitantly, I lowered my guns and dropped them to the ground with a clatter.

"What are you doing?" Junie growled at me.

I casually reached over, put my hand on the barrel of this gun and lowered it to the ground.

Luka smiled and nodded at me. We both understood. He could have easily parked himself 1000 yards down the garage with a sniper rifle and picked us off, or had those twin .50 cals primed and loaded when we burst through the door to saw us in half. But there was no respect in that. He was going to allow us to fight and die with honor, with a chance.

I reached behind my back and pulled out the knives Junie had given me. I held them at my sides. Junie, recognizing what was going on, pulled out a massive machete and held it in his right hand. He slipped a pair of brass knuckles onto his left.

Luka reached above his head and from behind his back and pulled out his massive katana sword. He flipped something on the handle and twisted. The blade split itself into two swords. He held them both at his sides like me, blades up.

Then he strode slowly toward us. We held our ground until he stopped about ten feet away. I squeezed the handles on my knives as tightly as I could.

"Are you injured?" he asked with his airy, light voice. The question caught me off guard. Why the hell would he care? Or was he trying to find my weaknesses?

"Not terribly," I said, never taking my eyes off of him. He looked at Junie.

"I'll live," Junie told him.

"Good. Then you still have a chance." He motioned with his head toward something behind him, but I refused to take my eyes from his. "I've programmed the coordinates of the Nest into it. But you must leave now. He's got quite the head start on you."

I blinked. "What are you doing?"

"Go get the boy. Mr. Cole is traveling alone with him. I have no doubt you can handle him. I can deal with anyone that comes through that door. Fear not for me."

My eyes took the chance and looked past him. An old, convertible Mustang sat ready to depart, right behind the Hummers.

"Why are you doing this?" I asked.

"Because it's right," he said flatly. He then pulled out a pair of those damn glasses from his pockets and handed them to me. "And because of this."

I took them from him and held them in my hand. *Could I trust him?* He nodded, encouraging me to put them on. "Will only take a second."

I had no choice. This was one man who did not partake in trickery or practice dishonesty. Besides, if he'd wanted me dead it would have happened already.

I put them on.

MONEY. IT WAS ALL about money.

It was quite simple really. Countries were going bankrupt all around the world. They couldn't support their own citizens anymore, let alone contribute to something like F.A.T.E. All of them could still provide the program fresh children, of course, just not money. A bit unsettling, I thought. F.A.T.E. could still be fully functional for a few more years, but after that it would be impossible without the full resources it was accustomed to. Their pleas had fallen on deaf ears.

F.A.T.E. had to take matters into its own hands to ensure survival. So a list was made of FIPs who met two specific criteria:

The first: The chosen FIP's death would be just big enough to get everyone's attention and thus get full funding back. Obviously, there weren't any future prime ministers or presidents on the list, but Nobel Prize winners? Sure. F.A.T.E. could then argue that luckily it was only that and not someone more important. Blackmail, in other words.

Second was that this: FIP had already created something worth a lot of money, *a lot of money*. It had to be something F.A.T.E. could steal and potentially sell: an insurance policy should the first part of the plan fail. When I called about Gareth's invention, his name went on that short list. He was deemed an acceptable loss and therefore so was I. It was nothing personal, it was just business. And it was all my fault.

I HAD THE WHOLE dirty story when I ripped the glasses off my face and shoved them into a pocket a few seconds later.

"Do you understand?" Luka asked me.

"Yeah."

"Then you must go now."

"What will you do?"

"They have used you, Ren Sharpe, as they have used me. I shall visit violence on them in ways they never thought possible."

Without looking back he said, "Best of luck, Ren Sharpe. I hope we meet again."

I watched him go a few more paces before sprinting toward the Mustang. I didn't bother with the door and instead jumped straight in. Junie limped to the passenger door, but when he put his hand on the handle, I shouted, "No!"

He flinched.

"Go to Emily." He began to shake his head but I kept going. "You got me here. You did it. I'm fine. This is my game now. I can handle Cole. You have to go to Emily. I'll come to you when it's over."

"I'm not leaving you. Not until it's done. That was the deal."

"Junie. It's done. Cole has Gareth. Just Cole. I've been dreaming of this for four years."

"And I've been dreaming of you," he stated. "I can't."

"I owe you my life. And I don't just mean today," I said. If he wasn't going to leave me then I'd make him. "Please, go."

Our eyes locked. We both remembered the promise we had made to each other so very long ago in the hospital. We could say those words once and the other would do it no questions asked, no arguments. One of us would go. Neither of us had ever said it, well, not really anyway. We'd jokingly used it all the time, but neither had ever called it in.

His lips tightened. "No. You don't get to do that, not here."

"I can. And I have. If you won't choose Emily over me then I will for you."

Leaving wasn't for me, it was for him. He was too good. Too loyal. He deserved better than me.

A crash made both of us turn. A flood of guards and Hunters came pouring into the garage only to be met by the twin blades of Luka.

"*Please*, go," I begged once more.

Wordlessly he turned and ran toward an old Chevy truck a few yards away. I fought back tears of relief as I checked the monitor in the car. It was displaying a map, with a small dot driving down a road. At the top of the screen it stated, *Distance to Target 7.62 Kilometers*, and the distance was slowly climbing.

When I looked up again, I was shocked by the number of bodies already around Luka. They stood no chance against him. He was a giant being attacked by ants.

I started the engine and felt it purr to life, vibrating at my feet. I heard Junie do the same in the truck. I slammed the car into drive. The tires spun out before catching and sending me tearing away at full speed.

Junie came flying up next to me. We swept past all of the other cars, motorcycles, and other fun gadgets before reaching the obstacle courses, fake city blocks, and then finally the hidden tunnel to the real world. The garage was kept on the bottom level and opened up through a cliff face a few miles away.

Luka had programmed the exit codes in for me so when I got close enough, the doors to the outside slid open. The cold night air slapped me in the face. It energized me, spurred me on as I flew out of the cave and onto the road.

Junie and I shared one final look as I went left and he went right. I watched him in my rearview until he rounded a bend and was gone.

The GPS showed me that I was gaining on Cole. How long I had before they reached this mysterious Nest place I had no idea? I only hoped I could catch them before they did.

Aside from the hum of the engine, the rushing wind provided the only noise on the deserted two-lane highway. No clouds and a full moon. The woods around me looked surreal in the moonlight. At any other time, it would have been beautiful. I suddenly found myself with the time to do something I absolutely didn't want to do. Think.

My brain, against my better judgment, began to go over all that had happened. It was not something I needed at that moment. I had do keep my focus. But alas, my brain has a mind of its own.

The whole situation sucked. Every part of it. And what made it that much worse (and I know how horrible this sounds) was that the F.A.T.E. Center was my home. Mr. S. was the closest thing to a father figure I had. Yes, he was demented, cruel, and a kidnapper of children. But he filled a role. He had betrayed me. I had been ripped from my life and forced into his, but I had believed in what my new life stood for, for what he stood for. So now I had nothing. It paled in comparison to everything else that had happened, all the lives that had been needlessly lost, but that betrayal still stung the most.

Fury soon took over leaving no room for anything else. The tears had stopped, and guided by hate, I focused on the path ahead of me. I was almost there.

I turned off the last real road and onto well groomed gravel. The car I was chasing was up around the bend.

I would be on it soon. It was time to bring the pain, to unleash the suffering that I had suffered. Cole would pay, as Mr. S. had paid.

I had to give it to my brain. While stupid and awkward most of the time, it had stepped up at this moment. It had allowed me a brief moment to wallow in betrayal, and then segued nicely into what I was feeling now, into what I needed to be feeling now. I was not about to lose Gareth. Not after all this.

CHAPTER 28
ALL KILLER NO FILLER

I caught up to Cole a short time later and flipped off the head lights. The best thing about old cars—okay the two best things about old cars—are big engines and no running lights. When I flipped them off I was invisible. Using the GPS and the light from the moon I kept about two hundred yards behind them.

I hadn't really thought of what I'd do when I got there. Shooting Cole or the tires could easily make the car swerve headlong into a tree ending in the classic Hollywood fireball. And I didn't know where Gareth was being held so ramming or sideswiping it was equally as unappealing an option as the first. No, what I had to do now would require a bit more finesse.

I had to channel my inner sneak again. It had been the hallmark of my earlier days before I toughened up. You needed a sneak? You needed clever? You went to Ren Sharpe. I needed to think like the fourteen-year-old me.

Figure out what she would do. *I* was more threatening, but *she* was more dangerous.

I looked around. Trees. Gravel road. Old Mustang. Pistols. Not much to work with. I looked at the GPS for help. It told me Cole had been traveling at exactly 45 mph for the last ten minutes or so. Not a mph higher or lower. That was a good thing. It meant he was relaxed, oblivious not only to me, but to everything that had happened at F.A.T.E. Had he been alerted to my escape I'm sure he'd be flying down this road. He was driving like someone without a care in the world because in his mind all was fine back at F.A.T.E. and I was unlinked.

And there it was. It wasn't much, but I had my idea. I think.

My distance to target on the GPS began to shrink. He was slowing down. On the GPS screen, his dot was approaching a line that cut horizontally across the road. On the other side of the line read the words *The Nest.*

Cole's car stopped at the border,

I turned my headlights back on before I rounded the final bend. I found myself staring down the road at an immense wall, at least twenty feet high, the tops wrapped in coils of razor wire. Where the road ran smack dab into the wall there was a gate bathed in large floodlights. The gate was flanked by a small guardhouse. A black BMW was parked in front of it. Cole was casually standing next to the BMW, talking with two machine gun wielding guards.

My sudden appearance drew an instant reaction from everyone. *Showtime.* The two guards pointed their guns at me. Cole stiffened, confused.

"Pull over, now!" yelled one of the guards. .

I pulled off the side of the road about fifty feet away from them, shut off the engine, and hopped out as if all was normal.

"Get back in the car!" yelled the other.

I raised my hands. "Whoa, whoa fellas, calm down." The look on Cole's face was priceless and I nearly blew it. "I'm here to help," I added.

"Stop moving!" the first shouted.

"Who sent you?!" the other demanded. He lowered his gun and pointed a flashlight right at my face.

"Who do you think?" I said sarcastically as I shielded my eyes from the flashlight and kept moving toward them. I stopped when I reached them, and turned to Cole. "Wassup. Been a while."

Cole eyed me, not entirely sure what was happening. I had to play it cool. I turned to the guard with the flashlight which was still pointed at my face. "Dude, seriously, can you turn that thing off?"

The guard turned to Cole, who gave the slightest nod. The flashlight went dark. The second lowered his gun too, but kept his finger on the trigger.

"Blake told me to come," I said before Cole could ask any questions. "Said I should be here. Thought it would be good for me."

Cole's eyes narrowed. "So you know who's in the car?"

I gave a fake yawn. "Some kid named Gareth? I don't know." I peered into the car, but it was empty. "He in the trunk?"

Cole nodded, his eyes on mine.

"Sooo." I looked around. "What's the hold up then?"

"Nothing." Cole pulled out a tablet from his pocket like the one I stole from Mr. S. "I'll call the professor and let him know we're here."

He gave me one last prying look. I raised my eyebrows like, *What?* He dropped his gaze and punched the screen.

Half a second later an obnoxious rap song, one I'd heard not long ago, blared from the tablet it in my pocket. *Busted.* Cole's eyes widened.

He opened his mouth, but before he could protest, I head butted him hard in the nose, sending him crashing to the ground in a heap. I spun kicked the first guard in the side of the temple, knocking him across the hood of the BMW and out cold. In the same motion, I whirled and grabbed the other guard by the vest, flipped him over my hip and slammed him onto the ground. A quick punch to the head and he was out too. Three seconds, tops, and I was back on my feet, pistol raised and pointed straight at Cole.

"Up," I said coldly.

"You broke my nose," he spat in a nasal voice, sniffing and spitting blood. Again."

"Up," I repeated.

He stood and dropped his hands from his nose. I backed away.

"Toss it," I said as I motioned at the holster on his belt. "Slowly."

Using only his bloody index finger and thumb, he gripped the handle of the pistol and pulled it out. I nodded and he tossed it at me. I grabbed it out of the air with my free hand and threw it into the woods behind me.

"Happy?" he choked out.

I pointed at his ankle with my pistol. "Not yet. And again."

He reached down, and once more, we did the same little grip-and-toss.

"Gareth, you okay?" I yelled.

I heard a muffled, "Yeah," from the trunk. My heart skipped a beat, "Get me out of here," he added. There was a thump.

At the moment, he was safe and out of the way. "Soon," was all I could muster.

"So, if you don't mind me asking, how'd you escape?" Cole asked. He took the tiniest of steps forward, trying to cut the distance between us. I matched with a mini step back.

"I had help from friend. And then from an unexpected one. Luka."

Cole blinked. He swallowed.

"He told me everything," I added.

Cole cracked a little smile. "Really?"

With my free hand, I pulled out the pair of glasses as I repeated, "Everything."

The glasses made Cole smile wider. "And you believe Luka? How do you know he wasn't lying?"

"Because he wouldn't do that. He's got too much honor."

Cole laughed. "Oh, and you know this because you know him so well? Ren, my dear, I've seen that man cut off a man's fingers knuckle by knuckle. He's no better than you or I."

"I choose to believe otherwise."

"So which truth do you think you know? Hold on, let me guess." He pretended to think hard before continuing. "How about the one where we say we found out Gareth creates a bomb that kills millions and we have to stop him. Wait, no, not that one. You'd probably agree with that." He gave me a studying look. "The money one." He raised his eyebrows, waiting for a response.

I kept as stone-faced as possible. I wanted to shut him up but he had me second guessing myself. He was winning.

"Yeah, that's the one. Governments are trying to cut our funding. We need more money. That's a good one." He rolled his eyes. "They keep stuff like that around to get people to do what we want, Ren. You think the people up top got together one night, had a few too many and typed out a nefarious plan on a computer and hit save? Give us all a little more credit, huh?"

"So if that's not the truth, tell me what is."

He laughed again. "No."

I pointed the gun a bit more assertively. "Then there's no point keeping you alive anymore."

"Guess not."

"I *will* kill you Cole."

"If I tell you anything, the man on the other side of this fence will do to me something far worse than death." He raised his hands and closed his eyes. "So just get it over with."

I hesitated. I'd never expected, nor wanted him to give up this easily. Where was the fight? What had happened to my tormentor?

"But know it won't change anything," he added. "There's a long list of others just like me. You should have blown that place up when you had the chance." The last part he said almost longingly, like he wanted it to be gone, wanted it over.

"And kill all those kids? Never. I'm not like you."

"And that's why people like me will always win." He paused and opened his eyes, "So what now, Ren?"

"Now? Now I do something I've dreamed about for four years." I tossed my gun into the woods behind me with the others. I dropped my knives to the ground. This was the moment I'd fantasized about since I was fourteen and had broken a kidnapper's nose. I charged. He was ready. We collided with a thud, but I was stronger, my adrenaline powering me on. I grabbed him by the shoulders, picked him up, and drove him back into woods. I slammed him, hard, into a huge pine tree.

Four years of pain, humiliation, and suffering were packed into every blow that I unleashed on my old teacher. He took it, and tried his best to fight back, but failed. He was no match for me. Not anymore. I had gone wild, all control lost. Cole, with his eyes shut and his hands raised high, was down on his knees, broken and destroyed. I was now one of the ones he'd warned us about. I had "turned." And he would be my first victim.

Wouldn't he?

CHAPTER 29
FAMILY REUNION

"Why didn't you kill him?" Gareth yelled at me over the roar of the wind.

We'd been driving in silence for nearly ten minutes, speeding away from the Nest in the Mustang. I didn't really have an answer. I still don't know why myself. Maybe it was pity, like Bilbo with Gollum.

"Maybe I'm getting soft," I yelled back, but with perhaps a bit of truth behind the sarcasm. Killing people to save Gareth, I could justify to myself. But Cole had surrendered. He had given up. There was no fight in him. There would be no honor in killing him, or so my inner Luka insisted. And honestly, I'd had about enough of death.

As I pulled off the gravel road and back onto the highway, I glanced at Gareth in the passenger seat. He was mine again. The monster inside was satisfied and neither of us would ever let this happen again. I'd been unable to go five seconds without looking at him since I pulled him out of the trunk and hugged him. Yeah, you heard that right, *I* hugged *him*, not the other way around. And I'd kept hugging past the point of normal, past the point of awkward, too. At one point my knees went weak. All the emotion, exhaustion, everything had finally hit me. But he'd held me up.

Needless to say, he'd refused to come with me until I told him what was going on. Knowing we had to get going, and fast, I gave him the five second, super abbreviated version and swore once we were safely away I'd be the open book I'd promised earlier. Which left us where we were now.

"I still don't know why we took this instead of the Beamer," he said.

"How many eighteen-year-olds do you know who drive that kind of car?"

"Tons," he lied with a smile.

I looked at him again and my stomach tingled. So wrong, but so right.

"Where are we going?" he asked.

"Junie's. Have to make sure Emily's okay. We made a deal."

"Who's Emily?"

"She's Junie's *you.* She's linked to him."

It took him a couple of seconds, but he got there. He was basically a genius, after all. "Is she in trouble?"

I shrugged. "They know Junie came for me, us, so they could go after her for payback."

"They'd do that?"

"I'm not putting anything past them at this point."

"Wow," he said under his breath. "With all that's happened I think you should consider tendering your resignation."

"Consider it tendered."

I pulled out the tablet from my pocket and tossed it to him. "Here. Play with this."

His adorable little nerd eyes lit up. "Whoa," he gasped, instantly immersed, fingers dancing.

I slammed the gas pedal. The car roared ahead. Further away from harm. Further away from this day.

THE GPS TURNED OUT to be quite handy. As Gareth found out, it not only functioned as a classic nav unit, but had full Internet, and provided real-time updates of the locations of all police officers and speed traps. With that knowledge we averaged about 120 mph, driving through the night and reaching Junie's in a little under nine hours at midmorning. Most of the drive was spent answering Gareth's questions. I told him everything. Okay, not everything. I left out a few memories, the really personal ones that were either too embarrassing, or about Junie, but otherwise I was an open book as promised.

As had happened the previous time, the closer we got to Junie's the more the butterflies in my stomach fluttered. But these weren't only the butterflies of seeing him. Others nagged at me. Like what would we see when we got to his house? Would there be a TAC team waiting to kill us? Had Junie even made it? Or was he dead on the side of the road having bled out? What if the block was all burned down, the result of a massive firefight between Junie and them? On and on it went in my head.

I took with the wheel with my left hand and gripped my pistol in my lap with my right as we made the final turn to Junie's street. I prepared myself for whatever I was about to encounter. And that's when I saw . . .

Blessed nothingness. Everything looked fine.

We passed a man mowing his lawn.

"Nice ride!" he complimented with a wave.

I waved back still scanning everything for a hint of danger but finding none. The truck Junie had taken was parked in the driveway. It was a little off center with one tire in the grass like it had been parked in a hurry, but that was understandable. I pulled in behind it.

Birds were chirping. The only other noises were the hum of the mower down the road, the sound of rustling leaves, unseen children in a nearby backyard laughing and squealing. All normal. Had Mr. S. called it a draw?

"Okay," I said. "We're clear."

Gareth popped up from the back seat. I'd had him lay down just in case.

"Looks normal, too normal," he said skeptically. He'd really taken to the idea that he was now part of the operation.

"Just stay behind me," I told him. "And remember what we talked about."

He nodded and kept a few paces back from me as we climbed silently over the car doors and made our way to the house. I made it up the stairs silently, but Gareth hit a loud creak. I looked back at him and shook my head. He grimaced, knowingly. I tried the handle. It was unlocked. The well-greased door swung open without a peep. Safely inside,

I drew my pistol. There was no need to search. If Junie was here, I knew where he'd be. I went straight for the basement.

As I made my way through the house I noticed how perfect it all was. The clean-up team had done a good job. All my bloody rags were gone and any broken windows or damage from the assault the other day had already been repaired. Like it had never happened.

The basement door was cracked open and the faint hint of blue light spilled through.

I looked back at Gareth and held up my hand. He nodded and hung back as I made my way down the basement stairs. It had all been so easy. So normal. Gareth was right. So when I reached the landing, looked in the room, and I saw *him*, I shouldn't have been surprised. But my gun was at my side. I started to raise it.

"Uh, uh, uh," Mr. S. said, waving his finger. His other hand held a pistol, shoved against a Junie's temple. Junie was kneeling on the ground: cuffed, beaten, bloody, and swollen. But he was still alive. He had duct tape across his mouth.

"Weapon on the ground, Ms. Sharpe."

My eyes were locked on Junie. He shook his head, but I did as I was told, placing my gun on the landing next to the first step leading up. Mr. S. motioned with his gun for me to come down the stairs. I did so.

"Knives, too," he added.

I placed my knives on the floor in front of my feet.

"Kick them to me."

I gave them a little kick, purposefully not hard enough to reach him.

Without hesitation he shot Junie in the shoulder. The impact made Junie lurch forward.

"No!" I yelled.

"Then stop acting like a child," Mr. S. snapped. He grabbed Junie by the hair and yanked him back to his knees.

"Please don't hurt him," I whispered. "I'll do anything."

Mr. S. raised his eyebrows and gave me a knowing look. "Anything?"

I frowned. "Not that."

"But that's what I want. *He's* what I want. Your FIP."

"I can't, no."

"Not even to save him?" he asked as he shoved the pistol hard into Junie's head.

"Please. Please don't make me choose. I can't."

"Here, I'll make it easier on you. You say you can't choose so I'll do it for you." He pulled Junie to his feet and dragged him over to the video screen on the far wall. The largest image showed Emily playing in the backyard with her mother. He shoved Junie's face into the image. "Here's what's going to happen if you don't give me who I want. I'm going to walk next door and put a bullet in *her* head."

Junie moaned in agony through his gag. Mr. S. kneed him in the ribs, knocking the wind out of him, and dropped him to the ground. He put his heel on Junie's throat to hold him down.

"I'm going to make you watch your precious Junie change. Watch him become the raging beast. After that you will either kill him or he *will* kill you. I'm guessing you'll kill him. Call it a hunch."

"Okay, okay."

"Good choice. Where is the stupid little boy?"

"Gareth," I said. "His name is Gareth."

"Why does his name matter?"

"Because you should know the name of the person who kills you," I said coolly.

BANG!

A small red dot appeared in the middle of Mr. S.'s chest. Then it spread out, bigger and bigger. His eyes bulged. He looked over my shoulder and shook his head as he clutched his chest and fell to his knees. He took one deep gasp and fell over.

I whipped around. On the landing stood Gareth, pale and shaky, clutching a pistol that didn't sit right in his hands.

"Only after I gave the signal," I said. "That was the plan. Did I give the signal?"

"Maybe . . . no," he stammered. "I'm sorry. I'm not . . . like . . ."

"Like us," I finished for him. I tried to smile. "We're really gonna have to work on what following instructions means later. Do you even know what explicit means?"

"Yeah, means not-plicit," he said, mustering a smile in return. .

"Nice shot by the way."

"Video games," he said, hurrying forward to hand me the gun as quickly as possible. He kept his eyes on Junie, avoiding the figure he'd just killed. "How'd you know I was there?"

I pointed toward the monitors behind Mr. S.'s body

and said, "Reflection. Sloppy work, kid. Lucky he didn't see you."

A muffled, "Hey!" came from behind me. I spun around and covered the distance two steps, then crouched down, and ripped off the tape from his mouth.

"I'm sorry, are you okay?"

"Been better," he said, choking for air. "Being your friend is exhausting."

I uncuffed him, carried him across the room, and laid him on the couch. I checked his wounds from earlier. They'd been patched.

"Did it myself when I got home," he said. "They're good," he added, taking my hands in his. "I'm good." He jerked his head toward Mr. S.'s crumpled body.

"He was waiting for me. All the cars have trackers. That's how he knew when you'd be here too."

"Is he alone?" I asked, hoping he was but fearing the worst.

"As far as I know," Junie said. "He screwed up and he knew it. This was a solo mission. Only a few people know about these side ops. This stuff isn't exactly sanctioned."

"Side ops?" Mr. S. was a well-documented Chatty Cathy, so I hoped Junie knew more.

"He's not the first," Junie confirmed, nodding toward Gareth, who was now snooping through Junie's gear.

"How many others?"

Junie shrugged. "All I know is they use them to fund something off-books called The Nest?"

I glanced at Gareth. But he was now preoccupied with a kit of micro cameras.

"It doesn't make sense to come for him. They got what they wanted when they broke him."

Junie shook his head. "Just the theory. The professor called while we were waiting. He said he couldn't figure it out and still needed the source. He needed Gareth."

"Professor?" It was the second time in the last twenty-four hours I'd heard this reference. I'd always assumed it was a Mr. S. alias . . .

"No clue. But I got the feeling Mr. S. was afraid of him."

Before I could say another word, Mr. S. emitted a deep, gurgling cough. Gareth spun around. I guess he wasn't dead yet. I crouched down next to him, not sure if I would just finish him off, and he looked up at me. Fear. Absolute fear. He was dying and he knew it. He reached out with a bloody hand, and I instinctively gave him mine to hold. I wasn't becoming soft. I'd always *been* soft. I wasn't afraid of showing the truth anymore, either.

"I'm sorry," he managed. "I really did like you." He pulled me closer and passed me a glass tablet. "He wants to speak with you." As I took it, his grip slackened and his eyes glazed over.

I held the tablet to my ear.

"Hello? Is this Ren Sharpe?" The voice was upbeat and pleasant, a dad's voice, like Mr. S.'s had once been.

"This is she."

"Good, good. And do you know who you're talking to?"

"The professor?"

"Excellent. Listen, Ms. Sharpe, we've gotten off on the wrong foot and I want to clear things up. I don't want to hurt Mr. Young, far from it. Oh, I did, I'm not going to lie. But now that I've seen what he's got inside his head I realize how wrong that would have been. He's a once-in-a-generation mind. As a fellow scholar, it's my duty to help cultivate it, ensure that it reaches its full potential."

"What if he doesn't want your help?"

"He does. He just doesn't know it. Understand this, Ren. I'm offering an end to this, a peaceful one where we all walk away alive and Gareth is safe from harm for the rest of his life. As his Shadow what more could you hope for, right? I can guarantee his safety, can you?"

I looked over at Gareth, who was handing Junie an ice pack. They were both alive, they were both safe. But for how long?

"But hang up this phone, turn down this offer, and the hunt will begin."

They must have sensed I was watching them and turned to look at me at the exact same time. And there was my answer. I'd lost my family once and had no intention of doing it again. Whatever was coming would come and when it did, it would have to go through me.

"Best of luck with the hunt."

I dropped the phone and ground it beneath my boot.